I0819568

The Silence of Bones

The Forest of Stolen Girls

The Red Palace

A Crane Among Wolves

Behind Five Willows

Behind Five Willows

JUNE HUR

FEIWEL AND FRIENDS
NEW YORK

A Feiwel and Friends Book
An imprint of Macmillan Publishing Group, LLC
120 Broadway, New York, NY 10271 • fiercereads.com

EU representative: Macmillan Publishers Ireland Ltd, 1st Floor, The Liffey Trust Centre,
117–126 Sheriff Street Upper, Dublin 1, D01 YC43

Copyright © 2026 by June Hur. All rights reserved.

Our books may be purchased in bulk for specialty retail/wholesale, literacy, corporate/premium, educational, and subscription box use. Please contact MacmillanSpecialMarkets@macmillan.com.

The publisher of this book does not authorize the use or reproduction of any part of this book in any manner for the purpose of training artificial intelligence technologies or systems. The publisher of this book expressly reserves this book from the Text and Data Mining exception in accordance with Article 4(3) of the European Union Digital Single Market Directive 2019/790.

Library of Congress Cataloging-in-Publication Data

Names: Hur, June author
Title: Behind Five Willows / June Hur.
Description: First edition. | New York : Feiwel and Friends, 2026. | Audience: Ages 13 and up | Audience: Grades 10–12 | Summary: "Set in eighteenth-century Korea, two teens secretly waging a war against government book banning find themselves irresistibly drawn together"—Provided by publisher.
Identifiers: LCCN 2025047618 | ISBN 9781250348081 hardcover
Subjects: CYAC: Romance stories | Censorship | Books and reading | Social classes | Government, Resistance to | Korea—History—18th century | LCGFT: Romance fiction | Historical fiction | Novels
Classification: LCC PZ7.1.H8645 Be 2026
LC record available at https://lccn.loc.gov/2025047618

First edition, 2026
Book design by Maria W. Jenson
Feiwel and Friends logo designed by Filomena Tuosto
Printed in the United States of America

ISBN 978-1-250-34808-1
10 9 8 7 6 5 4 3 2

To those who safeguard knowledge.

And to Eunji and Eunwoo:
I hope you'll always find the extraordinary in the everyday.

King Jeongjo (1752–1800) is considered to be one of the most outstanding and respected monarchs of Joseon dynasty–era Korea, known for his love for the people and his many efforts to reform and strengthen the nation. However, one of his policies (now considered controversial by many scholars) was his push for the restoration of a pure writing style, later referred to as *Munchebanjeong* (문체반정). Under this policy, fictional writings and the creation of fiction were officially banned, along with other restrictions.

The reasons behind this edict are complex. They include Jeongjo's personal distaste for novels, the political rivalry between the dominant Old Doctrine faction (Noron) and the Southern faction (Namin), and growing concerns over the influence of Western knowledge and Catholicism. There was a widespread fear that anti-state and anti-Confucian ideas could be hidden within novels.

This royal order banning novels was first declared in 1785 and reiterated in 1786, 1787, late in 1791, and once again in 1793.

The person, be it gentleman or lady,
who has not pleasure in a good novel,
must be intolerably stupid.

—Jane Austen

Chapter 1

Spring 1792

The countryside had exploded in a storm of colors—shimmering willow tresses, golden shoots of forsythia and bursts of flowering sansuyu trees, and purple-pink azaleas smothering the hillsides and valleys. Warm gusts breezed through the village, showering petals onto thatched rooftops and earthenware pots, drifting down withered streams and speckling the parched earth.

Drawing her veil over her head, Shin Haewon journeyed through the floral downpour, pausing now and then to turn her eyes skyward. A bird glided along the mountain ridges, and she found herself wondering how she must appear from such a height: a young woman walking alone, her jangot billowing like the wings of a silken green butterfly.

No one would see a criminal.

She clutched her travel sack tight beneath her cloak, enjoying the weight of books. What she had in her possession was breaking every rule in the ladies' etiquette manuals she had read growing up—as well as a few laws.

"Agasshi!" a shrill female voice called out. "Wait for us!"

Haewon slowed to a halt, raising a hand to shield her eyes from the sun's glare. "Hurry," she answered, "before the line at the fortress gate grows too long!"

"A lady oughtn't to walk as vigorously as you do, agasshi," the sixteen-year-old maid huffed as she finally caught up. "Besides, your elder sister cannot keep up. You know how delicate her constitution is!"

"Don't trouble yourself over me," Haewon's older sister said with a sweet smile, though a bead of sweat trembled at her brow. Her name was Yeonok—*Yeon* for "beauty" and *ok* for "jade"—but their family had long ago taken to simply calling her Jade. "I am in perfectly good health, Boram-ah. The fatigue has lessened of late."

Haewon linked arms with her sister, adjusting her stride to match Jade's. "Last time, it felt like an eternity just to get through the gates. And Five Willows was already crowded by the time we arrived."

"All the books I wanted were already gone."

Haewon patted Jade's arm. "We cannot allow such a tragedy to repeat itself."

"I don't know why your father permits you to visit Five Willows," Maid Boram grumbled. "Most ladies wouldn't dare visit a secret book-lending shop themselves; they'd send their male relations. And did the king not reinstate the edict banning all novels a few months ago?"

Haewon shrugged. "The authorities have long abandoned any real effort to enforce the ban. I doubt there will be much effort this time, either—"

"*Haewon agasshi,*" Maid Boram squeaked. "The way you

speak . . . it gives me such severe heart palpitations." Her hand fluttered to her chest, and she bore the aura of a scandalized middle-aged matron. "Novel reading is a dangerous business."

"Is it? I'm not afraid of a little danger." Haewon cast a smile at her sister. "It sounds rather thrilling, don't you think, eonni?"

As Maid Boram continued to lecture, they took a shortcut across a brittle reed field. The unrelenting dryness had returned this spring, and only the most resilient trees and plants had flowered. Even the stream yonder had thinned into a glistening thread.

Soon, Gyonam Village fell behind them. After their brisk walk, the outline of the fortressed capital began to emerge ahead. The Souimun Gate—one of the main entrances into the city—stood magnificent against the azure sky, and after what felt like ages of waiting, they were finally permitted through. A cacophony of sounds greeted them as they strolled down the streets of the capital: the squeals of pigs, the squawks of cooped chickens, and the piercing cries of peddlers hawking their wares. Endless rows of tables and mats presented by sweaty merchants were adorned with goods of all kinds, from wooden spoons and straw sandals to rolls of silk and glittering hairpins.

The capital never failed to invigorate Haewon. *Anything* could happen here. Destinies could be changed with the slightest brush of coat sleeves, the briefest of glances. And there was one place in particular, one secretive shop, that had become her safe haven.

Hoisting her travel sack higher, Haewon bit back a smile as she arrived before Five Willows. Anyone could enter the store selling secondhand Confucian texts, but only certain trusted patrons were permitted to explore the secrets behind it.

"Draw your veil closer," Maid Boram whispered.

Haewon did so as she stepped into the shop and made her way over to Merchant Hyoyang. The gray-bearded man was seated behind a table, glowering down at a book.

"Readers these days have no reverence," the merchant mumbled to her in greeting. His calloused, ink-stained fingers wagged accusatorily at the scribbles in the margin. "*Look* at the state of this borrowed copy!"

"Ajusshi, is your daughter in?" Haewon asked.

"She just returned from Myeongrye-bang District. Aigoo, aigoo, this is a disgrace!" he went on, clucking his tongue, flipping through the pages while shaking his head. "This book was in perfect condition just three days ago, and now look—someone has defaced entire pages with their comments and dog-eared the corners!"

Haewon expressed her sympathy, just as she did with every visit, and as usual, found that nothing she said could appease the merchant's outrage. Excusing herself, she led her maid and sister past the light crowd of patrons to the door at the far end, hidden behind a row of shelves. She knocked three times.

A wooden panel slid open, revealing an eye through the peephole. "Yes?" came a female voice from behind the door.

Haewon leaned in and whispered the code, verses from the great poet Tao Yuanming's work: "*This gentleman does not know where his people have come from / Also doesn't know his family's name / At the side of his house grows five willow trees / This is how he got this name.*"

"It's me," she added quietly. "I brought Jade and Boram, too."

At once, the door was opened by her friend Mistress Wol. She was a plain young woman with high cheekbones, a long slender nose, and a pair of intelligent and sensible eyes framed by jade-rimmed spectacles. Her hair was always tucked into a chignon, the style of a married woman, though Wol had never married.

"Come in quickly," Wol urged, a stack of books cradled in her arms. "Before you are seen."

They stepped into the secret shop lined with wooden bookshelves. Patrons hid in the dusty corners, browsing and reading like hungry mice.

"I'll be right over there; you go and speak with Wol," Jade said, her face glowing as she hurried over to the shelf holding romantic literature. Maid Boram trailed behind, nervously playing with her sleeve.

Finally alone with Wol, Haewon walked close alongside her companion. "You must have heard the rumors? I didn't think much about the edict being reinstated until recently," she whispered. "There is talk that it will be different this time. More serious, perhaps."

"Hmm."

"Are you not worried about the inspectors?"

"I confess, I am more concerned about book thieves finding their way in here. Do you know how many bookshops have closed down because of them?"

"Too many to count, I'm sure. So you are not concerned?"

"Of course I am. But there's no need to frown, Haewon-ah," Wol said as they ventured deeper into the maze of shelves. "We oughtn't be too worried. Some things will change because of the edict. Many will give into royal pressure, condemning novels in public while devouring them behind closed doors. Others will cling to their beliefs." Wol plucked two books from the pile in her arms and slid them into their rightful places on the shelves. "What will remain the same is the people's love for novels. Readers cannot be stopped."

She moved farther down the aisle, then paused again to shelve a few more books. "Besides, many government officials are in my father's pocket. We have purchased their protection. But never mind about politics and policies." Casting a glance back, she asked, "Did you bring them?"

Haewon lifted her travel sack. "I did."

Wol nodded, lengthening her stride while Haewon took her time, drawing in the familiar sight around her. Golden light streamed through the high-set windows, illuminating dust motes drifting in the air. Someone muffled a sob in the far corner, likely moved by a tragic scene they were reading. There came giggles from the opposite end as pages rustled. The shelves stood close enough to allow patrons a semblance of privacy, the aisles so narrow that one could not stretch their arms without bumping into books. And wherever one went in this shop, the comforting mustiness of aged paper warmed the air.

She loved this place.

It was her second home, and whenever she stepped inside the dusty, crowded space, a feeling akin to hunger curled inside her. Books upon books were stacked on the shelves, ten thousand lifetimes pressed between covers. With the turn of a page, she was no longer Shin Haewon. No longer the daughter of a family in financial straits; no longer a helpless sister witnessing an overwhelmed Jade, the government soon to force her to get married *quickly, quickly*; no longer the keeper of a younger third sister who was prone to recklessness. A page turned, and all fears and anxieties fell away. Her mind became sheer mountains and cliffs and the raging sea. This hunger awoke her even in the early hours of the morning, when the cold predawn light illuminated her room just enough. She would read with haste, turning the pages quietly, afraid to wake the household, and when the room turned golden, she'd feel full enough, just enough, to begin her day.

"How many copies did you manage to transcribe?"

Haewon glanced back at Wol. "Four."

"Only four copies in seven days? If you wish to make a respectable living from transcribing, you must work as quickly as my own scribes. They can complete four copies of a novel in a single day."

Haewon sighed. "Madam, your scribes needn't share a room with two sisters. Especially one like Yeonhee."

Wol let out a soft grunt as she pushed aside a reed veil, holding it as Haewon passed through. They entered a tiny transcription room where scribes worked tirelessly to mimic the printing press itself, the use of which was forbidden to any but the government. Once they were in the small, private adjoining room, Wol asked, "Do you still hide your work from your mother?"

"She knows," Haewon replied. "But every time I sit down to work, she calls me to help in the kitchen or insists I escort my sisters somewhere."

After setting the travel sack down on a table, she unwrapped five books, four of which were her painstaking transcriptions of Black Lotus's latest romantic adventure novel. She then stepped back to wait as Wol examined her work.

"You will keep transcribing, then?" Her friend adjusted her spectacles and flipped to the next page. "It's not easy work, as you have experienced. It will ruin your eyes and your posture in due time."

"And so will making embroideries and weaving mats to sell in the marketplace," Haewon countered, wandering over to the wall lined with narrow shelves. She brushed her fingers lightly over the spines of the books all requiring mending. "I make more transcribing books. I get to read as I do. You let Jade and Yeonhee borrow whichever books they like, and the only payment is that I transcribe a copy." Then with a little smile, she added, "It's not hard work to me. It feels rather like I'm carving a corner in my life. A small place where I am mistress over my own fate."

Like you, Haewon did not say aloud.

Wol was only a year her senior. She was the illegitimate daughter of a gisaeng who had amassed enough to pay off her debt and have her name removed from the gisaeng registry, regaining her commoner status. A few years before passing on to the next life, Wol's mother had married a wealthy merchant, whom Wol now called Father. The older girl, who claimed the freedom of a married woman without being married herself, had declared more than once to Haewon that she intended to devote herself to her first and only love: books.

"When you introduced me to novels," Haewon said softly, "I realized how small my world had been. There's so much more to life than what Mother and other ajummas talk about—marriage, childbearing, cooking . . ."

Wol shook her head. "Transcription work is also dangerous work."

"I know. But you once said so yourself, the authorities have long abandoned any real effort to enforce the ban. I want to believe that will not change, despite all the rumors."

"I told you that *last* spring. The edict was reinstated since then, and a ban is a ban. To go against His Majesty's wishes is . . . unthinkable to most. And yet, you still wish to transcribe?"

"I work under a pseudonym," Haewon reminded her friend. "What could possibly happen? Some archenemy, intent on my ruin, scours for my handwriting, uses it as evidence to uncover my identity?" She let out a soft, wry laugh. "Who would care to do that? I am but an inconsequential woman."

Wol snapped the books shut and set them aside. "If you insist, I will not deter you. Your writing is always neat, and the readers prefer your transcription work over that of other scribes." She set a stringed bundle of tarnished coins on the table next to Haewon. "One nyang for your hard work."

Haewon bit back a smile as she took it. Such a bounty could purchase a small luxury—a modest hairpin, perhaps, or a bit of fabric for new clothes. Her sisters would be so pleased with such a gift. It would be a welcome change from their relatives' castoffs.

"But most importantly," Wol added, "Black Lotus appreciates your transcription of her work. She says you make few errors, if any—" She frowned, then murmured, "That reminds me. I returned this morning from visiting Black Lotus."

Haewon shot her a glance. "You did? I remain astonished and greatly wounded that you know the identity of the author and yet refuse to tell me."

"Black Lotus made me vow secrecy, and I keep my word." Wol rolled her shoulders, massaging her right before continuing. "She has ignored every letter I've sent, so I went straight to her house and waited until she had no choice but to grant me an audience. It was as I feared. I, too, could not sway her—there will be no more books."

Haewon winced. "But . . . surely, with time, Black Lotus might change her mind."

"But will the readers wait for her?"

"*I* would wait. I could wait two, three years. Even a decade."

Wol laughed. "You would wait a decade?"

"I am a most devoted reader."

"Well, at least there will be you if Black Lotus ever decides to write the last volume." Wol riffled through a drawer full of papers, then set a small booklet before her. "Here, to cheer you up. You can make a copy of this book catalogue if you'd like."

Haewon gasped, delight rippling through her. These catalogues allowed her to have a comprehensive idea of what new books had been published. Such knowledge was why fellow readers sought her out for recommendations—and made her feel particularly useful. Every patron of Five Willows knew that Shin Haewon could share all of the best and recent trends.

"Where is this catalogue from?" Haewon asked, barely able to hide her glee.

"Our broker purchased it from a bookshop on Liulichang."

"Liulichang," Haewon whispered, a little wistfully.

Every Joseon reader knew of the famed bookselling district in the empire across the sea, Qing China's emporium of the most sought-after books.

"Make me a list if you see any books not yet widely known or introduced to Joseon," Mistress Wol said.

"Even at a glance I can tell you there will be over a hundred volumes to include."

"Then a hundred we will request. Last time I requested over a *thousand*. I can't make this shop survive on the popularity of a few local authors like Black Lotus. I split her manuscript into as many volumes as possible." Then to herself, she muttered, "Perhaps I ought to have waited until she actually wrote an ending . . ."

Haewon expelled a dramatic sigh. "Everyone is waiting for the tenth and final installment. They have no idea, do they? That they may have to wait a decade for the last volume, if it ever happens at all?"

Wol's lips thinned into a grim line. "I have readers hounding me daily. Those who've read the ninth volume always tell me they're in sheer torture. Some even lose appetite for days when I warn them that Black Lotus might never finish this series. I have an entire drawer reserved for all their letters begging Black Lotus to continue writing." Wol reached under her spectacles, rubbing her eyes. "I pity the readers. She never answers them, so I have stopped sending them. And I pity myself for the barrage of frustrated customers I must endure daily."

Haewon bit her lower lip, pushing a strand of hair behind her ear. Everyone knew that Black Lotus was secretive, even going so far as to order that her original manuscripts be destroyed once transcribed. Black Lotus had never responded to a reader.

None, that is, except Haewon.

Chapter 2

The chamber was quiet, save for the steady rustle of paper as Minister Yu reviewed a stack of letters spread across the low table before him.

Seojun tugged at the stiff collar of his robe, all too aware of the envelopes. Each one bore the name of a distinguished household, sent by parents of eligible daughters who inquired after his father's health and hinted at interest in a union between their families.

"You are a prime target in the marriage market," Minister Yu observed, his tone as solemn as a war strategist. "We must select your bride with care. Marriage is not merely a personal matter but the binding of two households, and of great consequence to our descendants."

"I understand, Father."

"Therefore, everything concerning your prospective bride and her family will be investigated. A focus will be placed on the moral behavior of your future in-laws. All family secrets must be uncovered."

The weight on Seojun's shoulders grew heavier, but he kept his posture rigidly upright.

"Matchmaker Okshi has interviewed each family, but most have failed to satisfy me," Minister Yu said with great condescension. "We cannot have you marrying into a family with any ties to the Southern faction, or with any roots in the Gwanseo region. And especially not one with daughters known to roam about the streets in broad daylight.

"There is, however, one family of note: The Minister of Rites has a daughter who is perfect in appearance, character, and position. She is said to be most superior to any other young lady. She has excellent needlework; she is skilled at meal preparation and managing a household. She is perfectly obedient, perfectly virtuous. And doesn't talk too much. A great sin in any woman," continued Minister Yu, who had been speaking since Seojun's arrival with barely a pause for breath. "She will bring honor to our household. When I die, you will inherit this entire estate and she will be a trustworthy mistress of it all."

Slight movement caught Seojun's eye. He glanced down and watched as an ant crawled across the silk of his robe, the gold-threaded floor mat, then across the immaculate floor. Alone, and entirely lost in the expanse.

"You are quiet, Son." Minister Yu's voice prodded his attention upward. "Speak. What is your opinion on this matter? You cannot reject every inquiry of interest."

Seojun tugged at his collar again. He couldn't tell his father what exactly was on his mind at the moment. The thought of marriage was merely another note on his growing list of obligations, and the lowest priority of all. His primary concern was his sister's happiness. As for his own . . . he had long ago put it aside.

"The opinion of children ought not to matter," his father barreled on. "I could very well choose a wife for you. Have I given you too much say and spoiled you? How long will you continue to turn the proposals down?"

"I would prefer to consider marriage after I pass the civil service exam—"

"That will take *years*, and I do not have the luxury of such time! My health has grown frail over the winter, and I wish to see a grandson before my death."

Seojun felt the collar of his robe tightening around his neck, and he glanced back at the ant, now traveling with quiet determination across the golden squares of sunlight. The shadow of a bird fluttered past.

"It is said that a son's foremost filial duty is to wed the bride chosen for him by his parents," Seojun said, voice low. Since birth he had been taught that filial piety was the root of all virtue. He could not simply wander wherever he wished. "I will meet with the Minister of Rites, if that is what you want."

"But that is not what *you* want," Minister Yu said, frustration edging his voice. He expelled a heavy breath and straightened his three-tiered hat of black gauze. "Return to your studies. I will write to the Minister of Rites regarding this matter."

Head bowed, Seojun retreated from his father's chamber. Once the servants drew the door shut, his rigid shoulders drooped. Attendants scurried away as he stalked down the hall, and he held his composure just long enough to unlock and enter his study.

He tried not to slam the sliding doors shut, then began to pace.

And pace.

What did it matter if he married now? Marriage was just like any other rite or ritual. It was simply another step in the ordered progression of life. And even if he married now, his bride would be no more than a guest in his house—a guest he would hardly ever see. He had passed the entrance exam for Sungkyunkwan Royal Academy in the first rank. He would enter the academy next month. And once enrolled, he would live there, only permitted to return home on the eighth and twenty-third days of each month.

He tugged at his tight collar once more, then sat before his low table, his heart thundering as he mindlessly flipped through the book he had to study. He had planned on finishing his review of the *Book of Documents* by the end of this month.

But he couldn't focus.

The words shifted under his eyes, took on wings, and flew away—

Close your mind to distraction, he reminded himself, having been disciplined to focus on his studies since the age of five. *Focus on the Way. On propriety, on structure and order, on pursuing virtue . . .*

His hand ached to pick up his brush and write stories instead. To wrestle with his thoughts on paper.

Against his better judgment, he found himself crossing the room to the red pinewood chest. He unlocked its small double doors and stared into the deep recess where his unfinished manuscript lay hidden alongside a stack of letters from Magpie. He had forced himself to abandon these pages for weeks. But now his hand reached, fingers hovering over the words he'd written.

Everything in him contracted with pain. He wanted to write. The desire was like a demonic possession, haunting every corner of his mind, leaving him restless and without appetite despite his every effort to resist. If he believed in shamans, he would have traveled to the farthest reaches of the kingdom for an exorcism, to eradicate the hunger before his secret ruined his entire family.

He shoved the chest shut, then fastened a lock through the metal ring.

Once the oppressive pull to write began, he knew focus would be impossible. He knew he would sit before his desk to study, but no matter his efforts, his attention would remain fixed upon the pinewood chest.

It was no use.

Seojun snatched up his hat and donned it, the long jade-beaded string bumping against his chest as he strode out of his study and locked the door behind him. He needed to escape. The walls themselves seemed to be closing in around him.

"Namgil-ah," he called out, and at once his young manservant scurried over from down the hall. "Bring me my horse."

"Where are you going, doryeonnim?"

"To the House of Bright Flowers."

"The gibang house?" Namgil's voice pitched high as they crossed the courtyard. "Did you not turn down the invitation for this evening, doryeonnim?"

Seojun's old friend Byeongho had finally returned from exile, the punishment his parents had imposed after he had failed the civil service exam yet again. Though illegitimate, he was a direct descendant of royalty and had been granted a rare exception to take the exam, a privilege most in his position were denied. But no matter how many times he took the test, he had failed. Now, with his father's passing and the mourning period over, Byeongho had wasted no time in summoning his friends to abandon their studies and join him at the entertainment house.

"It will be a small gathering," Seojun muttered, "and I am in desperate need of distraction."

"Begging your pardon, doryeonnim, but you look truly unwell. Perhaps you should rest today—"

"I am soon to be married."

"Oh." Namgil blinked, then scratched his head. "Well . . . I'm certain you will be very happy. And whom will I be addressing as mistress of Myeongwoldang one day, may I ask?"

"My father hopes it to be Mistress Deokkyung."

Namgil's brows shot high. "I have heard of her. Who has not, I suppose. They say she possesses a beauty so exquisite that flowers are made to feel ashamed."

"Indeed, so I have heard . . ." Seojun murmured. He'd spotted her in a palanquin three days ago, window open, her eyes peeking out at him. Their gazes had locked. A sheepish smile had curved her pink lips.

Mistress Deokkyung was, he supposed, quite beautiful. But in truth, darting silver-scaled fishes and the little wildflowers flourishing across the fields and forests moved him more. He had such a deep fondness for fishes and flowers.

I know the flowers by their names.

Sunlight slanted across the brim of his hat, blinding him for a moment. Words from Magpie's letters continued to beckon, words from the scribe whose friendship had embraced him in his darkest hour.

Forsythias, sansuyu, plum blossoms, pear blossoms, apricot flower, mugunghwa, the blossom from heaven . . .

He shook his head.

He had stopped writing to Magpie, just as he had to stop writing novels. He had to disassociate himself from what his father called "vulgar matters."

Running a hand down his face, Seojun stepped out of the compound, then gazed beyond the road at the sun illuminating the capital. The bright sky loomed large, empty and lonely. He remained lingering under the eaves of the mansion gate for a moment longer—until he looked down and was startled to find a stray mutt sitting by his feet, looking as lost as he in the vast city.

Seojun swept aside his robe and crouched by the creature, so thin with prominent ribs, white coat tangled and dirty. Gently, he reached out his hand, and the dog scampered closer. Its wet nose trailed his palm, tail wagging in frantic delight.

"Namgil-ah," he called out as his manservant approached, leading his horse. Seojun took the reins, then paused before mounting. "Find some scraps for this creature, then give him a good wash. Cleanliness and perfection is expected here at Myeongwoldang. Father tolerates nothing less."

As the very words left him, he felt an uneasiness coil deep within his chest, a troubling thought that kept him awake some nights.

What would his father do if he ever learned the truth, that Yu Seojun was Black Lotus?

Chapter 3

The Five Willows secret book-lending shop had become a second home not only to Haewon, but to many others. After leaving Mistress Wol's little workroom, she rejoined her sister and wandered the shelves, all the while observing the quiet hum around her.

Patrons of various ages flipped hungrily through pages of prohibited books by Joseon and Chinese writers, of Catholic literature and controversial history books. Most of the customers were men, many of whom were husbands or brothers sent by their female relations to borrow a book for them. But there were also a few bold girls, like the pair standing a few paces away, who came of their own accord, their maids wringing their skirts nervously, urging their mistresses to hurry.

"It isn't proper, this place! And these books . . ." Maid Boram pulled one from a stack, and her eyes widened as she stared down at the title: *The Tale of Lady Jeong and Her Forbidden Desires*. She nearly dropped it. "Good heavens! Who would dare *read* such lewd tales?"

Haewon suppressed a laugh. "Boram-ah. More than one *very* proper noble lady has ended up in financial ruin from borrowing novels such as these." Her smile dimmed as she glanced at Jade, whose eyes were pinned, unfocused, on the page of a book, as though her mind was somewhere adrift. Somewhere troubled.

"What is it?" Haewon asked, though she already suspected.

Her sister remained silent, gripping the book tight. She was not one to voice her troubles freely; she would rather bear them alone than burden others.

"Come." Haewon guided her sister deeper into the aisle, away from Maid Boram, who had picked up *The Tale of Lady Jeong and Her Forbidden Desires* again and was sheepishly flipping through it. "Tell me."

"It's nothing." Jade hesitated. "It's . . . it's silly."

"You're thinking about the marriage edict," Haewon whispered.

Jade's shoulders tensed. Of course, as Haewon had already guessed. It was why she had insisted on bringing her sister to the bookshop, to pry her away from their mother's fussing.

For months now, government officials had been making their rounds, interrogating unmarried men and women, compiling names. The decree had been announced last year: All unmarried men and women who had entered into spinsterhood—over twenty-nine years old for men, twenty-four for women—were required to wed. The order stretched across all five districts of Hanseongbu, and Jade had been named among 281 spinsters in the capital.

An edict on marriage, so soon followed by a ban on all forms of fiction writing . . . it was all too much.

Jade attempted a smile, her doe-like eyes lifting to meet Haewon's. "I oughtn't to be so distressed, I suppose. I still have one month to become betrothed." Her smile faltered. "And twenty days after that, I must marry, or Father will be punished."

Haewon racked her mind, searching for a way to comfort her sister.

"Villagers say the drought will end when all the spinsters are married," Jade went on softly. "Even the shamans claim it, and the government must think so, too. It is my duty to marry . . . But you see, Haewon-ah, I believe I have read one too many novels. Marriage determines the course of a woman's life, and I'll have little say in it. This is simply how it is and yet . . . I find myself terribly unhappy."

Helplessness sank into Haewon's stomach. Of the two of them, Jade was the romantic. She was the one who had picked up novels first, who had introduced Haewon to Wol and this bookshop, to this world of fiction where she could go anywhere, be anyone she wished to be. Jade was the one who had told her, in words that had left a deep impression: *Follow your heart . . . without breaking too many rules.*

She had no idea how to help her sister in this moment. She could not protest before the palace gates. She could not find for her sister a gentleman who might love and cherish her. She could do nothing . . . except one thing.

"Books are the best cure for a troubled heart," Haewon declared as she continued to browse, then stopped at *The Tale of Hong Gildong* and pulled it carefully from under a stack of other books. Like all volumes in circulation, the cover was wrapped in sambae, a sturdy hemp fabric. She flipped through the pages, oiled with sesame extract to keep them from tearing so easily, and ran her finger over the paper. "You should borrow this today. Everyone in Joseon has read it except you. Go bring it to Wol, and I'll transcribe it as payment as usual."

Jade looked at it hesitantly.

"I've spoken with other readers," Haewon said, pressing the book into her sister's hands. "They say this book makes them feel powerful no matter how hopeless their circumstances. Hong Gildong was an illegitimate child, forbidden even from calling his own father 'Father,' his fate determined before he had any say in it. It's a book about defying the impossible, about overcoming, no matter the odds. And there's magic, too, so fantastical—"

She stopped mid-sentence.

A finely dressed woman had stepped into view, garbed in a short and fitted pink jacket glimmering with flower prints, and a voluminous skirt of multilayered sheer red fabric. She was a gisaeng entertainer, recognizable by her large, conical bamboo jeonmo hat. A veil flowed from the wide brim, like black smoke that offered only glimpses of her red lips and a pair of disapproving eyes. "You are the Shin sisters," she said, her diction sharp and crisp. "I saw you last time by the creek."

Haewon blinked, then glanced uneasily at Jade.

"Yes, we were there," Jade said. They had gone to where gisaeng entertainers were bathing to retrieve their sister, Yeonhee, who had befriended many of them.

The gisaeng's red lips thinned. "I came to return a few books, and then I saw the pair of you. You are fortunate that I would even bother to stop and warn you. Yeonhee is at the gibang house. At the House of Bright Flowers."

Slowly, Haewon shook her head. "You must be mistaken."

"Wh-why"—Jade's voice wobbled—"why would Yeonhee be there—"

“She is there,” the gisaeng said, voice clipped. “And you have to retrieve her before she ruins your family’s name.”

Haewon felt weak at the knees. A woman’s reputation was as brittle as ice. One false step, and she could be plunged into the frigid depths, swept away into endless ruin.

And her entire family would drown in it.

Chapter 4

HAEWON HURRIED WITH ONLY ONE SHOE ON AND COULD NOT say when she had lost the other. Perhaps it had slipped off when she stumbled over a jutting stone in the road, or when she had veered off the path to take a quicker, alternate route, leading her maid and sister down a small hill and across a trickling stream.

But one shoe was gone, and quite frankly, she did not care.

"Your family is doomed," Maid Boram gasped, holding Jade's arm as they scurried down another path. "Do you remember Lord Yi Eun's family? There was a rumor of impropriety circulating—a mere *rumor*!—that his niece-in-law was seen flirting with men other than her husband, and *that* was enough for the family to do away with her. The men tied her up and tossed her into the river!" Boram quickly dabbed Jade's perspiring forehead with a handkerchief, then her own. "I *told* Yeonhee about this so many times. And yet still she decides to do something this reckless!"

As her maid spiraled, and as Jade grew paler from panic and exertion, Haewon tried to focus on her steps. As unbearable as her younger sister sometimes was, Yeonhee was family, and family was Haewon's entire world, the beating center of her being.

She could not let her family fall apart. She could not.

The House of Bright Flowers rose ahead of them, like a shroud of large, creamy-white magnolias in full bloom. In any other circumstance, she would have gazed in awe upon the majestic establishment, with its sturdy pine structure and flowing eaves, a beauty of lines that harmonized with the surrounding mountains and river. But all she felt was sheer terror as she strode around, surveying the area surrounding the walled compound.

That silly, *reckless* girl.

"What are we to do, agasshi?" Maid Boram cried. "Shall—shall I climb over the wall? S-search for her? Though, I do think I twisted my ankle a little—"

"She's our sister," Haewon whispered, her attention landing on a small gate where servants were passing in and out. "She's our sister, so she is our responsibility. You wait here, somewhere nearby."

"I—I—" Jade tried to catch her breath, still clinging to Boram's arm for support. "I will—go with you—too."

"No, I'll be quick. You both stay here in case . . ." Haewon searched her mind, anything to convince Jade not to follow. "In case Yeonhee comes out."

"Very well," Maid Boram blurted, tugging Jade toward a cluster of trees. "Be careful, agasshi!"

Haewon kept her veil low over her head. She didn't even know what to say as she approached the gate. But as it happened, no words were required. A few servants eyed her curiously but shuffled back to let her pass, mumbling, "Are you the new girl? Just head into the main house and ask for Madam Seolhwa."

Haewon passed through what seemed to be the servants' courtyard, which was connected to the next by a low gate, and the House of Bright Flowers opened before her in all its glory. It sprawled luxuriously across the courtyard, a vast wooden structure rising from a stone foundation, its latticed doors marching down the wooden terrace, each one a gateway into secrets exchanged between noblemen, whispers of clandestine dealings and conspiracies. It was an exclusive house a common man could only dream of entering. Here nobles intermingled with some of the most highly educated gisaeng, women known for their arts, for the ability to entertain, fan dance, and hold intellectual conversations. A world, a gilded cage, into which her sister had wandered.

A scuffle of hurried footsteps approached. Haewon quickly tucked herself behind a pillar and watched from the shadows as a posse of young women in colorful silk gowns appeared, fluttering their fans, whispering and giggling among themselves.

"I heard Lord Yu might come. The girls have placed a bet."

"A bet on what?"

"Winning a kiss from him."

Snickers ensued.

"I have a feeling he'd make an excellent kisser—"

"*Hurry*, the gentlemen will arrive soon!"

Their fragrance wafted by Haewon in a rush, like an armful of sweet-smelling flowers. Then they were gone and she was left in further panic.

The gentlemen will arrive soon . . .

The sun had begun its descent. A servant was already hurrying down the veranda, lighting floor lanterns. A wave of pressure and tense excitement charged the grounds as another crowd of girls hurried by with trays of liquor bottles, a rush of footsteps stormed down a hall, doors opened and slammed shut, and gisaengs warmed up their instruments, the earthy timbre of flutes trilling while someone pounded on the soribuk drum. In mere moments, the evening's revelry would begin: dancing, music, and drinking all night. Officials had likely abandoned their posts by now, moments away from spilling into this space. Once they arrived, it would be impossible to search discreetly.

Haewon hesitated for the barest moment, then hurried up the stone steps onto the veranda that wrapped around the establishment. She snuck through a back door and into the hall, which was blessedly empty. All she could hear was her own racing heartbeat and words that seemed to float on the melody of a distant gayageum being played.

Do not boast of your speed,
O blue-green stream running by the hills

She had never stepped foot in an entertainment house before, but she had read the poems written by famed gisaeng entertainers. Words always soothed her, and more than anything now, she needed to be calm. She knew, from observing her mother, that rarely could any good decision be made when one's emotions were running high.

Once you have reached the wide ocean,
You can return no more.
Why not stay here and rest,
When moonlight stuffs the empty hills?

She tucked the veil tighter around her face and paused before each hanji-screened door, which were thin enough for her to hear any murmurings within. But there was nobody. She pressed onward, cold perspiration clinging to her back. Then, at the farthest door, she heard a snort followed by a muffled giggle.

"He has read the *Seonggyoyoji,* too, and he frequents bookshops as well! Our minds are so alike it is incredible!" came the whisper of a familiar voice, followed by more giggles. "We are both passionate, curious, and unafraid. He is as fascinated by Western teachings as I am. He says, 'The more unorthodox it is'"—the girl's voice lowered in mimicry—"'the more intrigued I am.'"

Haewon bit her lower lip as she inspected the hall, reining in her anger, her outrage. She gripped the brass handle so tight her knuckles ached, then slid the door open and entered. Yeonhee and a gisaeng entertainer were before a low table, staring at her over a drinking bowl filled with liquor.

With deadly quietude, Haewon said, "Put the wine bottle down. We are leaving at once."

Haewon then shot the gisaeng a glance, and it took a moment for recognition to dawn—it was Yeonhee's childhood friend Jongbi, who had been sold to the gibang house. The news had shaken Gyonam Village for months, and the parents had since then been all but shunned. "We must not be seen or recognized," she said, less sharply this time. A lump of sadness had formed in her chest. "You will not say another word and follow me—"

"We can't leave yet—I promised we'd wait for Lady Sunghyun," Yeonhee cried. "She promised to tell us more about the teachings from the West; it claims all people are equal. Equal! Can you imagine that? Apparently in Catholic gatherings, men and women sit *together*! They believe that the highest noble to the lowliest servant are all equal in the eyes of the Heavenly Father. Of course, I don't believe in this Heavenly Father, but imagine such a life! A life in which we are free to live like men!"

Haewon heaved out a breath, then shook her head. "Right now is not the time or place to be discussing reform. We need to go."

"There are gisaengs who have attended these gatherings," Yeonhee chattered on, "and I need to hear more. Don't you see how important this is? It's for all those girls in our village that we tutor, who live with their eyes downcast, who believe that the sole purpose of their existence is to marry and bear sons—!"

"And make it their sole purpose to worship this Heavenly Father from the West instead? Foolishness. Come, *now*. If you don't, you'll be ruined. Our whole family will be ruined."

"Aigoo, Older Sister." Yeonhee waved her hand, her breath reeking of rice wine. "There is no need to be so dour."

"Perhaps you should listen to your elder sister," Jongbi nudged.

Finally Yeonhee staggered up to her feet. Then she swayed, tripped, and before Haewon could reach her, went stumbling to the floor, and there she remained. "Oh . . ." Yeonhee blinked, looking dazed. "I think I drank a little too much."

Anger returned with violence, boiling under her ribs, threatening to spill over. Haewon tried to hold it in, but it came steaming out through the cracks in her composure. "What is the *matter* with you?" she hissed through clenched teeth.

She grabbed her sister by the arm and tried to drag her to

her feet—then her stomach leapt at the sound of approaching footsteps.

Firm, heavy footsteps.

And more than one pair.

Swiftly she hoisted the inebriated girl onto her back, securing her arms around her sister's legs as she stood up.

"Let's go," Haewon ordered, casting frantic glances at the door. Whoever was in the hallway could pass them by, but it was a risk she couldn't take. "*Quick.*"

They hurried toward the window, which the gisaeng cracked open and climbed through first. Haewon shoved Yeonhee out to her, her sister landing in the grass with an undignified thump.

Then Jongbi cried, "Your sister's veil!"

"She must go without—" Haewon paused. Words from a ladies' etiquette manual prickled at the back of her mind: *A girl without her veil invites ruin.* "Very well, I'll get it. You help my sister hide, and ensure that no one sees her."

Haewon rushed around the room, her heart beating in quick, painful stabs. Finally the bright green silk snared her attention. Her sister's veil was on the floor by a folding screen, and she had left her money pouch there, too. Haewon grabbed both, then froze as the doors slid open.

She lunged behind the folding screen, squeezing into the shadows.

A second passed.

Then two.

Then an eternity.

It was a party of men in conversation, voices muffled under the roar of panic in Haewon's ears. As her heartbeat slowed, the pounding in her ears eased, and she was able to hear bits and pieces.

"This small gathering has turned into a rather large one... Lord Yu looks absolutely displeased... I didn't think everyone would come... No, I didn't intend for this to be a literary gathering like old times, but you all have brought your books! Except Lord Yu... He is positively glowering. Ha!"

Haewon listened, heard the clinking of wine bottles, the gisaeng entertainers joining the conversation. She was too focused on devising an escape plan to listen, until a familiar name was mentioned.

"Everyone is talking about the ban being reinforced," one gentleman said. "Did you hear King Jeongjo's criticism of Black Lotus?"

Haewon straightened.

"That is old news. The author's works have become so well loved among the populace that the king has designated Black Lotus as the newest culprit behind the corruption of the writing culture," another gentleman replied. "If I recall correctly, His Majesty said Black Lotus's work was 'rough, coarse, and inelegant.'"

Haewon knew the rest, criticism she'd perhaps taken too personally. *The whole book is more suited to heathens than to intelligent, respectable people.* She waited to hear the opinions of those beyond her hiding place. If they were in agreement with the king, then she was hiding from not only strangers, but strangers she loathed.

"Some say," another scratchy voice chimed in, "it was the king's distaste for the writings of those like Black Lotus and Yeonam that led to the reinforcement of the edict in the first place."

"No, no," came a fourth voice. "I heard it was because ancestral tablets were broken by Catholics a few months ago. That's what sparked it. You know the fear—that there's Western teachings hidden in the pages of novels. And as fear grows in the government, the laws will grow harsher, too. And Black Lotus's works do have a rather unorthodox streak to them, don't you think?"

"Oh, quite unorthodox!" a high-pitched male voice replied. "You can sense the author's curiosity regarding Western ideas, but I never once sensed anti-Confucian or anti-state sentiments in his work—"

"You refer to Black Lotus as a man," someone noted. "Do you really think the author is a man? There are so many conflicting rumors."

As the men discussed, Haewon wished she could join the conversation. Most female patrons she'd spoken with were convinced that Black Lotus was a woman, and they all quoted the same line from Black Lotus's fifth volume as evidence: *Give her a novel, a window to look out, for the walls that hide her are too high to scale.* No man could write with such understanding.

"*I* have no interest in Black Lotus's identity," another gentleman brightly declared. "I like to read without seeking a thorough understanding. I read merely out of habit. So whether Black Lotus is a man or woman, I have no thoughts on this matter."

"How like you, Young Master Byeongho," someone said. "You have no thoughts on most matters."

Chuckles arose.

"I am, however," continued this gentleman named Byeongho, "very curious to know what Lord Yu must be thinking so quietly in his corner. Tell us. What are your thoughts on Black Lotus?"

Silence fell.

A silence so complete, accentuated by a rumble of laughter in the next chamber.

Everyone, it seemed, was holding their breath.

She *had* to look.

Haewon shifted, ever so slightly, to peer through a hole in the folding screen. Others before her must have hidden here to spy—on what, she didn't wish to know. She followed the direction of the stares, and her attention settled on a lone figure standing near the latticed window—the same one she had shoved Yeonhee out of. The setting sun cast deep shadows across his sculpted, imperious face and silhouetted his graceful figure. He was tall and had broad, well-shaped shoulders that no scholar had any business possessing.

Lord Yu finally glanced over his shoulder. "My thoughts?"

His voice sent a little shiver down her spine, so low and rich, threaded with a husky warmth. But the strange sensation she felt vanished as he spoke on.

"The writings of Black Lotus, and those like him, are stories we enjoyed in our youth. Writing we ought to grow out of. Novels like the works of Black Lotus are anti-ideology; they stir up one's emotions, make us change our thoughts and beliefs. Black Lotus's works, in particular, are more frivolous adventures than they are stories with moral lessons behind them. His Majesty realized this; he recognizes the danger in such unorthodox books and knew it would make us stray from the Confucian way."

Her ears burned. Irritation flared, hot smoke curling in her chest. And she resented how silent the party remained.

"You all ought to exercise more caution," Lord Yu went on. "It is reckless, gathering here to discuss forbidden novels. I've heard that the king has already dismissed five officials who were caught reading the like."

"It is why we are gathered *here*," a gentleman countered nervously. "A house of secrets."

"And do you truly believe secrets remain so?" Lord Yu turned to stare out the window again, as though thoroughly unimpressed by his company. "If you continue to read writings by literary rebels, the king will inevitably find out."

Haewon held back a scoff. She had never heard anyone speak like this, going on and on despite the great discomfort of others. With such frankness, so little worry about offending. He must be rich and powerful, for she noticed such people tended to be very blunt. They never needed to accommodate the feelings of others.

So caught up in outrage, as though Lord Yu had offended *her* personally, Haewon didn't notice the passing of time—until she heard, somewhere outside, a loud hiccup followed by her sister calling out for her. "*Eonniiiiii?* Where *are* you?"

Haewon clamped her hands over her mouth. She had moved ever so carefully, her knuckles only just barely brushing up against the screen. But as though she had kicked the screen down, Lord Yu turned to stare in her direction.

Her eyes widened as he wandered over to the side of the room, close to the back where the folding screen stood. Standing where he could fully see her.

And he was staring directly at her.

Chapter 5

Little in life surprised Seojun.

His days followed a monotonous rhythm, each one blending into the next, like an endless, unchanging landscape. But when he found the girl hiding behind the folding screen, wide-eyed and ghostly pale, a jolt of shock struck him. Like the time he'd been thrown from his horse, slammed to the ground, winded and breathless. One could never brace for such moments.

"What are you doing there, Seojun?" Byeongho called out.

Seojun regained his composure. There was utter terror in the eyes of the girl before him. A look he had witnessed before in his own sister.

"Nothing," Seojun replied, moving away from her. "Nothing at all."

He tried to ignore her as he stared blankly out the window, though his attention kept slipping back to the screen. Why was she hiding? Surely there were only two reasons for anyone to hide: She was either seeking safety, or spying.

A moment passed by. Tension locked his shoulders, his every limb.

He could try ignoring her; it would be far simpler to do so . . . but he had never mastered the art of looking away, of brushing aside matters that bothered him. And she very much bothered him. He was much too aware of her—he could sense her anxiety burning through the screen.

Seojun ran a hand down his face and glanced around at his peers, who were lost in an impassioned debate about whether the printing quality of Joseon or Qing books was superior.

"Books made in Joseon are heavier compared to books from Qing," Byeongho observed, flourishing his fan. "One really can't lie down and read, and we're forced to sit upright. Some of you argue that such a posture makes you more moral, but heavens, I should *love* to read while lying down—"

"Gentlemen," Seojun murmured.

The chatter stopped at once and all eyes turned to him.

"The weather is pleasant today," he continued calmly, wearing his mask of perfect indifference. He cast a quick glance at the screen, which he swore had trembled again. "Let us move the discussion out to the pavilion. Byeongho, didn't you mention earlier that you fancied some music and poetry reading outdoors?"

"Yes . . ." Byeongho idly aired himself with his fan. "I meant in the summer—"

"The day is fine. Let us all proceed outside."

The young gentlemen exchanged glances and peered past him out the window. They seemed to be simultaneously observing the stray blossoms on otherwise bare branches, trembling in the chilly gust of wind. But one did not disregard a member of the Munhwa Yu clan, the son of a leading Noron faction leader. To disagree with him was unwise; to argue, unthinkable.

Everyone exited the chamber.

Seojun strode out, feeling the woman's gaze still prickling

his back. He didn't understand why he was assisting her, but he couldn't dislodge the thought of his sister from his mind, similarly hiding in the women's quarter for a second year straight, too afraid to face the unkind world.

Or perhaps the girl in hiding wasn't even a woman.

"Perhaps it was a dokkaebi," Seojun muttered under his breath as the doors slid shut, "playing tricks on me."

"What's that?" Byeongho replied, then added with a good-natured grin, "You've only said ten words since your scolding. Did you just utter your eleventh?"

Seojun couldn't form a response, still too disoriented. For a moment, he considered returning home, but his manservant—who had joined him here after feeding and washing the mutt as requested—was nowhere to be found. It occurred to him, too, that if he left the House of Bright Flowers now, he would only be met by his father's lectures on his return home.

Abandoning his party at the pavilion, Seojun wandered past the lantern-lit courtyard and out into the garden, where shadows had deepened as purple clouds drifted across the brilliant fuchsia sky. Flowers perfumed the air, and the sound of music and laughter faded into the back of his mind as his gaze strayed over to the open window. It was the one he'd stared out of moments ago, while his acquaintances had discussed forbidden books. He froze as realization dawned on him: The girl had heard everything.

If she repeated what she knew . . .

You are too fearful, Byeongho would have insisted, brushing aside any concern with a wave of his fan. *The censorship was reinforced two times already, and the police never bothered once to raid a single shop!*

But Byeongho didn't understand. Times had changed, and Seojun had sensed a new, growing fervor in the royal court that was determined to root out all subversive thinking.

While Seojun held no official position himself, his father was the Minister of Justice—not directly in charge of censorship, but the one who determined punishments. And his father's acquaintances often stopped him in the street for idle conversation, uncaring of how much they let slip.

Such as how the king would not be so forgiving this time.

His Majesty believes that to eliminate unorthodox teachings, one such official had shared with him, *we must first eliminate trivial literature.*

What disturbed Seojun most was all the uncertainty. Not one reader or writer knew if the threat was real, if the punishments would truly be harsh.

Some, like Mistress Wol of Five Willows, had taken every precaution at Seojun's warning—keeping her secret book-lending shop hidden, allowing only trusted patrons through. Then there were Byeongho's friends at the House of Bright Flowers, speaking freely of novels and the ban, convinced the government wouldn't be able to control the situation even if the king did forbid fictional writing.

But history, he knew, repeated itself. And the last wave of censorship under the previous ruler, King Yeongjo, had been a bloody one.

Seojun gripped his hands tight behind his back, walking the

grounds, hoping to outpace the building sense that calamity loomed in Joseon's future. That the ban on fictional writing was a signal for worse things to come—

His thoughts stilled.

Light, quick footsteps sounded from across the garden, and when he looked, he spotted a stray figure hurrying through the shadows. And to his horror, he realized she was coming straight toward him.

He took a hesitant step back but she was before him too soon, her features illuminated by the light of the pink sky. There was nothing extraordinary about her. She had a straight nose, thin lips, and a pair of ordinary brown eyes in an angular face. She was very common looking, passably pretty at most.

"Thank you, nauri." The stench of liquor rose from her clothes.

He held back a grimace and took a swift measure of her. By her veil and the silk of her dress, she was either a gisaeng or a lady—he assumed the latter. No gisaeng would wear a castoff with ink-stained cuffs, an outdated jeogori jacket, and a hem worn thin. It was indeed a rare sight, finding a respectable woman in a gibang house, but not unheard of.

"You were the girl in hiding," Seojun observed.

"I was." She dipped her head. "Thank you for assisting me."

"There's no need to thank me. It seemed a predicament of your own making."

A muscle twitched in her jaw, but she kept her lashes lowered, gaze fixed on the ground. "It wasn't of my own making. But thank you nevertheless." She shifted, about to take her leave.

"There were voices outside the window earlier. Your sister,

I presume," he said coolly, watching as the line of her shoulders tensed. "Did you bring her here?"

She didn't answer, but he saw a flicker of hesitation. He pressed on. "It is your duty to keep your younger sister from falling into such impropriety. Instead, you've encouraged her. Allowed her to indulge in a place where no respectable woman would venture—"

"I am a complete stranger to you, and yet you speak very plainly," she said, her face flushed, her jaw tightened. And then—much to his astonishment—she looked up. Her eyes lit with a glint of steel, and a smile tugged at the corners of her lips. "But let me assure you, nauri, that protecting my sisters has been my duty for eighteen years." She tilted her head a little. "I was also taught never to shrink from defending myself when wronged. And you, nauri, are very wrong about me indeed."

She turned on her heel, walking too sharply for someone who was intoxicated. Perhaps she hadn't been drinking after all.

Just as he opened his mouth to summon her back—he had more questions—she stopped and whirled around.

"Oh, and one more thing, nauri," she said. "You claimed that Black Lotus and those like her will not be remembered by the ages."

He felt ice trickle through his blood at the mention of Black Lotus. Of *himself*. A pseudonym he'd thought of while staring outside his study room, watching lotuses bloom from dark, muddy waters. "I did . . ." he managed to say.

"Well, I beg to differ."

He feigned a look of indifference, even managing to arch a brow. "You beg to differ?"

"Black Lotus's work speaks to justice and social reform. It is *not* frivolous—"

"So you are a reader of forbidden novels, too," he murmured, glancing around to ensure that they were alone. He dropped his voice low, his words for her ears alone. "His writings are of a most unremarkable quality. Any attempt at conveying something meaningful is buried under vulgar tales about nothing of real importance."

"Very well, you say her books are completely frivolous," she whispered. "I suppose they are, in that sense."

Her admission stung. "See, you admit it, too—"

"And they are awe-inspiring, beautiful, and"—her voice trembled—"and they bring me such *joy*!"

Everything in him quieted at those words, and the way she had spoken them. The deep love, the reverence. She spoke with a passion that could set the stars ablaze.

"Perhaps history will not remember Black Lotus. But *I* will remember her."

Seojun never lost his composure, yet he felt his grip slipping. His voice rasped slightly as he said, "I'm not sure you ought to be declaring in public that you are a reader of such books."

She cast him a disdainful glance. "Everyone reads novels these days." Her eyes glittered in the skylight, like stars on a darkened sea. And then she mumbled under her breath, so quietly he was certain the words weren't meant for his ears, "Only the miserable sort does not."

He didn't know whether to laugh or scowl as she stalked off, shoulders straight, bearing an aura of a most proper young lady. It was then that he noticed one of her shoes was missing, her socked foot stained with blood. Then he noticed the bundle of a second veil, which, he realized, she had been clutching behind the screen. She must have remained to retrieve it for her sister, who had fled.

This young woman had not come for entertainment. She had run here, so fast that not even a missing shoe had caught her notice.

He discreetly moved to the little side gate, staring out at the open road cloaked in the growing darkness. He watched as she joined three other women. The veils shrouding the girls fluttered, like an illusion that hid the mischievous spirits underneath.

And then they were gone.

He had a feeling she would never forgive him for that slander, but that was of no significance. He doubted they would ever meet again.

Chapter 6

SEOJUN FOUND HIMSELF IN A STRANGE MOOD AFTER THE goblin-girl's departure.

He tried not to think of her, but his thoughts kept straying. His writing had brought her joy, a remark that had induced the most unsettling sensation in him. Was it simply enough for one's writing to bring delight? To lighten the burden of another for a moment's time?

No. He forbade himself from indulging in such thoughts. He would keep his vow, to never again pick up the brush to write fiction. The written word was meant to increase morality—that was what his elders had taught him. One's writing was meant to preserve the worldview embedded in classical Confucian literature. Yet no matter his painstaking efforts, Seojun found that nothing he wrote could ever emulate the classics, nor capture the exquisite stories that called to him. His work was a mere glimpse, a shallow imitation, a constant reminder that his writing had fallen short. That *he* was inadequate.

The king had spoken the truth. The works of Black Lotus were indeed "rough, coarse, and inelegant." His work was vulgar. Seojun was unaccustomed to such humiliation, and reluctant to stray any further from the Way.

"My lord!"

Seojun tensed, pausing on his way back inside the House of Bright Flowers. When he looked to see who had accosted him, his irritation sharpened.

Inspector Wuyeong was a man of a slight, spidery frame, with a perpetual smile pinned onto his hollow-cheeked face. A smile born from a groveling habit.

"My lord." Wuyeong wove through the crowded courtyard and bowed, swift and all too low, with a reverence that seemed excessive. "It has been some time since we last crossed paths. I have heard much of you since then. There is no family in all of Hanyang who does not speak of your virtues."

"And my father never tires," Seojun said dryly, "of praising your unwavering devotion to righteousness."

Wuyeong's face lit up. "He is too kind. Truly I do not deserve such high praise! But I shall do my utmost to one day be worthy of such exaltation, and treasure his words as I continue to execute my present duties—which, I might add, is the *very* morally significant task of investigating into the distribution of illegal novels."

"Indeed?"

"You will, I trust, agree with me when I say that diligence is of utmost importance in our effort to repress prohibited books. The underground literary market, my lord, is vast and complex, and every day the number of book peddlers and bookshop owners multiplies," Wuyeong explained with great eagerness. "Everyone wants to read such unorthodox books these days. Novels that hide dangerous ideas that, inevitably, lead young people to criticize elders and disregard moral law! Indeed, I am sure you would not deign to read such filth."

Oblivious to Seojun's growing coldness, Wuyeong chattered on, as though meaning to impress him. "And in my effort to put an end to novels, I've already discovered the true identities of two of the most popular authors."

Seojun frowned. "Which ones?"

"Munmuja is Yi Ok—some lowly scholar you wouldn't know. And the other author, Yeonam, is the pseudonym for Pak Chiwŏn. Your father knows him and was greatly shocked by this news."

A muscle worked in Seojun's jaw. "And . . ." he said with a measured tone, "who is next on your list?"

"Dongim, for one." Wuyeong's lips twisted. "His lewd literature is popular among wives, so much so that I might argue these readers are committing adultery in their hearts. And, of course, others. Chojeong, Black Lotus, and the like."

Seojun was not surprised. His father, who knew nothing of his son's own writing, had said as much in passing. He'd simply wished he had misheard.

"Well," Seojun said, keeping his voice mild and even, "I wish you all the luck in your endeavors."

After a few more moments of painful pleasantry, both gentlemen exchanged bows, and Seojun finally managed to extricate himself. But his relief was short-lived as he maneuvered himself through the large crowd, a gathering of the wealthiest and most powerful men in Hanyang. Such men flaunted their superiority by their dress, their manner, and their glittering gisaeng companions. The spectacle was overwhelming, and Seojun could not take more than a few steps through the mass before someone would stop him for a shallow conversation. Though he did not intend to scare them off, his silence did so.

He felt drained and miserable by the time he retreated to the private room, only to witness the agitating sight of novels abandoned on the table by Byeongho's friends. It was like leaving stolen goods in plain sight for a police raid to find.

After collecting them all, Seojun stacked the books behind the screen, into two low towers. He hesitated before a familiar title. *Yeolhailgi.*

With his vow to never write fiction again, he'd sworn off reading it as well, for he'd always been one to try to follow the rules. He had managed to resist for months, but to love something one ought not to love so desperately . . . it hurt. Like a wound festering within him, a love that had come to feel more like self-loathing. But the brief encounter with the inspector made Seojun pick up the novel out of spite and open it.

The scent of old pages rose to greet him, stale and earthy. A few more pages whispered, and his world disappeared.

The worries, the irritations, the overbearing presence of others, they all disappeared. He was still there, in a chamber filled with the echoes of distant laughter and music, but his mind could slip away. It was his favorite book, written by one of the very authors whom Wuyeong had so proudly targeted.

Seojun slipped to the section titled "Dogangnok."

He read as the author Yeonam traveled beyond the borders of Joseon, explored Qing, and arrived before an open field, the type of which could never be seen in his homeland. Seojun became Yeonam, followed his gaze across the fields of Liaodong, seeing the

rising, straightening his collar. "I would have left, and you wouldn't have had to wait on me all this time."

"According to the servants, you haven't been sleeping well of late, and so I didn't wish to wake you. Besides," he said, his eyes lifting slightly before skittering away. "There was much on my mind."

Seojun sighed. "There seems to be much on both our minds these days."

"Doryeonnim, if there is any way that I can ease your concerns," Namgil said, more eagerly than usual, "you must say it. Is it the marriage you are worried about?"

Seojun stepped around his peers, strode down the corridor, then walked out into the quiet morning, the air chill and moist with the scent of the dew-dampened earth.

"It must be so," Namgil pondered aloud, still continuing with his earlier line of conversation. "The thought of marriage must indeed be weighing upon you, but I wouldn't worry, doryeonnim. You will fall in love and find that love is—" Namgil expelled a little sigh. "Love is so sweet, and she will become your entire world. You'll want to do *anything* to keep her happy."

"You know something about love?" Seojun raised a brow at the manservant, who was his equal in age. "You never told me you had a sweetheart. Do I know her?"

Namgil turned red. "I am but a lowly servant. I dare not bother you with—"

"You know I've always liked your stories."

Namgil let out a nervous laugh but spoke no more. With nothing to distract his thoughts, Seojun felt his shoulders grow heavier as they traveled back to Myeongwoldang. The residence was as silent as a casket, the hush deep and undisturbed as he strode through the interconnected courtyards. Only a few servants were awake, pausing in their tasks to bow as he passed. His father had likely already departed for the Ministry of Justice, where he would remain until evening.

As for his sister . . . she had long since lost track of time. Days blended into nights, nights into days; she woke when the household slept and slept when they woke. The mere thought of her weighed on him further.

"Find out for me if my sister has finished reading all her novels," Seojun said as he approached his study. "I'll borrow more if that is the case—"

He froze.

The lock usually fastened on the handles of his study room's double door dangled. It was hanging open.

Impossible—he was certain he had secured the door. He never left his home without ensuring that this entrance was locked.

At a sudden movement, he shot a glance toward a pillar, and recognized the figure trembling in its shadow: his sister's personal attendant.

"Maid Daebi," he called out, keeping his voice calm.

She stepped forward, and he studied the girl, wondering what she was doing lurking about the men's courtyard. Suspicion flitted through him as he glanced back at his door. Was she a thief? But what was there to steal? A maid would do better raiding her mistress's chamber, full of trinkets and silk, than his own, used only to study for his exam.

"What are you doing here at this hour?" he inquired.

"Mistress Gwideok couldn't sleep." She offered a nervous smile, revealing the gap between her two front teeth. "S-so she sent me out to find a b-b-book for her to read . . ."

"And you entered my study?"

She flinched as though he'd struck her. "No!" she cried. "Oh, I wouldn't dare, doryeonnim. I came to see if you were awake; you always have books to lend to Mistress Gwideok. But then I saw the lock hanging open like that and became afraid."

Seojun studied the maid, who was growing paler under his scrutiny. Beads of sweat dampened her brow. She had her hands held behind her back, not politely before her.

"May I see your hands?" he requested.

"Of—of course, doryeonnim." She hesitated, then stretched to hold her palms out before her.

"Turn your hands around."

She did so. Darkness lined the crescents of her nails. Then he noticed the dirt on her sandals and on the hem of her skirt, and a trail of it down the veranda and across the courtyard. His curiosity piqued, he followed the trace of dirt, the two servants scurrying behind him.

"What is it, doryeonnim?" Namgil asked. "What is the matter?"

"I heard . . ." Seojun observed how the trace of dirt led to a bed of crushed flowers, and took note of the scuff marks along the wall. "I heard that Housekeeper Myeongsu is militant when it comes to cleanliness."

"Sh-she is, doryeonnim," Maid Daebi replied, her voice shaking.

"Then how is it your nails are lined in dirt?"

"I was cleaning spring greens."

"This early in the morning?"

"I was cleaning it last night, then—then accidentally fell asleep."

"Indeed? And why would the personal maid of my sister be made to clean spring greens?"

Splotches of red stained her cheeks. "Kitchen Maid Aji is my dearest friend, she was overwhelmed with work, so I offered to help—"

"There is dirt in your nails," Seojun bit out. "Dirt across the courtyard. And someone has broken into my study."

"Perhaps, doryeonnim," his manservant said cautiously, "perhaps you simply forgot to secure the lock. And as for the dirt, perhaps . . . perhaps it was the stray mutt you asked that I bring inside."

Seojun frowned. He had never forgotten to secure his door before. "Perhaps you are right . . ." He wrestled with this possibility for a moment longer, but an uneasiness settled in his bones. He turned to the maid once more. "Did you hear or see anything while in the kitchen?"

Her delicate brows knitted together. "I did briefly wake up to sounds of a clatter and a thud. But then I heard nothing more after that."

"And at what time was this?" he asked firmly. "What time did you hear this 'clatter and thud'?"

"I—I can't be too sure. But it was shortly before the great bell rang at dawn."

Only moments before his arrival . . .

After dismissing the maid, he returned to his study and stared down at the lock. Absentmindedly, he reached for his keys only to find them missing.

His blood went cold.

The keys he carried everywhere. The keys no servant ever touched. The keys that remained on his person at all times, except when he slept, and then he kept them hidden under the false bottom of a document box.

He pulled the lock free from the handle, slid the door open, and stepped inside.

His study appeared as though a storm had blown through. Scattered papers littered the floor, bookshelves stripped of their contents, heavy volumes cast aside. A pale porcelain jar rested on the floor, miraculously unbroken. And the second lock—the one securing his red pinewood chest—also hung open.

He stared at it with incredulity.

Two locks. Both undone. It was impossible—he could think of no other way to describe this circumstance, but that it was, truly, *impossible.* His locks were turtle locks, their hard shells a symbol of their impenetrability; there was a reason why they were referred to as "secret locks." Each held riddles that had to be solved before they could be opened, a multilayered series of tumblers, latches, and pins, each requiring precise manipulation.

The thief would have had to know exactly what to do.

His pulse pounded. He forced himself forward and tugged open the small double doors of the red pinewood chest.

Shock carved a hollow into his chest.

His entire manuscript was missing.

Chapter 7

By early afternoon, Haewon came to the conclusion that worrying would not solve the conundrum in which Yeonhee had placed their family. Grabbing her veil off the hook, Haewon stepped out of the house and slipped her feet into her sandals.

"We are ruined!" her mother's shrill voice rang, echoing through the open windows of their humble abode. "If rumors spread, their chances of marriage will all be ruined! My dear husband, what, tell me, what am I to do with three unmarried daughters? Every family gathering, your brothers and sisters scold me so for raising such unruly girls! And if they learn of *this* incident? Oh, simply thinking of how cruel and mean they will be to us! My poor heart—it is already difficult to breathe!"

Her mother hadn't stopped wailing over the gibang-house incident since their return the night before, and chastising Jade for not keeping a closer watch on Yeonhee. When Jade, holding back her tears, had fled the house, Mistress Myeongok had turned her wrath onto Haewon. But now, her father had returned from his walk and he had become the newest target of her scolding.

"You *must* speak to Yeonhee," Mother called after her husband, following him in and out of his study, down the hall, and around the house. "She ought to be rebuked!"

"Yeobo," came her father's voice, as tranquil as ever, "I fear that my powers of rebuke have long since been exhausted by Yeonhee's recklessness."

"But our daughters' reputations, *your* reputation, is at stake! What is the point of studying for the civil service exam, when the lives of your girls are in shambles? Did you not hear what Yeonhee said? She shared with me a most shocking account, thinking it quite *funny*. Are you listening? She said that Lord Yu—*the* Lord Yu Seojun!—was witness to this embarrassing affair! And his family is close to royalty—that is what all the villagers say! One word from him, and everyone will be whispering. Scandalmongers will delight in this gossip, and soon all of Joseon will know of Yeonhee's indiscretion!" Mother declared all in one breath. "You will soon die from old age, and I from a broken heart. How will our girls fend for themselves when we are gone?"

"Everything will work out in the end. It always does," Father continued in his usual, unperturbed manner. "Besides, I've always believed that you have a special talent for managing our silly daughters and their . . . adventures. I will trust your wisdom in dealing with this matter."

Haewon couldn't stand to hear any more. She hated how helpless it all made her feel.

Catching up her skirt, she quickened her steps, and soon she was running, her heels striking hard across the dirt road. *Do not run*, she could hear Maid Boram's phantom voice. *It is unladylike to run!* Haewon ran faster, for if she did not run, she feared she would cry from frustration.

There were too many rules a woman had to live by. Too many strings attached to her—her mind, her heart, her very soul—forever pulling and pulling at her. It was all horribly unfair. Lord Yu and his ilk entered the House of Bright Flowers as they pleased, while Yeonhee only snuck in under the cover of her silk veil, and her mother had spent the entire day weeping as though the world were about to fall apart. Because if word spread, their world *would* fall apart.

Haewon ran until her skirt was coated in dust, her chest heaving for air, needles shooting through her lungs with each breath. Her mouth felt dry and her face was flushed, but she refused to cry. Whenever she did, her eyes puffed red; Jade would see and the burden in her heart would double.

Wiping her brow, Haewon made her way up the slope. As she'd expected, she found Jade sitting on the hill overlooking a stream, the hill they'd always retreated to whenever they wished to escape the house.

"Eonni," Haewon called out breathlessly. She collapsed onto the grass next to her older sister. "I knew I'd find you here."

Jade sat with her knees drawn up, watching the women below. A small crowd of them chattered as they rolled and pounded their laundry in the shrunken stream, its waters thin and slow from the drought. Nearby, Yeonhee swung carelessly on a creaking geunettwigi swing, her voice carrying over the breeze as she ordered Maid Boram to push faster.

"I don't know how Yeonhee laughs like that, so unworried," Haewon remarked. "She's convinced the rumors won't spread. She says hardly anyone saw her at the House of Bright Flowers."

Jade didn't respond. She always responded.

Peeking at her sister's face, Haewon frowned. "You look miserable. What is it?"

Jade remained quiet for a moment longer. Then, softly, she said, "When the government official visited last week, he said that when a woman lives a moral life, word spreads about her, as word might spread about precious gems, and it would be—" She sniffled, then dabbed at her nose with a handkerchief. "That it would be natural for such women to receive marriage proposals from honorable families." Her fingers twisted the cloth. "But I am unmarried at five and twenty and I feel it is somehow my fault. How will I care for you all, should rumors spread—"

"You are unmarried because no match was ever good enough for Mother," Haewon pointed out. "Besides, I think Yeonhee is right. Rumors won't spread."

"How can you both be so certain?"

"Lord Yu, that gentleman from the House of Bright Flowers. He seems the type to dislike idle gossip. In fact, I doubt he enjoys conversation at all." Haewon forced a smile. "And as she shared, few saw Yeonhee at the gibang, and those who did are her friends."

But the frown remained etched into Jade's brow. "There's something else," she whispered, then hesitated. "You said, when you went to fetch Yeonhee, you heard her mention a gentleman."

"Yes."

Jade took a breath, then looked away. "I read her journal."

"What?" Haewon couldn't hide the disbelief in her voice. "She'll *murder* you."

Jade's face burned a flaming red. "The moment you mentioned she was speaking with a man, I knew she was hiding something. I had to be sure. As the eldest, I feel responsible. I don't want to see Mother and Father hurt. Please, don't tell her, but . . . look."

She pulled a slip of paper from her sleeve and handed it to Haewon. "I found a letter in her journal, pasted onto the most recent page. I copied it exactly."

Tense and uneasy, Haewon took the letter.

Dear Mistress Yeonhee,

I write this in haste before my acquaintances join me. It was a pleasure conversing with you. Indeed, I must agree that no two minds are as alike as ours.

Your insights on Western teachings and class reform were most compelling, and I would be honored to continue our discussion. Should you wish to correspond, you may send your letters to Clerk Gonghwe of Hanseong City Administration on Yukjo Street, to whom I have entrusted my letters during my brief stay in the capital.

With great respect,
Your admirer

Haewon stared at the words. Just to be certain she hadn't misread, she read it again. Yeonhee—her little sister, the plump-cheeked child she'd piggybacked until she had fallen asleep on her shoulder—was flirting with a man. This felt like opening a door she was never meant to look behind. An unsettling sensation crept over her: a realization that, no matter how well she thought she knew someone, she never truly did.

"This is serious," Haewon said.

Jade nodded. "I think Yeonhee will write back. And if this

continues, what then? What if this turns into a love affair? What if he doesn't offer for her hand? She is only sixteen—"

Both sisters yelped as Yeonhee suddenly plopped down beside them. "My ears are itching. Are you whispering about me? I told Jade to stop moping. You agree with me, do you not, Haewon eonni, that rumors will not spread?" she asked, her veil falling from her head and pooling on the grass as she wove flowers into her hair.

Haewon grabbed the veil and threw it back over Yeonhee's head.

"There's no man in sight." Yeonhee threw her veil back off. "Who ought I hide myself from?"

"You can't always do whatever you wish," Haewon snapped.

"You're still upset with me, I see. It seems you are in need of a reminder: I *didn't* go to the gibang house to associate with men. I told you so already," Yeonhee said with great forbearance. "I went there to meet my friends—"

"Are you going to keep associating with *him*?" Haewon demanded.

Yeonhee blinked.

"When I went to the gibang house," Haewon said, "I overheard it all. You met someone there."

"Oh yes. I spoke with a man, and I'm not ashamed," she said tartly. "I enjoyed talking to him. There's no one in this village who understands me, no one else who cares about these things."

Jade frowned. "These things?"

"The world outside of eligible bachelors, outside of gossip," Yeonhee said sharply, and her voice rose with frustration. "Everyone here is fixated on marriage, on these silly edicts, while the world beyond is shifting. Interest in the Western teachings is growing like wildfire, and did you know it is Joseon women who are spearheading the Catholic community? And at court, the factions continue to clash in their never-ending fight for power. A river of blood will flow. And yet Mother only weeps about Jade's lack of a husband." She huffed. "I'll go mad if I must remain confined to this little village."

Jade sighed. "Who raised you to be this way?"

"I want to be known," Yeonhee said fiercely. "To be respected. To be—" She faltered.

"To be what?"

"To be . . . more."

Silence filled the space between them, muffling the distant sounds of splashing water and laughter.

"You need to be careful," Haewon said at last.

"Your time will come," Jade chimed in solemnly, yet still she sounded sweet and gentle. "You'll marry soon and leave this village."

"My time?" Yeonhee's face reddened. "Mother says I cannot marry until Older Sister marries, but Jade is nearly six and twenty! How ashamed I should be if I were not married before then."

"*Yeonhee!*" Haewon snapped.

But Yeonhee bolted to her feet, as though wrenching herself free from her sisters. And the girl staring down at them was no longer the pudgy baby sister Haewon had once adored; she was gone, and in her place was a fiery young woman who would not be contained.

"I will not stay here and—and—sew and cook my life away like I'm told to," Yeonhee said, eyes burning. "I will not settle, as you both have, for a dull and ordinary life."

"You need to stop speaking with this man. And you need to stop associating with those interested in heretical ideas," Haewon urged. "It's dangerous."

"You want to control me," Yeonhee shot back, "yet *you* transcribe illegal books that are tantamount to treason!"

"That is different—"

"Is it?" Yeonhee scoffed. "Everyone in Five Willows knows the only transcriber who dared to copy the Catholic manual is Magpie."

"Haewon *transcribes* it," Jade swept in to explain. "That does not mean she believes it. And Haewon has done her due diligence in remaining discreet. She writes under a pseudonym. Your sister understands that to ruin herself would mean to ruin her entire family. Something, I fear, you have yet to fully grasp."

Yeonhee's fire sputtered. She sank back down onto the grass. "I do grasp it," she said miserably. "And I do care for you, my sisters." Her lashes lowered, and she plucked absentmindedly at the grass. "Believe me. I won't be reckless. I won't see him again, or write to him. All right? So don't tell Father."

Haewon held on to the sight of Yeonhee, feeling torn. It felt like her duty to tell their father. It physically pained her, and how much more must it agonize Jade, who had never kept secrets from their parents? And yet, Haewon cherished her sisters more than anything. They had raised one another.

Long days when their mother lay abed, grieving, after their little brother had passed. Their father locked away in his study for hours. It had been just them, the three Shin sisters. Playing in the red sunset. Whispering under the covers long after the candle was blown out. Sneaking out barefoot across the dewy grass to see the full moon, laughing and whispering, screaming and running when they spotted a snake in the reeds.

We are sisters, they'd declared together, an oath Haewon had strung together for them. *We are bound to one another by blood, by the deepest affection. No matter what, we swear an oath of lifelong comradery.*

A naive promise made as children.

Now she looked at Yeonhee and thought of that promise.

"Very well," Haewon whispered. "I'll trust you."

Jade hesitated, her face so pale she looked about to be ill. Her brows were knotted, and dark emotions shifted in her eyes. At length she let out a sigh of defeat. "Please, do not get yourself into further trouble, Shin Yeonhee. You must promise me this."

Yeonhee nodded. Wilted flowers clung to her hair as she pulled the veil back over her head. "I promise. I truly, truly mean to keep my promise this time."

Chapter 8

A DAY HAD PASSED SINCE THE BREAK-IN, AND SEOJUN HAD scarcely found his bearings when his father—who'd learned of the incident through a servant—summoned him to give an account to a police investigator. Seojun shared what he could, fabricating a tale about how his box of coins had been stolen, while carefully omitting any mention of his missing manuscript.

Once the investigator left, Seojun quietly began his own inquiries. He questioned Maid Daebi again, along with nearly a dozen other servants who had been awake when the crime had occurred. One by one, they confirmed the same unsettling thing: Not a single person had witnessed or heard anything. It was as if the thief had slipped through the estate like a ghost. How was this possible? The questions swirling in his mind soon became a tangle, impossible to grasp the longer he brooded over it.

Seojun rode out of the capital that day to clear his thoughts. Before long, he reached the open field surrounding Hwasadang and spotted Byeongho, the estate's owner, who had sent him a note that morning expressing his intent to practice archery. Several targets had been set up accordingly, yet it appeared his friend had long since lost any will to shoot.

"You've come at last," Byeongho said in greeting, lighting his smoking pipe as Seojun dismounted and tethered his horse. "I know I invited you to join me, but you will have to practice on your own, I fear. My shoulder is already throbbing in pain after a couple of shots." There was a long pause as Byeongho considered him for a thoughtful moment. "You know, you look positively awful. Another lecture from your father?"

"Far worse," Seojun muttered, and proceeded to explain the break-in to Byeongho, whose brows shot higher with every detail. When Seojun finally finished, Byeongho took a long puff from his silver smoking pipe and said ponderously, "So someone stole your keys, broke in, and took the entire manuscript. Who else knows of your writing endeavors?"

"Not many. The only people who know are my sister, Wol, and you."

"But why would they steal your manuscript? To sell it? I suppose book thieves are rampant these days . . ."

Seojun took a narrow band of leather and wrapped it snug around his left wrist. With a final tug, he secured the wrist guard and snatched up a bow. "Perhaps they were book thieves. It could also be for the handwriting."

"To somehow prove your identity?"

"That's the only other reason I can think of."

"But prove it to whom? And why?"

"Handwriting is like a signature." In one smooth motion, Seojun drew the bowstring to his ear and found himself wishing he could maneuver this puzzling case with as much ease. "Perhaps they have a mind to blackmail me."

"Your family *is* immensely wealthy. I would blackmail you, too, if I had no morals." Byeongho drew lazily on his pipe and blew out a cloud, watching the smoke drift into the clear blue sky. "And you believe the theft of the keys occurred at the gibang house. You returned there, did you not, on the morning of the break-in? I remember seeing you when I was about to leave the house myself."

"It was to inquire if anyone had discovered a pair of keys."

"And did you find it?"

"No." Seojun steadied his focus, narrowing in on the target, and released the arrow. It cut through the air with a sharp whistle and hit the target with a resounding *thud*. But he was still not satisfied. He felt no calm. His shoulders remained as tense as a rock. "I also spoke with Madam Seolhwa there, to see if anyone of suspicious character had been seen on the premises. But she couldn't recall anything."

"It seems like you've walked straight into one of Black Lotus's vignettes," Byeongho said with a grin, "full of convoluted mystery and thrills, seedy characters and an intelligent investigator—but who will be the investigator? The police? You yourself?"

Seojun took up another arrow and aimed, but concentration was difficult as thoughts swarmed in his mind. "I don't wish to draw too much attention to the break-in; it could invite speculation," he noted, then frowned as he recalled information he'd uncovered earlier.

"What is it?"

"The house was ransacked without anyone hearing a thing, not even the gatekeeper, who was resting nearby," Seojun said. "Although . . . Maid Daebi claimed to have heard a clatter and a thud."

"So she heard something no one else heard," Byeongho repeated. "Intriguing."

"Books were tossed around—surely that would have made some noise. Alerted someone. But no, only she heard. And no other rooms were disturbed. Nothing else was stolen but my manuscript."

Byeongho pursed his lips. "It's almost as though the culprit *wants* you to know his intent."

"I inspected the gates and walls."

"And?"

"At first I thought a thief had scaled the outer wall to enter. There were footprints crushing the flowers, and dirt on the tile capping the wall. But there were no corresponding marks on the other side. No scuff marks at all. No crushed plants to suggest someone had stood there. The tracks were all made from within the mansion."

"What are you suggesting?"

"The scene was staged. This was not a break-in, but really, a breakout. And there is one detail that leaves me utterly bewildered." Lowering his bow, he glanced at his friend as he voiced the question that had plagued him all day: "How did the thief manage to open my locks? To open the first, the thief would have had to find the keyhole hidden at the bottom, behind a sliding panel. Then unlock the outer body, pull out the inner mechanism, and slide aside another panel, all while inserting the key at precisely the right moment. He would then have had to turn the key at a full rotation to make the lock finally give way. He opened both, with two different unlocking mechanisms, before anyone took notice of him. It's impossible."

Byeongho shrugged. "I've heard of master locksmiths. Or maybe a servant saw you opening it a few times."

Seojun remained unconvinced, but all possible explanations eluded him. He was completely and thoroughly bewildered.

"Well, I am quite sure you will find the culprit. You always get your way." And with this, Byeongho sprawled out under a pine tree, retrieving the book he'd left abandoned on a rock nearby. "Here, let me cheer you up before you snap that bow in half, as you appear on the brink of doing. Listen to this poem," he called out as he flipped the book open.

Pining for each other, we can meet only in dreams;
Yet while I rejoice to see you there, you rejoice to see me here.
If we are to dream of each other on a night to come,
Let us set out at the same time to meet on the road.

Seojun raised his bow again, determined this time to find his equilibrium. "'Meeting in Dreams' by the gisaeng Hwang Jini." He steadied his breathing, aimed, and released, watching as the arrow struck the target once more.

"Of course you know. What book or poem has Yu Seojun not read?" Byeongho expelled a wistful breath. "You know, if I ever meet a girl whom I pine for so painfully that I would write poems about her, I would marry her right away, even if she were a gisaeng or a servant girl."

Seojun sent him a puzzled glance. "What?"

Byeongho grinned, placing the poetry book aside again. He

stretched out, one hand tucked under his head, the other holding his pipe. "I would, you know."

"It would be illegal," Seojun said flatly. "Intermarriage between classes is forbidden."

"I would elope with her, of course."

Seojun grunted. "You would marry for something as mundane as love?"

"Mundane? Love is the closest thing to the heavens."

Shaking his head, Seojun set aside his bow to examine his loosened wrist guard. Normally his manservant took care of securing it, but Namgil had disappeared this morning, another mystery that had left Seojun bewildered. At least Byeongho's concern was simple enough. "Gentlemen do not marry for love. Marriage is an alliance between two families—"

"You can be such a bore, sometimes, Yu Seojun. So you can imagine my surprise when I saw you alone with a lady at the House of Bright Flowers," Byeongho pointed out, a conspiratorial note in his voice. "You were in the garden, staring at her with such *piercing* attention. Perhaps your heart is not so immune to the finer feelings as you make yourself out to be?"

"I would hardly call her a lady," Seojun muttered.

"She's a gentleman's daughter. I recognized her, one of the three Shin daughters. She's always out and about, going on long strolls and bribing her maid with sweets to escort her." He smiled. "The eldest daughter is known to be a great beauty. I've only ever seen her from a distance, though."

"The girl I spoke to was no great beauty." Seojun continued to thread the leather strap through a loop, his thoughts drifting back to that night. Back to the girl who had stared at him in silent challenge. With one aggressive tug, he finally resecured the wrist guard. "So she must not have been the eldest."

"The youngest daughter, in particular, is known for her youthful vigor and reckless friendships with heretics. And the mother!" Byeongho declared. "Oh, the stories I have heard. I get a good laugh the more I learn about that woman. She is like a butterfly that only seeks flowers and does not care for the dangers of wind and dew. Such a delightful family, don't you think?"

"The family sounds more like a thing of nightmares."

"At least they could never bore me—you know I despise being bored. Sometimes I wonder how we ever remained friends." Byeongho took a puff of his smoking pipe and heaved out a sigh, more clouds forming before his lips. "Never mind about me, I'm more concerned about you right now. This investigation . . . it's quite troubling, isn't it? Someone knows who you are. They must. Why else would they take your manuscript and nothing else?"

The gravity of the situation returned, and the bow now felt ten times heavier in Seojun's grip. He'd usually had an answer for everything, until now. "I haven't the damnedest idea."

"You're certain no one else knows of your identity as Black Lotus? What about that scribe—Magpie? You practically grin like a fool whenever you mention your correspondence with him."

"I do not grin like a fool."

"Oh, of course not! Lord Yu Seojun never smiles. Except, of course, when he's reading letters from Magpie. Mysterious creature, that one."

"I doubt Magpie knows my true identity." Seojun re-nocked an arrow, slower this time. "And even if he did, he would have kept it secret."

"How can you be so certain?"

Seojun fell silent for a moment. "There are very few people I don't find irritating, and fewer still whom I trust. Magpie is one of them."

"You trusted him *that* much? What on earth did you two write about?"

He drew back the arrow, just as words from their very first correspondence filled his thoughts. Words that were burned into his memory.

Dear Black Lotus,

I am Magpie, the scribe whom Mistress Wol entrusted with the transcription of your work. I have diligently washed your writing away after completion, per your request. I hope you'll forgive me the liberty I'm taking of writing freely to you.

He readjusted the aim of his arrow.

I have been eagerly transcribing and following the journey of the main character Scholar Hong for the past nine volumes of your work.

I do hope you will keep working on it, and if you have the next volume but feel uncertain about it, you and I can go over it together. I would be happy to review a selection of your compositions before transcribing them for the public.

His grip on the bow tightened as he tried to hone his focus.

Words are no good whatsoever to capture how I feel. There are few peaks in my life, and transcribing your work has been the highest of all. Thank you for everything. Your writing makes me very, very happy.

His focus wavered.
The arrow flew wide and missed the target entirely.

Chapter 9

For the next few days, Haewon waited, feeling as though her family teetered on the brink of ruin. Yet by the end of the week, she realized that by some great fortune, no rumor had spread of Yeonhee's indiscretion. Her family had been spared from irrevocable disgrace—for now.

"You see, yeobo," Scholar Shin declared to his wife over their meal of soup, barley, and fish, "everything worked out in the end, as I said it would."

Haewon was determined to believe her father; what good could come from tormenting her mind with what-ifs, from living life fearing what lay around the bend in the road?

The dark cloud of anxiety finally lifted from her, Haewon found herself in particularly good spirits the next morning. The house was blessedly empty, which was rare, and so Haewon took advantage of it. She reached for her notebook kept at the bottom of a chest. It had a heavy cover with thick red stitches along the spine, binding that was as sturdy as the strings of a gayageum. She opened it, then paused. A dried flower she had placed between the pages was missing.

That was odd.

It must have fallen out the last time she'd opened this notebook.

Shaking her head, she flipped through the book of letters from Black Lotus, to the very first letters she'd received.

Dear Magpie,

She still felt a frisson of excitement, recalling when she had first received the letter, how she had crawled across her thick blanket bed to show Jade, her voice and hands trembling. *Black Lotus wrote back!* She'd suppressed a squeal. *She doesn't reply to* anyone *except Wol!*

My apologies for the delayed response. Firstly, why this bird sobriquet? I am of the understanding that one's hoching is often based on one's hometown, or signifying markers of where one lives. Secondly, to answer your question, it is impossible to write. I keep thinking to myself . . . Why should I write at all?

Since you wrote freely, allow me to write freely, too.

Each time I pick up my brush, I am guilt ridden, thinking, "What a waste of time this is!" How can I continue writing a work that is of so little value? It will not stand the test of time; I am certain of that.

So why should I keep writing?

We only live one life. I have my mind bent on learning, on continuously cultivating myself. I want to live correctly. And this desire to write feels like the young antlers of a deer. They grow out of its own body and ultimately threaten the deer's life. How can they not be troublesome?

Hence, while your offer to be of service to me and my work at this time I greatly appreciate, I shall not need to trouble you, although it is comforting to know that I may write to you.

Please burn this letter after reading.

She had, following Black Lotus's request, burned the letter—though only after transcribing the contents into her notebook. Haewon hadn't realized, then, that their correspondence would become a space in which they could reveal their true selves to each other. She perused letter after letter, some no more than a brief note, others that spanned pages. She paused before one of her favorite ones:

Dear Magpie,

You asked whether I actually visited the places I've written about. To answer your question, I am nearing twenty and have not been to any of the places like the Nakdong River or the West Lake, or anywhere at all, for that matter. I imagined these real places while staring out at the little lotus pond that can be viewed outside my residence. Imagination has become my escape when life becomes unbearable, as you yourself shared.

Growing up, I only studied the classics, but when

I saw the world map again in my later years, I realized I was the frog in the well who sees only a portion of the sky and thinks it knows the universe. And then I read *Yeolhailgi*—have you read it? It moved me to tears. And that was when I felt gripped by a need to write, like I was being possessed by a ghost.

Indeed, I remain a frog in a well, writing about a universe I will never see in its entirety. But I see glimpses of it above my dark and dreary enclosure, and it sets a burning in my heart, a painful humility and awe that the universe cannot be fathomed by any man—or frog—but how I want to try.

I am filled with sighs as I write this.

Please, burn this letter, too.

She set the notebook down as a new concern wove through her thoughts.

Something Yeonhee had said continued to bother her; she had equated transcribing to treason. It wasn't that Haewon hadn't considered the danger of transcribing books. She had been very aware. She had even written to Black Lotus about her concern, wrestling with her guilt on paper. She had, nevertheless, continued her work.

She had confessed to have transcribed *Chugyoyoji,* the first Catholic catechism, and *Seonggyoyoji.* Nearly a dozen copies of each, all circulated and returned tattered and worn. She had shared about having found both books outrageous, offensive and yet fascinating. To confront foreign ideas had been like peering over the walls of her own enclosure. She didn't need to agree with the teachings, but surely there was no harm in *knowing* that the world was vast and complex, filled with places that were unfamiliar to her and ideas that were different from hers.

She had therefore chosen to transcribe such works for this simple reason. Was it still wrong, though? What if some ideas were, indeed, *too* dangerous?

The etiquette books she'd grown up reading would have agreed that it was. Pages after pages had warned her not to think for herself, and certainly not to create. *It does not befit a woman to actively compose poetry* was a line from such a book, carved into her memory, *let alone to circulate it outside of home.*

The authors of etiquette books would have, without a doubt, trembled with outrage if they knew what she was doing. For what she wrote was far more scandalous than poetry.

I wonder the same thing, more often than I care to admit, Black Lotus had written in response to her concerns. *I fear it as much as you, perhaps even more. Am I committing a moral transgression? Ought I to stop? I have no answers, but I promise you this: If ever you are discovered, if the world turns against you, write to me at once. You will never be friendless. You will never be entirely alone.*

All concerns drifted away, as they always did whenever she perused Black Lotus's letters. Pressing the notebook against her chest, Haewon fell back against the thick blanket, warm in the pool of sunlight. The window was open, and the cool spring breeze carried in the sound of birds.

"And neither will you, Black Lotus," she whispered. "You will never be friendless."

Chapter 10

THE FOLLOWING WEEK, WITH THREE TRANSCRIBED COPIES OF Munmuja's newest stories prepared, Haewon convinced Jade to visit the Five Willows bookshop, with Maid Boram as their escort. She was convinced that if Jade remained home a moment longer, her sister would surely spend the entire day moping about her future.

A government official had arrived earlier to rebuke Mother for rejecting every suitor as unworthy of Jade, to the point that no matchmaker would even consider the Shin household anymore. He warned that if Jade did not marry within two months, Father would face punishment, and the official himself would be dismissed from his post and haunt their doorstep for the remainder of his life.

"Do not fret," Haewon said as they entered the secret book-lending shop. "It will turn out fine. Everything works out in the end, as Father always says."

"I'm sure it will." Jade smiled, but it did not reach her eyes. "I feel cheered up already, being here. Go on now. You have books for Mistress Wol."

"I'll be back with you soon, I promise!"

Haewon walked down the aisle, nodded to a few familiar patrons as well as Mistress Wol's thug-like assistant, then slipped into the narrow passage leading to the scribes' workroom. Her mind was so full of concern for her sister that she didn't hear the heavy footsteps until she nearly collided with a gentleman.

Startled, Haewon glanced up, and her eyes landed on Lord Yu, his imperial features shaded by the brim of his gentleman's hat, the jade-beaded hat string swaying as he quickly stepped aside, pressing up against a shelf of books. The passageway was too narrow for two.

"Begging your pardon," she whispered as she squeezed past him, her traitorous silk dress brushing against him like a caress. The proximity was absolutely excruciating.

As soon as she passed, she glanced over her shoulder and watched as he straightened the stack of books behind him. She waited for him to turn his eyes and look her way, for his brows to lift in recognition, but he didn't. His dark eyes didn't look at her, not once. Instead, he seemed lost in thought, brooding, as he stalked off.

He was gone now, but Haewon couldn't move.

She felt anchored to the spot, staring at where he had stood moments ago, her heart thrumming a wild beat. Perhaps her heart had recognized him: an enemy in another lifetime. A smile played across her lips at this thought, then fell away as another seized her mind.

Quickening her steps, she crossed over to Wol in the adjoining room. She set the stack of books down a little too roughly. "You know him?"

Wol readjusted her jade-rimmed spectacles. "Whom?"

"The gentleman who left a moment ago."

"Vaguely. He was explaining why a book he borrowed was . . . stolen. Someone recently broke into his residence."

"He reads novels? He doesn't seem the sort."

"And you know what sort of man he is?" Wol examined her, rather curiously. "How do *you* know him?"

"It's a long story, and all you need to know is that he isn't the sort I would want to further my acquaintance with."

"Is that so," Wol murmured. Then she waved a hand. "Leave the copies you transcribed. I'll review them in a moment. I spent the whole day fixing Scribe Im's mistakes," she grumbled, running a finger across squares of paper pasted over a page. "I've received enough complaints from readers and cannot possibly send such copies into circulation. With this many errors, they will demand their payment back. Oh, and before you leave—the Buddhist monk I told you about, from the southern provinces? He sent another boxful of tea. I set some aside for you."

"You excel at distracting me from the matter at hand, as usual," Haewon said, even as she walked over to a side table and gleefully took the bundle wrapped in cloth. "This one?"

"Yes."

Haewon had grown fond of tea ever since Wol had introduced her to it, though it was now difficult to come by. With Buddhism suppressed and smoking on the rise, tea had fallen out of favor. Everyone smoked—her mother, her father, even Yeonhee—but she couldn't stand it.

She raised the bundle and breathed in the deep, earthy scent, with a pleasant bitterness at the back of it. Her very soul sighed with delight, but she wasn't so entirely seduced as to forget why she'd stormed over here in the first place. "So you know Lord Yu only vaguely," she began, keeping her voice light, "yet you let His Lordship into the back quarter. You never let just anyone in here."

Wol remained quiet for a long moment, then replied cryptically, "I know his family well. I often visited my wealthy aunt, who dwells in his neighborhood."

"Oh?"

"There is a saying that wealthy families lose their fortunes in three generations, but his family has maintained a good reputation over the course of several."

"I am hardly surprised," Haewon scoffed. "I barely know Lord Yu and one can tell he has an *impeccable* reputation."

"It's not what you think. His father, Minister Yu, and their ancestors have always lived frugally, yet were always known for their generosity. The Yu family made sure that no one living within their vicinity died of hunger. It is this strict teaching that was passed down from generation to generation, instead of wealth itself."

"So he is the perfect gentleman," Haewon said, unimpressed.

"Well, I really must finish editing this manuscript." Wol peered at Haewon over the rim of her spectacles. "I'll find you later, if you're still here."

Haewon knew a dismissal when she heard one. She returned to the main area of the secret book-lending shop and went from aisle to aisle, searching for her sister—as well as a new book to read. Truly, there was no joy quite like the pleasure of searching for her next read. Her pulse leapt, like she was wandering among countless doors, each one leading to a different world, and she was allowed to *choose* which story to fall into.

Unlike her, all other readers were only given a three-day borrowing period with the book of their choice; each loan cost a small fortune, but it was still more affordable than the staggering price of attempting to purchase a novel. Haewon had seen women offer their precious jade bracelets, rings, silver hairpins, rolls of silk, or brassware—precious items kept as collateral until the books were safely returned. Then they would have to pay a tenth of the book's price for borrowing. If not for Mistress Wol and their agreement, Haewon was certain that she might have lived her life never picking up a single novel in the first place. She would have had to rely on public storytellers—

Her thoughts quieted. Her steps faltered.

Through the gaps between books, she saw Jade speaking to a gentleman dressed as colorfully as a peacock, and she was addressing him as "Young Master Byeongho." They were talking about how he had seen Jade once or twice in Gyonam Village; he lived near it.

As they conversed on, Young Master Byeongho grinned down at Jade the entire time, head bowed as though attempting to catch a fuller glimpse of her face. And he seemed intrigued by her quiet reserve. And terribly quiet she was. Jade rarely spoke, each response barely more than a murmur. One might assume that Jade was indifferent to the man, but Haewon knew better. For her sister, the truth of her feelings was often nestled in the space between words, and Haewon could see Jade's feelings now in the flush of her cheeks, paired with the suppressed smile quivering upon her lips. Her eyes glowed, as though a great happiness, so uncontainable in its nature, were bursting within her.

Before Jade could spot her, Haewon quickly moved farther down the aisle, closer to the window. The sunlight here was warm and lulling. She had barely slept the night before, rushing to finish transcribing the third copy for Wol. And now she found herself pleasantly sleepy in the heat. Closing her eyes, she tilted her head back, her eyelids heavy as she listened to Jade's laughter.

She thought of all the love stories she had hunted down together with Jade, stories from two centuries ago when Joseon women were portrayed as more proactive in their romances. Stories where women made choices, pursued the men they loved, and refused to be passive in their own lives . . .

The scent of sandalwood drifted around her, rousing her from her thoughts. She opened her eyes and found herself staring at the gentleman who stood frozen before her. He had a book in hand and his hat dangled behind him by its black chin strap, as if he thought himself in the privacy of his own home. It wasn't seemly for a gentleman to be hatless in public; it was a sight far too intimate.

"Lord Yu," she said in a small voice, "what a pleasant surprise."

Chapter 11

Look away.

He ought to have walked past, ought to have ignored the sight of her standing between the shelves, lost in a daydream. But he had faltered, recalling the young woman who had spoken of books with a passion that had burned into his memory. All thoughts of decorum faded as he'd watched her, the dust motes drifting between them in the golden sunlight.

Look away.

His pulse now quickened as she glanced up at him with those luminous brown eyes. The warm brown of a summer forest, with flecks of light speckling the earth in tiny explosions. He reluctantly admitted to himself that he'd been wrong in his initial judgment. He found her quite lovely now—

Not, of course, that it was of any significance to him.

"Lord Yu?" she repeated when he did not answer.

He wrenched his gaze away, and yet just as quickly, he looked at her again—only to find her watching him, color rising on her cheeks. A rosy blush that made her lovelier still. And despite their apparent mutual embarrassment, she tilted her head to the side and a mocking smile tugged at the corners of her lips.

"You look positively scandalized by the sight of me, nauri," she said.

"I—" He was rarely, if ever, at a loss for words. But it took him a moment now to find them, grappling with his own silence as he donned his hat. He'd taken it off earlier, thinking himself alone in the back of the shop and wanting to somehow ease his headache and the growing sense of frustration over the break-in. But all thoughts had vanished the moment he'd laid eyes on Mistress Haewon.

Clearing his throat, he tried to speak again. "I wasn't—I wasn't expecting to see you here."

Her smile sharpened. "Nor I you."

"I came with a friend," he said in needless explanation. "Who, it seems, is very taken by your sister."

She darted a look toward the pair, and as she did, Seojun noticed a little bird embroidered onto her veil. The mark was small enough to go unnoticed at a glance.

"That gentleman speaking to my sister . . ." Alarm sounded in her voice. "Is *your* friend?"

He shifted his attention back to her. "Yes."

"*Your* friend. I see . . . And how do you know my sister?"

"I caught a brief glimpse of her at the House of Bright Flowers."

Her cheeks paled, clearly a night she was loath to recall. "Thank you for your discretion."

He knew that now was the perfect time to bow and excuse himself. She wasn't his concern. Yet he remembered his own sister, and how brittle a woman's reputation was. "I would strongly encourage your parents to arrange for a female teacher to instruct your younger sister as soon as possible," he cautioned. "With lessons from etiquette books such as *Nechik*, so your sister might be inspired to strive for moral perfection." *And save your family from further ruin,* he did not add.

Her smile remained polite, but there was a bite to her voice as she said, "But of *course* this is your advice, nauri."

He slid a glance down at her. "You seem so sure of who I am."

"I can read people as easily as that very book in your hand," she declared, then looked away, as though expecting this to be the end of their conversation.

It *ought* to be the end. She was unmarried, and he was fully aware that their conversation had turned inappropriately long. Yet he was so curious.

"Then what do you make of me?" he asked.

She turned and blinked up at him. A shade of pink swept across her cheeks again, deepening under his scrutiny. He wanted her to squirm. To strip away her bravado. He expected her to meekly retreat from his challenge, to let out a sheepish laugh and, at most, mumble a nervous non sequitur.

"You would allow me to speak plainly?" she asked instead, catching him off guard. "My frankness, nauri, has left village boys in tears."

"You could never make me cry, Mistress Haewon."

As though hearing the test in his voice, she peeked up at him with a mischievous glint. If they were sparring, then he had struck, expecting her to falter, only to find her already braced to strike back.

"My understanding of you is this," she mused, tilting her head in thought. Her veil had slipped a little, baring the loose strands that had fallen from her braid. Her hair was that of an adventurer who'd just stepped off a ship after surviving a storm rather than of a proper young lady. "You are the most perfectly civilized man, the most perfect gentleman the kingdom has ever known. You move and breathe according to the rule. You are superior to most and therefore have no tolerance for errors, though your one failing is your inability to relate to those beneath you."

"Your judgment of me is most severe," he replied, unable to look away. She had remarkable nerve, which he found—much to his chagrin—oddly charming, too. "And this, I presume, is your final verdict?"

"Yes. And I am rarely, if ever, wrong in my reading of people," she remarked. "Though, I did err in one matter. I didn't think you would ever deign to pick up a novel. I thought you found them to be a frivolous waste of time."

He stared down at the book in his hand. "My opinion hasn't changed. But my elder sister is a voracious novel reader, and so here I am on her behalf . . ."

His attention strayed. The golden beam of sunlight had dimmed. The window, once aglow, had turned a somber shade of gray.

"Perhaps it will finally rain," he whispered, half to himself.

In the growing darkness, so sudden and abrupt, the shadows cloaked the shelves and swelled tight around them, as though they were the only two people in the shop. Her veil had slipped further, this time falling around her shoulders as she glanced up at the high-set window, wide-eyed and smiling.

"I hope it *pours*," she said, her delight humming in the narrow space between them. She seemed to forget herself in this moment, speaking more freely now. "The drought has gone on for far too long. For months! Or has it been an entire year already? I've always been so fond of the rain. When I was a child, I would walk right outside and imagine myself standing beneath a waterfall. I'd open my arms and feel the rain on my skin, breathe in the smell of the damp earth—"

She turned her eyes to him, strands of hair falling down across her rosy cheeks, a visible pulse beating against the side of her throat as their gazes locked. He felt a warm rush through his veins, and a strange, most peculiar tightness in his chest. A breathlessness he couldn't explain.

Clearing her throat, she abruptly looked away and tugged the veil back over her head. "I'm not sure why I'm telling you this . . . You came here looking for books for your sister. I could offer your sister a recommendation," she said with an unnatural cheerfulness. "All ladies in this shop know to come to me. Is she interested in love stories?"

"No," he said, his voice rough.

"History? Travel books? Those are widely favored."

He needed to stop, to stop engaging her in conversation, to stop being so curious about her—

"She prefers books about Joseon," he answered stiffly, "written by Joseon authors."

"Then . . ." Haewon moved farther down the aisle, and he followed her without a thought, noticing her height for the first time: two heads shorter than him. If he held her, her cheek would only reach his chest. Not that he felt the slightest temptation to hold her. He had not the slightest, burning inclination to do so. He froze as she turned to him.

"I'd recommend *Taekriji*," she offered. "It means 'A record that helps people choose where to live.'"

She flipped through the pages, and the shadow cast by her veil had deepened over her face, making her expression unreadable.

"The author, Lee Junghwan," she continued, "was a scholar from a prestigious family of southern descent. He rose quickly in the bureaucracy but was expelled from court after a factional dispute. In 1728, he was implicated in the Rebellion of the Throne and deprived of his position. Wandering the country with no way to make ends meet, he asked himself, 'Where can I live without starving?' And so, *Taekriji* was born."

He found his head bowed, listening to her in genuine interest and wishing she could speak on for a great deal longer.

"Lee Junghwan traveled across Joseon, analyzing the land—topography, climate, resources, transportation, even human sentiment—and made judgments about which places were worth living in." With a glimmer of a smile, she added, "My sisters and I devoured it, arguing endlessly over where we'd choose to live, if ever we had to move. I think your sister would enjoy this book immensely."

"I'm sure she will," he said, accepting the copy she offered him.

Suddenly, hurried footsteps thumped down the aisle, breaking whatever spell he'd fallen under, followed by a sharp voice.

"*Everyone* must leave at once!"

Seojun, along with the other patrons, peered out from between the crowded shelves to see Mistress Wol. She stood tall, her jaw tight and her arms locked around a stack of books like a dragon guarding its precious treasures.

"I've just received word that a raid is underway at a bookshop down the street," Wol continued, her spectacles askew on her nose. And despite the firmness of her voice, there was the slightest tremor to her hands. "I do not believe they will trouble us, but it is best to err on the side of caution. Leave now." She looked prepared to herd everyone out when her gaze landed on Haewon, and remained on her, even as patrons knocked by her. "You're still here?" Wol cried. "I thought you had already gone!"

"I was always here," Haewon said, the confusion audible in her voice.

"I spoke to your sister moments ago. I was so certain you'd left; my father swore he saw you leave the shop!"

As Mistress Wol urged Haewon to leave now, warning her to be on the lookout for officers, Seojun turned to frown at the bookshelves. A raid? Surely this couldn't be a raid ordered by the king. His father's cronies at the Ministry of Justice were light-lipped around him . . . If the king had ordered such extreme measures, he would have known.

"Nauri? *Nauri.*"

Wol spoke, but her voice didn't register. His mind remained on the books. Stacks upon stacks of books glorifying Western teachings, Joseon novels written in secret, and Chinese novels smuggled across the border. All books King Jeongjo criticized for promoting vulgarity and disorder. At length, he looked to find Wol watching him, eyes clouded with worry, and there was no Shin Haewon by his side.

"Where did she go?" He looked around, scanning the shop for her green veil, but there were at least a dozen ladies in identical colored headdresses pushing through the crowd.

"You should leave, too," Wol warned, and Seojun peered down

at the bookshop keeper, his sister's longtime friend, once more. "If your father hears of this—"

"Whoever instigated this," he said, voice low, "it is likely to destroy the Catholic books in circulation. You ought to remove them, if you have any care for your shop."

Wol scoffed as she turned to examine her curated collection. "Once I remove those, what will be next? All novels that contain any traces of unorthodox ideas? I will have nothing left to lend out then."

A deep rumble of thunder shook the window frames. The sound of heavy rainfall pummeled the roof, as though the sea itself were spilling down from the sky.

Wol paled and grabbed Seojun's sleeve. "I do have one favor to ask."

"What is it?"

"Could you ensure that both Shin sisters make it home safely? You, of all people, should want to keep Shin Haewon safe."

"I'll go find them but . . ." Seojun frowned. "What do you mean by—"

Before he could finish his question, Byeongho appeared beside them, snapping open his fan to air his face. He looked to have not a care in the world, watching as the last of the patrons scrambled out of the shop. "There was a customer reading a book I wanted to borrow. Perhaps he's left it behind. Now, what is it you were both talking about? Find whom?"

"The Shin sisters," Wol replied.

Byeongho hummed in response, then froze. "The Shin sisters? Do you mean to say that the lovely young lady I was speaking with—is lost? But she was with me only moments ago—" Another deep rumble shook the shop, and his eyes widened. "I am entirely at a loss, but I'll go with you, Yu Seojun. I'll help you find the ladies."

Outside, rainwater sluiced down from the eaves like waves crashing against coastal cliffs. The moment Seojun stepped out to retrieve his horse, which was tethered to a post, the downpour soaked him through. Byeongho mounted his own horse, and soon they were off, leaning low against the explosion of rain.

"We should look around this area first, to make sure they're not still here!" Byeongho shouted over the piercing thunder. "Then head in the direction of their home. Gyonam, the first village beyond the Souimun Gate."

Seojun nudged his heels into the horse's flanks, spurring the creature into a gallop. "I have a feeling," he called out loudly, "that we'll find them perfectly safe in their home."

"What?! I can hardly hear you in this torrent!"

The sky had darkened as they searched the vicinity, the capital drowned in blue-gray light. Rain came down in gusts, driving people into nearby shops. Market stalls quaked, their fabric coverings billowing loose. Merchants scrambled to retrieve their goods. Children danced about and farmers laughed. When Seojun and his companion reached the western gate, a drenched guard waved them through, looking delighted himself as the parched earth took in deep gulps of the long-awaited downpour.

Everyone was likely celebrating, especially the king, perhaps sagging into his dragon throne in sheer relief.

But as Seojun sped out of the fortress, he could think of nothing other than Mistress Wol's strange remark: *You, of all people, should want to keep Shin Haewon safe.* Why on earth did she believe Shin Haewon was of any particular significance to him? His foolish heart had, indeed, quickened at the sight of her—just as foolish hearts were wont to do in the presence of the lovely and charming.

But after today, he was determined to put her from his mind. She was a lady who ought never to have caught his eye to begin with. A young woman of no social consequence.

A nobody.

Or at least . . . that was what his father would have him believe.

Chapter 12

"EONNI?" HAEWON CALLED OUT, CLUTCHING THE VEIL SHE'D discovered along the forest path. It was her sister's; she was certain of it. Jade had embroidered a small plum blossom onto hers, as she had a magpie onto Haewon's. "Eonni!"

In the mad rush of patrons escaping the bookstore, Haewon had yelled out to Jade their plan when she'd finally found her sister. They would meet by the large rock they always passed on the way home if they were separated. And sure enough, she'd lost sight of her sister almost immediately in the flood of people spilling into the overcrowded marketplace. And when Haewon had arrived at the rock, it was to find neither Jade nor Boram—only the veil.

Haewon continued to search the periphery, her sandals sinking into the wet earth, then walked along the path that wended through the thickly wooded hill. It occurred to her that Jade might have slipped in the rainfall, a heavy torrent that had calmed into a trickle only moments ago.

"Eonni!" she continued to call out as she carefully searched the hillside, anchoring her balance on protruding roots. She finally reached the foot of the slope and frantically made her way through the tangle of bramble and branches, hoping to find nothing—no missing shoe, no shred of silk fluttering on a branch. She truly hoped Jade had simply abandoned her veil and had continued homeward.

So caught up in her thoughts, she was unaware of the tramp of hooves until the earth beneath her trembled. It was then she realized she had wandered out of the forest, back onto a road—right into a horseman's path. She was about to clear the way when she slipped in the mud, and all too soon, a great shadow swept up high, horse hooves striking out from the mist.

A choked cry escaped her as she scrambled back, watching wide-eyed as the horse pranced backward, legs thrashing the air. Haewon quickly dragged herself to the side of the road, her back scratching against a prickly shrub, and there she sat with her heart pounding. She'd nearly had her bones crushed—

Her attention fell from the horse's empty saddle to the man curled up on the earth, his cerulean-blue robe stained red.

"Lord Yu!" she cried, hurrying over to his side. His face was pale with shock as he clutched at his arm, his sleeve torn and bloody. Next to him was a sharp slab of granite. "You are hurt—let me assist you." She crouched low. "Here, lean on me."

"That's unnecessary." His jaws locked with determination as he rose to his feet, but within moments, he was curling forward, his back tensing in pain. "I didn't see you," he said through gritted teeth, and then was considerate enough to add, despite his injury, "Your sister is well. We found her with your maid. She was too faint to travel all the way home, so Byeongho took them to his residence nearby. His mother also resides there."

Relief rushed through her, and all her focus returned to the gentleman before her. "Please, lean on me—"

He ignored her again, the stubborn man, and staggered toward a nearby tree. He leaned heavily against the trunk, his lips pale and perspiration gleaming on his brow. Still, he managed to summon his horse with a single breathless command.

"Jeolyeong."

The creature snorted, nervously pacing back and forth.

Haewon hesitated for only a moment, then cautiously approached the creature, an animal several times her own size. "I'm sorry for scaring you," she whispered, laying a steadying hand against its side. There was, she noticed, a constellation of seven small white spots along the horse's hindquarters, like the Bukdu Chilseong—the seven stars of the northern sky. She smoothed her hand across its silken coat a few more times, watching as the horse finally caught its breath.

Once the animal had stilled, Haewon walked on, leading the horse out of the blue drizzle, until she could tether the reins to a branch.

A horse was easy to calm; she had done so countless times, for her family's horse was easily spooked. But as she turned to Lord Yu, she knew a greater challenge remained.

"Your arm is injured," she pointed out.

"Yes," he answered, staring down at the blood oozing out between his fingers. "I am aware of that."

"I can stop the bleeding, if you would permit me."

"You needn't."

She wiped aside wet strands of her hair. "I am only asking to tend to your wound. You needn't look so afraid of me, nauri."

"I'm not afraid of you," he said dryly.

"If you do not stop the bleeding," she said, "you might pass out, and then what am I to do with you?"

A muscle worked in his jaw, then he wrenched his gaze away from her. "Bind me up then."

Letting out a breath, she knelt before him. She took the ornamental paedo tied to her coat string and used the knife to cut a strip from the hem of her skirt. His muscles tensed as she reached for him, moving aside his bloody hand to examine the wound. It did not appear to be life-threatening.

She proceeded to wrap the fabric around his arm, mindful of the pain she might cause. But as she smoothed the bandage into place, her gaze flickered past the torn sleeve and stilled.

An old scar, oddly shaped, carved into his bare arm. Then another. And another. She followed their path up to where they disappeared under what remained of his sleeve, then up to his shoulder, where his loosened robe had shifted just enough to reveal the faintest glimpse of yet another scar disappearing behind the curve of his back.

Her fingers hesitated.

Where could a man like him have suffered such wounds? And so many? His body, surely, had been guarded as carefully as a crown prince's, tended to with the same reverence by those who raised him—

No, she was determined not to wonder. She was *not* curious about Lord Yu. She forced her gaze away, and as she searched for a distraction, she realized she had never expressed her gratitude. "Thank you," she said, "for coming all this way and assisting me and my sister."

"It was nothing," he replied, staring straight ahead, his expression taut. "Besides, to recognize a duty without carrying it out is mere cowardice."

She bit her lower lip. Lord Perfect, it seemed, spoke in rules and proverbs. *Of course* he had just quoted the *Analects* to her. He was every bit the proper gentleman she had imagined him to be.

He was truly insufferable.

Truly.

And yet . . .

She glanced up at him through her lashes, and her traitorous heart did a little skip. Raindrops escaped through the canopy, streaking down the hard lines of his face, on his lashes like the finest of crystals, nothing boyish about him at all. He looked so stern. Too stern for someone so young.

"You've done this before," came his deep voice, startling her attention away.

"Beg pardon?" She sounded breathless.

"I said, you've done this before. You've tended to wounds."

She forced a smile. "When you have a sister like Yeonhee, many times. She once fell off a swing and broke her arm. Another time she fell into a well and broke her ankle; thankfully it was winter so the water was frozen." She continued to recite the many incidents until he looked almost overwhelmed, then she added quietly, "And my two sisters have done the same for me. They have always come to my aid in times of difficulty. It is what family does—nay, it is what any decent human being ought to do. Be there for one another."

In that moment, a lonely shadow flitted across his features. "Is that so?"

"Don't you have anyone like that?" she asked, careful to keep her voice casual. "Someone who is there for you? Your father or mother, perhaps?"

"My mother is deceased. My father—he's in mourning and has trouble even caring for his own self."

"You mentioned you had a sister. Are you close to her? Perhaps I've met her, if she's visited the bookshop before?"

He watched her for a long moment, his gaze inscrutable. And then, without a word, he looked away and proceeded to examine his bandaged wound, as though he could not be bothered to answer her simple question. Never had she been so coolly dismissed, and she almost wanted to laugh. His arrogance was astounding, and his opinion of her quite clear: He didn't think her worthy of conversation.

And, quite frankly, she didn't care.

If he couldn't bother to be amiable, then she refused to try to be pleasant, either.

Chapter 13

Alone with her in the forest, his mind had turned to the consistency of gruel. He couldn't think. Words escaped him. And when he finally did, he had spoken with burning clumsiness. The mere recollection of his response to her, when she had thanked him for his assistance, left him mortified. He had, of all things, quoted the *Analects,* as though he were a dull, gray-haired schoolmaster.

He couldn't understand why she had such an effect on him.

He had always prided himself on perfect composure, but he felt overly self-conscious before Mistress Haewon.

"Here, step on this rock and you'll be able to mount," Seojun said once he managed to untether his horse. "I'll escort you to Hwasadang now that the rain has stopped."

"I will walk, Lord Yu," Haewon declared. "I refuse to sit in your saddle while you hobble next to me. My legs work perfectly fine."

"If you walk, it will take us three times as long. And don't you wish to see your sister sooner?"

"You told me my sister is safe."

He trained his gaze ahead, warmth gathering under his collar as he muttered, "We'll ride together then."

"Together?" she blurted, sounding as scandalized as he felt.

Then her tone turned almost taunting. "Of course you are aware of the rule, nauri: Namnyeo-chilse-budongseog. 'Boys and girls over the age of seven mustn't sit together.' You are the perfect gentleman and I would hate to ruin you."

Her repeated use of the term *perfect gentleman* was starting to grate on him. "We've already broken that rule a long while ago. I've already touched you."

She froze, her eyes widening, the flush on her cheeks deepening.

"When you assisted me with the bandage," he rushed to clarify, his own face burning.

A tense silence thickened in the rain-soaked air. He couldn't bear the thought of her walking, drenched and cold, while he rode on horseback. But she was right. There was etiquette, and there was also the pain in his ankle, growing sharper with every step. No wisdom from the Five Classics could offer guidance here.

"Walk then, and I will follow," he said, then added politely, "if you please."

"I need to visit my home first. To inform my parents."

"Your sister will want you with her."

She seemed hesitant. "Very well, I suppose I could send a note instead . . ."

The journey that followed, he imagined, would be mortifying, with him on horseback and a lady shivering as she traveled on foot. But Shin Haewon seemed to have come to the decision to ignore the circumstance—and him—completely. Soon, she seemed lost in her own thoughts as she walked in long strides, skipping away from puddles, hopping over rocks. His own taut limbs eased as he watched her. He followed the direction of her gaze—at the hills, a smudge in the mist; at the drying reeds that swayed like tresses of unbound hair; at the way light fell across the shape of the earth.

"You look captivated," he murmured, "by the sight of a nearly flooded land."

"It's not so bad as the flood two years ago. Look at the way the sky reflects in the waters on the road."

His horse tromped through a particularly large puddle, and he cursed, steering the horse away to keep from splashing muddy water on her. But she continued on, voice light. "Like riding through clouds."

She was a puzzle to him; each new angle of her face seemed to reveal something unexpected. From the side, he caught the faintest curve of her lips, ever so slightly tilted, as if she was secretly amused by something. *What is on your mind?* he wanted to probe. *What so entertains you?*

Then some thought darkened her face, and her smile fell.

"What is it?" he asked, before he could catch himself.

She stayed quiet a moment, then said, more to herself, "I hope the officers leave Five Willows alone. That book-lending shop is like a second home to many, and the only home to Wol."

"Wol's father, Merchant Hyoyang, has given government officers a share of his profits in return for protection," Seojun replied. "But with this edict being reinforced, I suppose no bookshop owner can truly feel safe. No one knows just how severely the law will be enforced."

"If at all," she said hopefully.

"If at all," he echoed.

He tried to focus on the road again, but his gaze strayed back to her. His mind was turning. And he realized, with some irritation, that he was searching for questions to ask her. He was curious; he wanted to know her. And his curiosity, his traitorous curiosity, refused to be held back.

"At the bookshop," he said, "you mentioned you are an expert at recommending books."

"Yes," she replied warily. "Yes, I am."

"What book would you recommend for me?"

Her brows arched, and the dark clouds in her face cleared. "Is this a challenge, nauri?" The corners of her lips twitched into a hint of a smile, her thrill ill-disguised. "You think, perhaps, that I couldn't possibly recommend a novel that would pique your interest?"

"If you would like to take this as a challenge, then yes, it is a challenge."

"What are you interested in?" she asked, with a look in her eyes he'd come to recognize—she was preparing one of her thorny jokes. "Well, whatever your interest, I would certainly recommend the works of Yeonam to you."

He held back a smile.

"In particular, I would recommend *The Tale of Kwangmun.*"

Yeonam's books were characterized by satirizing the hypocrisy of the yangban; the tale she'd recommended was about a morally pretentious nobleman, whose conduct was contrasted by that of the righteous beggar Kwangmun.

"I doubt you'll read it, though," Haewon said.

"I promise I will."

She let out a single laugh, a delightful sound.

"Do you doubt me, Mistress Haewon?" he asked.

"Entirely, Lord Yu. I have absolutely no faith in you." She snapped her gaze back to him, another impish smile curving her lips. "After *The Tale of Kwangmun*, I would recommend the works of Munmuja." Her expression turned genuine, seemingly determined to make a case for it. "Most consider Munmuja's works inferior compared to Yeonam's. But I think Munmuja is a rare talent, one of those writers who exists only once every few centuries. There is something about his writing that feels so . . . free. He writes for the joy of writing itself, unlike most writers."

"The joy of writing itself . . ." Seojun whispered, his chest constricting. Her words made him want to pick up his brush again, to write, to take flight from everything he knew—yet in that exact instance, the heavy hand of his father weighed him down. "The aim of writing," he said, repeating the words he'd grown up with, "should be to increase morality."

She arched a brow. "Indeed? So one cannot write to simply express . . . life?"

Seojun felt compelled to speak on, to convince *himself*. "The ancients claimed that a society's character can be seen in its writing style. And these days, with this storm of sensational novels that make no attempt to shape a moral society . . . how can we preserve Confucian order?"

Bemusement twinkled in her eyes as she studied him, so intently that he had to resist the urge to look away.

"You are, Lord Yu," she said softly, "a man of absolutely no surprises."

He considered her for a moment, unsure what she meant by

this. She had a peculiar way of being charmingly sweet in tone despite her sharp words.

"I, myself, have a deep fondness for Confucius and his works, particularly the *Analects*. And since you *insist* that all writing must shape a moral society," she pressed, "then I might argue that if you examine Munmuja's works—the most free-spirited book in bookshops—you will often find morality *is* there. The theme of his writing is that everything changes and goes away. Nothing remains. Honor doesn't remain, reputation doesn't remain, it is all fleeting. So you see, I think you still ought to try reading one of his books." She let out a sigh. "I ramble. I am boring you, nauri."

Not at all, he caught himself thinking.

Chapter 14

Every respectable young lady was surrounded by a neighborhood of meddling ajummas, older women who considered it their communal duty to involve themselves in her affairs. But it seemed the rain had kept the villagers indoors this afternoon.

Haewon clutched her damp veil around her head nevertheless, grateful for the anonymity and for hiding the blush that refused to leave her cheeks. In the silence following their conversation, she'd found herself thinking back, agitated by his earlier words. She couldn't believe Lord Yu, of all people, had suggested they share a saddle. That she sit perched *between his thighs*. Heavens above, the mere thought left her feeling overly warm and restless. She walked faster, and Lord Yu matched her pace on horseback, his posture perfect, his expression far too severe for her liking.

"We're almost there," Haewon said, and she tried to fix her attention on the giwajip house up ahead, with its black-tiled roof and flared eaves.

Hwasadang was a residence that Mother declared must be four times the size of their own home, a compound holding two courtyards. Haewon now remembered her mother gossiping about a young man nearby who had finally left a parent-enforced exile at a Buddhist temple to return to this modest estate after his father's passing. If her mother were here, she would have sworn that the talisman she'd purchased from the shaman had brought Jade and the young man together.

"You mentioned you were friends with Young Master Byeongho?" Haewon asked, determined to be conversational.

"Yes," Lord Yu replied. "Since childhood."

Haewon still recalled the look in Jade's eyes, that glazed, dreamy look, as though Young Master Byeongho were the only man in the entire world. Nothing might come of this encounter . . . or perhaps it was the beginning of Jade's great love story.

Unless Lord Yu intervened.

"I'm relieved that my sister is well and safe," Haewon said, searching for a way to elevate her sister. "Jade is the best sister one could ask for."

"I'm sure she is," he said, sounding perfectly indifferent.

"My mother was too busy in the early years with caring for our ailing grandparents, so my sister took pity on me and Yeonhee and tutored us."

He flicked a glance down at her. "She instructed you both?"

"Indeed." Haewon stepped around yet another deep puddle in the road. "Jade collected excerpts from Kim Manjung's *Madame Sa's Conquest of the South,* and *The Tale of Lord Zhuge,* and other beautiful and worthy sayings of the ancients. She made us copy these texts, and so we did, mimicking her own hand. My sister's handwriting is extremely beautiful. All the other women in our village seek to emulate her."

"And did you?"

"I did. Her handwriting is a treasure, and mine is—uniquely mine."

Haewon continued on her campaign, boasting of how her sister was skilled in food preparation and knew how to brew soy sauce and wine, how she always took care of the seasonal outfits for the entire family and prepared elaborate meals for the ancestral service, sparing no means or effort.

"My sister takes pleasure in every kind of womanly work, doing everything with great dexterity, and bringing each task to perfection," Haewon said, a little out of breath now. She peeked up at Lord Yu from under her veil, wondering if she was doing a good job of convincing him that her sister was most worthy. "And, as I shared, her handwriting is very elegant. A skill to be prized in any young woman."

When she looked ahead again, she realized she had run out of time: They were already before Hwasadang House. Its rooftops gleamed under the sunlit rain, beads of water slipping off the eaves. Somehow, in what had felt like only a brief conversation, they had crossed through an entire forest and an entire field. It was like the earth had flown beneath her as they spoke.

"Lord Yu!" a voice called out.

A manservant hurried toward them, waving an arm, his familiarity with Haewon's companion evident. "My mistress said you both might be arriving. The little gate is flooded—come this way, through the main entrance. And here, nauri, I'll take your horse to the stable."

"Lord Yu is wounded," Haewon pointed out, before she could stop herself. "He will need assistance."

Lord Yu cleared his throat, visibly discomforted perhaps at how intimate her concern might have seemed.

The servant flicked her a curious glance before nodding. "Yes, of course."

Haewon gripped her veil tighter as she followed the two into Hwasadang. Wind whistled across the muddy land and whipped by her, turning her drenched veil and dress into sheets of ice. A shudder ran down her spine. How desperately she longed to see her sister, to slip into warm, dry clothes and put this ordeal behind her.

"You're injured, too, I see," Young Master Byeongho said to Lord Yu as he hurried over to join them.

He bowed to Haewon. "Looks to me you both had a little *tumble* in the forest," Byeongho observed, then paused as the words left his mouth. A beat of silence followed. His ears flushed as he darted a glance at her, then back to Lord Yu. "I—I mean, you must've had a *fall*. A proper fall. Down a slope! That's what I meant—"

"I fell off my horse," Lord Yu said dryly.

Haewon blinked. She had no clue as to why both gentlemen had turned red.

"Well then," Byeongho said, still looking rather appalled with himself, "it's a wonder you escaped with just a limp and a cut to the arm. I'm sending one of my servants to fetch a nurse and physician."

Haewon suddenly remembered her parents. "Could your servant send a note for me, too?" she asked. "My parents are likely waiting anxiously for us."

"Yes, yes, of course." Young Master Byeongho still looked flustered. "Ehm. There's paper and writing utensils in the room where your sister is resting. I'll tell the servant to wait—no, I am being silly. You're here already."

He summoned a servant and quickly sent him off with an order. A moment later, he ushered Haewon over to the veranda, where the servant had prepared a low table with writing utensils.

"I will send your note off instantly," Young Master Byeongho promised. "Your parents will be reassured that your sister is in good hands. My family never turns away a traveler, and we have more than enough room in the women's quarter for your sister to recover, as long as she needs."

He flicked a nervous glance around as Haewon began to compose a quick note. "Very pleased that you are unharmed, Mistress Haewon," he said, his back respectfully to her. "If you are uneasy out here in the sarangchae courtyard, you can go write in the women's quarter."

"No, I am fine," Haewon replied, writing quicker. "I'm nearly done."

"Shall I bring a folding screen? To offer you some privacy?"

She forced a smile up at him. The man was making her more anxious. "I am fine." She waved her hand to shoo away his concern, and the brush slipped from her hand and splattered onto the floor.

Lord Yu came over in a few long strides, picked it up, and set it before her. He paused there, his eyes on her handwriting.

"You write in the palace women's style." He frowned, and there was a strange note in his voice. "Few do."

"My aunt is a palace woman who was dismissed due to illness. She taught my sister. Why, does my handwriting not meet your approval?" she asked testily. But her teasing smile melted off her face when she looked up at him. His dark eyes bore into her, almost accusatory. It was intense and demanding, as though she had declared something preposterous to him, something outrageous.

Young Master Byeongho let out a little laugh. "My dear friend, you will frighten poor Mistress Haewon away with that scowl—"

"I have a question," Lord Yu said, his voice gruff. "What is your favorite flower?"

Her lips twitched at this peculiar question.

"Name it." Desperation edged his voice. "Please."

She had too many favorites to choose from, and this hardly seemed the place to list them—in the middle of a courtyard reserved for men. Yet, at his insistence, she began counting them off on her fingers, then paused. "No, indeed, I cannot name them. Anyone who knows me well knows that I love common wildflowers. They are the most inferior of flowers to scholars, who prize the plum blossom over all others, but I love them. They bring me such delight on my walks."

"Excuse me," he said, a little weakly now, as he abruptly turned. She watched him walk off alone, brushing his friend's remarks aside, looking a little dumbstruck.

She couldn't help but wonder how it was possible that the sight of her writing could make a man look so ill.

Chapter 15

SEOJUN STARED BLANKLY INTO THE NIGHT. HE DIDN'T NEED TO charge home to the pinewood chest to reinspect the letters. He knew. Too often he had traced the strokes of Magpie's writing with the pad of his finger. The handwriting was like stringed pearls—exquisite, delicate, and precise. A writing style that rivaled his in power.

Dear Black Lotus,

He closed his eyes, Magpie's letters as clear to him as memorized verses from a cherished poem.

I am quite convinced that this letter will offend you, and in my hopes of this not becoming a source of unforgivable enmity, I am sending you a pressed flower. So many are in bloom, and so colorful, even from a glance I can tell what they are. My favorite ones are many. Forsythias, sansuyu, plum blossoms, pear blossoms, apricot flower, mugunghwa, the blossom from heaven—dansim, baedal, asadal. But my most favorite are the common wildflowers, for they bring me such delight on my walks.

I digress. I have spent the days reflecting on what you shared.

The words flowed, and with each sentence, Seojun felt the panic in his chest tighten. Magpie's handwriting, like Shin Haewon's, bore the rigid style of the palace that few women outside the royal service used. He had always found it peculiar, assuming Magpie to be a gentleman, that he would write in such a style, but had attributed it to the fact that it was customary for women to teach boys how to write. He had thought, perhaps, that a retired court lady had instructed Magpie on writing. But what stood out most was the distinct yet subtle flare to their style, one he had recognized instantly. It was the kind of difference only someone intimately familiar could discern, like recognizing the voice of a dear friend in a crowded room.

You wrote that you are discouraged to write, that you feel your work will not impress the heavens. But what is meaningful? Must one's work emulate the classics to be a work of significance? Must your work be cherished by generations to come to be significant? Is the spring not beautiful, even though it is fleeting and soon forgotten?

Life is difficult, and your books are like shelter in a storm. Isn't that enough to be meaningful? Forgive my audacity, but I must defend your stories, which have brought me so much joy.

Letter after letter, exchanging thoughts on writing and books. Over time he'd come to look forward to Magpie's letters; they had become the peak of his day. He would study hard, carry out his duties to his father, and reward himself at the end by shutting his books, drawing out a sheet of paper, and pouring all his thoughts into his response.

Dearest Magpie,

It was all part of the joy of book writing—and of life itself. Joy was only made complete when shared. And what joy he had felt in the world they had built for themselves, letter by letter, a place to be their truest selves, two like-minded frogs trapped within their well, pondering the universe, freely and unafraid. A world he had never wished to leave.

Dearest, dearest Magpie,

Their letters had become a safe space for his heart to breathe. And now those very letters left his heart pounding with an erratic force that terrified him. A cold sheen of perspiration gathered on his back. His limbs wouldn't stop shaking. Were these indeed Shin Haewon's words?

He lowered his head into his hands.

The dozens of letters they'd exchanged, the memory of them, now came falling around him, pale letters fluttering like wings in the night.

Life may feel tangled and impossible to grasp, but also life is very simple . . .

. . . We flourish, and then the wind blows and we are gone, and its place remembers it no more. When I am gone, the world will remember me no more. But I am not afraid. Life is fleeting and therefore how precious . . .

. . . You say your ancestors would be ashamed of you, of your writing. May I speak plainly? I send yet another pressed flower, hoping not to offend you . . .

. . . May I speak even plainer? I find myself constantly asking for such liberties, but only because I feel that I have found a kindred spirit. I hope I do not presume too much by saying this, but though we have never met, and perhaps never will, it feels as though I have known you for far longer . . .

As the candlelight dimmed, and darkness consumed the room, the letters remained as vivid as specters in his mind.

Chapter 16

Haewon stood in the women's quarter before the open window, arms folded against the damp breeze. She had never stayed the night away from home. It had always been the center of her universe—no matter how far she wandered, she always returned to her parents before nightfall. But here she was, alone with her sister, in the residence of a family unrelated to them. It was such a strange, unsettling feeling, to have *too* much freedom.

The entire afternoon, in fact, had been spent in a manner far too unrestrained.

Chewing on her lower lip, she stared out at the shadowy garden as her thoughts meandered through the haze of events—her path crossing with Lord Yu, the crowds fleeing Five Willows, the dismal escapade through the rain . . . and Lord Yu again.

She was ashamed at how frequently she thought of him. She had tried to push him from her mind, but a single remark of his refused to let go.

No one knows just how severely the law will be enforced.

At the time, she had dismissed his words, clinging to a desperate hope that the worst would not come to pass. But now, in the stillness of night, they sent a chill down her spine.

No one seemed to know what the consequence would be for possessing, transcribing, and distributing illegal books. But

Haewon knew for certain that regardless of how merciful the king's punishment might be, what would amount to a mere slap for a gentleman could prove fatal to a lady.

Perhaps the freedom she'd enjoyed in transcribing anonymously was not a good sort of freedom, but a dangerous recklessness.

Haewon finally pulled the window closed. She'd only meant to open it for a little fresh air, but now her fingers were cold, and her blood felt even colder.

"What is worrying you?" came Jade's voice behind her.

"Oh, nothing at all." Haewon glanced back at her older sister, who was reclining weakly on the silk bed mat, her lips and cheeks pale. She didn't want to dampen Jade's spirits, and she tried for a few moments longer, but then the words came bursting out of her. "I used to be so concerned about the book thieves. Their greed knows no bounds, stealing from bookshops until they're forced to close. But now I'm worried about the edict," she confessed. "I kept brushing it aside, but this time it feels different. Don't you think?"

"It does," Jade whispered, her brows puckering with worry. "Poor Mistress Wol, the bookshop is her entire heart. She spends such a great deal of time curating her collection, and the patrons are like her family. They come and bare their souls to her while borrowing their books, and she truly cares for each and every one of them."

Haewon sighed. There was nothing she could do to help, and she was in a predicament herself. "An edict is an edict, after all. Perhaps I should stop transcribing . . ."

Jade struggled up into a sitting position. "Why would you say such a thing? You love transcribing. I have never seen you happier than when you do it."

"No, I have thought long and hard about it, and I really should stop. If, in any way, a literary censor discovers that I am Magpie . . ."

Jade shook her head. "There are so many such copies in circulation, why would the authorities bother with the transcribers? It is the authors who are writing the 'dangerous content,' I should think."

Haewon paused before a white porcelain jar on display, moonlike in shape, and glared at her faint reflection. "Perhaps you are right. But I don't want to do anything that will ruin your prospects of marriage—"

"You are worrying needlessly. I forbid you, Shin Haewon," Jade said, her voice solemn and yet still sweet, "do not stop transcribing books for my sake."

"But—"

"I always said to follow your heart."

"So long as I do not break too many rules. I'm very much afraid transcribing is starting to feel like *too* much rule breaking."

"Come here." Jade touched the floor before her. "Sit with me."

When Haewon sat before her sister, her skirt puffing up around her, Jade took her hands and squeezed them gently. "Do not be as apprehensive as those soldiers of old," she said softly, "who mistook for sounds of attack the cry of the cranes and the rustling of the wind. Fear makes us see things that are not truly there. What you are doing is not wrong. I think it is brave, and it is necessary. You said so yourself, books give our minds wings. Knowledge ought not to be feared."

Haewon swallowed, her heart tightening. Perhaps Jade was right, and she was worrying too much. Her tense shoulders eased as she whispered, "You, my dear sister, are too sweet, kind, and generous."

Jade gave a weak smile, but it faded quickly. Her lashes lowered, and her voice turned into a fragile whisper. "Sometimes I'm tired of being sweet, kind, and generous. I envy you, Haewon; Mother rebukes you for being obstinate and headstrong, but I admire that. You always speak your mind. I wish . . ." Her eyes reddened, as a thought seemed to constrict her. "I wish I could be like that. To say what I truly feel."

"And . . . what is it you truly feel?" Haewon asked, studying her sister's face. Jade never unveiled her deepest thoughts easily, but Haewon had learned to read her sister's face like the words on a page. "You are thinking about Young Master Byeongho."

A flush crept to Jade's cheeks. "Is it that telling?"

"You've been telling me since I arrived how kind and amiable he was when he found you in the forest," Haewon said, grateful for the diversion, "and how his *strong* and *masculine* arms scooped you into his embrace."

The flush deepened. "I really wish you wouldn't remind me—"

The door slid open and Maid Boram stalked in with a rattling tray of herbal medicine. "Remind you of what, agasshi?"

"Never mind," Jade whispered.

Maid Boram let out a tragic little *aigoo* as she sat before Jade. "I truly can*not* endure your family, mistress! The Shin sisters are always getting into trouble! Misfortune follows you three wherever you go! After this, I will resign. I was hired to wash laundry, not to *be* washed away as I nearly was while assisting Mistress Jade here!" She huffed.

"I'm sorry, Boram-ah," Haewon said, "it cannot be helped. We are all three of us very unlucky. Didn't the shaman say so herself?"

At least once a month Boram complained about wanting to resign. She wasn't an indentured servant, like most in Joseon, and could leave whenever she wished. Haewon would have helped secure a better position for her, and with a good reference, if she ever decided to leave. She never did, though.

"So what is the plan?" Boram asked. "Are we to stay here longer? Did Mistress Myeongok write back? What did your mother say, agasshi?"

"She is rapturous that Jade is too ill to return home immediately," Haewon said with a humorless laugh, "and the nurse also advised that Jade rest the night."

"I am merely exhausted from the cold and travel," Jade murmured. "I feel terrible that we must burden this household with our presence—"

"Oh, you needn't feel terrible at all," Boram said. "All the servants are whispering that Young Master Byeongho is beside himself with concern, constantly pestering the maids to check on you. I think, agasshi, that he is *delighted* to have an excuse to fuss over you."

Once Boram finished administering the medicine, she stood up with the tray and took her leave. As soon as they were alone, Haewon snapped her attention to Jade, grinning.

"Did you hear that?" Haewon couldn't hide the thrill in her voice. "Perhaps Young Master Byeongho feels the same way about you."

Jade fidgeted with the hem of her sleeve. "Do you really think so?"

"Tell me more. Tell me everything now about how you feel."

Jade hesitated a moment, then said, "You should have seen his smile; it was so kind and warm. And what is more, I feel like myself with him. I was sharing all my favorite novels, and he said he would read any books I wanted him to. Even the romantic ones! And throughout our entire time together, he was so attentive. Oh, Haewon-ah, I finally understand those lines in books, about how the whole world seems to disappear before his gaze. I felt that."

"It's not impossible, you two. Young Master Byeongho's mother seems to like you. She even asked you to come visit her when you are recovered."

Jade let out a weak laugh. "She and her son are simply being kind. It might not mean anything much."

"Well, then you must meet him a few more times until things are certain. He'll recognize how deserving you are of his love. I'm sure of it."

"How do I meet with him? There is less than a month until the official comes to ensure I am betrothed. It's not enough time to wait, in the hopes of encountering him enough times to win his heart."

Haewon sat still, arms crossed, deep in thought.

"You look like a general planning a military campaign," Jade noted with some concern.

"Well, this *is* a campaign, and I want you to be victorious." Haewon set her shoulders and gave her sister a determined look. "You must seize your destiny. It is the only way."

"What?"

"You said so yourself: You have no time. You will have to make a gamble. Would you, even before being certain of your feelings for Young Master Byeongho, wish to become betrothed to him? Or would you rather wait for Mother or the government to choose a husband for you?"

Jade hesitated. "The official wishes to match me with Master Pyeongtaek—"

"The village *bully*," Haewon spat, "who is a bachelor because his betrothed broke with him at the last moment to marry someone *not* poor and prone to violence." She shook her head. "Edict or not, I will not let anyone trifle with your happiness."

Jade's lashes lowered. "But . . . but what should we *do*?"

Haewon rose to her feet and began pacing. She was absolutely clueless as to how to make this possible, but as her thoughts turned, her mind kept returning to what had moved her own heart: Letters from Black Lotus. They had made her come to love Black Lotus as a dear friend. Letters could move hearts—surely they could move Young Master Byeongho's, too.

"There are love letters in *The Tale of Unyong*," Haewon said conspiratorially. "You should write such a letter to Young Master Byeongho."

"Write to him?" Jade cried. "Me, an unmarried lady, write *openly* to an unmarried man? My dear sister, have you lost your mind?"

Haewon shook her head, pacing faster. "No, you must write him a letter. Secure his affection. I know it's early, but you only have less than a month to get engaged, and you might never have the chance to see him again."

"But to write him a letter . . . even before I'm certain of his own feelings for me . . ."

"You must guide his heart. It is decided. Write him a note," Haewon said, then quoted one of the letters from *The Tale of Unyong*. "Tell him you think of him, love him, and you yearn for him so desperately that . . . *my heart has grown restless, my spirit has dissipated, and my mind cannot be easily appeased. It seems as if my bowels have been severed . . .*" Haewon placed a hand dramatically over her heart as she recited, fluttering her lashes. "*I could not sleep, although I lay down, and I could not swallow any food although I tried to eat—*"

Jade looked horrified. "I could never write that to him." She shook her head, looking demoralized. "I could never imagine such a love. Can you?"

"I have no interest in a love that is capable of severing a man's bowels." Haewon snorted. "I have enough to worry about without a man starving to death because he is so madly in love with me."

Thoughts of the bookshop raid, and Yeonhee's accusation about her transcription work, flickered to mind. But she stomped them away. She would focus on Jade for now. "Yet I can see you being loved in such a way one day."

"No . . ." Jade smiled lightly. "No, not I. I can't imagine ever inspiring such passion in any man. I've told him nothing about my feelings. I've barely even encouraged him, or hinted at my affection for him."

"That is why you must write him a letter. I'll deliver it." Haewon hurried to the window and peeked out. "The women's quarter is locked for the night. I'll discreetly deliver it tomorrow morning."

She walked around, finding paper, ink, and writing tools. "What should I write? You dictate and I will write it down."

"I . . . I . . ." Jade covered her face, now bright red, shaking her head. "I'm not sure what to say."

"Close your eyes. Imagine yourself alone. And just tell me what is in your heart." Haewon's grip on the brush tightened, determined.

Jade would have her love story.

She would make sure of it.

Chapter 17

EVERY RESPECTABLE LADY HAD BEEN TAUGHT AT A YOUNG AGE that chastity was her most precious possession. She was to remain wholly pure, pristine and untouched for her husband, preserved like a prized flower. For a lady to then exchange private letters with a man unrelated to her was beyond improper. It was ruinous, and Haewon knew that if she attempted to entrust Maid Boram with such a task, the girl would likely cast the letter into the fire. She would have to deliver the letter herself, and with utmost caution.

Haewon kept her veil low as she stepped outside the following day, Boram tailing behind. Servants, upon questioning, had shared that Young Master Byeongho had gone out to survey the property and his tenant farmers. Her hope was to find the young master alone in the open, and to slip the love letter into his possession without Boram noticing. Instead, Haewon found him stretched out in a pavilion that faced a vast field, a book over his face.

"They say archery is meant for leisure," he said, voice muffled. "But watching you, I can't help but think you're punishing yourself. Truly, it's sheer torture to witness. What is bothering you?"

"Nothing."

Haewon's gaze swiveled onto the young master's companion,

the young man with an arrow aimed across the empty field. His focus was so intense he seemed not to register their arrival.

She and Boram gawked as Lord Yu drew the arrow back with such elegance and ease. One could only imagine what tremendous strength was required to pull the bowstring and hold it steady. He did so with effortless control, it seemed. But then the slightest tremble of his bandaged arm told her he was in some pain, a pain he resisted as he released the arrow. She watched as it flew and met the target board, joining the cluster of others.

He reached for the next, then stilled at the sight of her. His gaze held hers, intense and unwavering, as he slowly lowered the bow.

"Whatever is bothering you, it kept you up all night, didn't it?" the young master's muffled voice spoke on. "I heard you pacing about until dawn. You've lost all appetite and look entirely too distracted. You're thinking about *her*, aren't you? Though, I wager, not nearly as often as I find myself thinking of Shin Yeonok . . . 'Jade,' as she prefers to be called—"

A squeak escaped Boram.

Haewon flung a horrified glance at her maid, just as the young master bolted up. The book fell off him with a *thud*.

"M-Mistress Haewon!" he cried.

Haewon inclined her head, hoping the veil hid her shock. "My maid and I were just out for a stroll," she remarked as she and Boram began inching backward in retreat. She tried to sound conversational, like she hadn't overheard anything at all. "Your injuries, Lord Yu . . . I hope you are recovering well?"

When he didn't reply, appearing sickly pale, she rambled on, her pulse pounding at the base of her throat. "The morning is cold and damp, so I hope you will be careful of your health, gentlemen. Now, if you will excuse us."

At once, Haewon maneuvered her maid around, and they quickly retreated to Hwasadang. Her plan to deliver her sister's letter was entirely abandoned.

"Agasshi." Her maid peered at her intensely once they were in the safety of the women's quarter. "Did something happen in the forest when you both were alone?"

Haewon, startled out of the shock, looked at her maid. "I told you, nothing happened."

"He didn't—he didn't make any untoward advances?"

"Of course not!" Haewon bristled. "What a preposterous assumption, Boram-ah."

"But when the young master said Lord Yu was thinking about someone, I'm so certain the woman in question was *you*."

"If Lord Yu thinks of me at all, it is in judgment. All he does is look down his nose at me whenever we are together. Whatever the case." She gave a wave of her hand, brushing Boram's silly concern away. "You must have heard, too. The young master *is* in love with our Jade—!"

A crinkle formed between Boram's brows. "But did you not see the way he was staring at you? Indeed, he appeared as though you were . . . someone very dear to him, agasshi."

"Me? Dear to *him*," Haewon echoed, feeling so dumbstruck she nearly laughed. This was absurd! Lord Yu had shown absolutely no sign that he held her in any esteem. She was certain of this; she could always trust her good judgment on these matters of the heart. "Even if the young master was referring to me, it's of no consequence. Haven't you heard the way gentlemen converse in private at the bookshop? Men will often tease one another, boasting, and saying what they do not mean. They say such things to amuse themselves, not because they are true."

"Well then, I wouldn't wish you to embarrass yourself, agasshi . . ." Her gaze flicked to the letter in Haewon's hand. "I hope that is not a love letter to Lord Yu."

Haewon looked at Boram, aghast. "I would never write a love letter to Lord Yu. Goodness, Boram-ah, how silly do you think I am?"

The maid let out a dramatic sigh and grumbled, "Silly me, to think you might ever marry a great man like him."

"I assure you, I take no interest in great men. Especially great men who actually believe they are great at all."

"Besides," Boram went on, as though she hadn't heard a word, "Lord Yu, so the servants whisper, is to be betrothed to the Minister of Rites's daughter. A rare beauty, it is said."

Haewon stilled at this. She oughtn't to feel anything but indifferent to this news. She had no reason to care; he meant nothing to her. Yet Boram's words pressed into her like a blunt knife. It was the strangest feeling—a feeling better left unexamined. "A perfect match for him, I am sure!"

For the rest of the afternoon, Haewon kept the letter safely tucked away as her sister—looking elegant and ethereal even while ill—conversed with the young master's mother, who seemed quite enchanted by Jade. Then, by nightfall, as Maid Boram was busy brushing Jade's hair, Haewon drew out the letter and stepped outside. If Byeongho was as besotted as he seemed, surely he would linger near the women's courtyard, hoping to catch even the sound of Jade's voice, especially since they were leaving for home the next morning.

Or had she read too many novels? Were men not like those in *The Tale of Sim Saeng*, where a single encounter with a beautiful woman would leave an upright scholar standing outside the lady's home for days, wasting away with lovesickness?

Haewon strolled through the courtyard, which was closed in by a high stone wall that shut out the rest of the world. A place where proper young ladies grew up, often never seeing much beyond.

"Please," Haewon whispered, halting before the wall. "Please be near."

She was so desperate now, she found herself hoping that she could *will* the young man to show up. That if she *wished* strong enough for him to pass by, he would.

As though her prayers had summoned someone, Haewon was greeted by the sound of hurried footsteps. She quickly ducked into the shadows, hiding behind a wooden pillar under the eaves. There, she watched as a female servant unlocked the gate that connected the two courtyards. The girl scuttled in, balancing a small table loaded with bowls. She hesitated, considering the unlocked gate behind her, but when the table nearly tilted, she hurried forward instead and disappeared into the shadows.

Now was her chance.

Holding the letter tight, Haewon moved toward the open gate. A door was meant to be walked through. Young Master Byeongho might be lingering somewhere near . . .

And yet, she could not.

Liberty was peril. The etiquette books had tied a delicate noose around her ankle, holding her in her place. *Chastity, respectability, and honor are everything; they measure a woman's worth, her family's worth.* She had read too many of these books to naively hope that, if caught outside the women's quarter, anyone would understand that her intentions were pure.

A sigh escaped her as she continued to stroll aimlessly. At least the courtyard was a pleasing sight to behold. White plum blossom trees, mountain peonies, and azaleas released their fragrance and sweetened the evening air. A chorus of birds called from the east. Rain had come and gone throughout the day, and the remnants of the previous shower dripped from the eaves like crystal threads.

Haewon found herself standing paces away from the gate once more, staring at the glimpse of the men's courtyard beyond—a vast dirt yard and the rippling silhouette of flared-roof structures. She was about to turn, then froze as she caught sight of a tall male figure. His back was to her, brooding as he paced in and out of view. She knew, almost at once, that he was not the young master.

Flee, her heart thrummed.

She wanted to dart away like a rabbit. But she could not move.

The moon rose higher, outlining his broad shoulders, his lean waist. Then he turned slowly. Their eyes locked. The color drained from his face. Something like fear flitted across his expression.

"Mistress Haewon." His voice was so low and deep, her skin pebbled.

"Someone must have forgotten to close the gate." She nervously wandered over and put her hand on the gate as though meaning to shut it, but she was once again rendered immobile. He was right across from her now, and his gaze fell onto the letter in her hand. Without thinking, she instantly snatched the letter behind her.

"A letter you would rather hide," he observed. "It is for Byeongho, I presume."

Her eyes widened, and he strolled closer.

"The servants whisper that your sister has less than a month left until the government's expected betrothal date. With such pressure, I'm sure there's a growing desperation to secure her a suitable match."

"I'm not sure what you mean," Haewon said, but didn't sound very convincing even to her own ears.

"Allow me to deliver it." He held out his hand. She stared at it. Those were not the hands of a boy or a frail scholar. They were the hands of a man well-versed in wielding a bow. "Mistress Haewon?"

She remained still, reluctant to deliver the letter into the clutches of the antagonist. For that was who he was. A man who might attempt to intervene in her sister's love story before even giving it a chance to blossom.

"I didn't mean to overhear, earlier," she said slowly. "Forgive my boldness, but is it true that the young master is fond of my sister?"

"It is true, though it makes no difference how he feels."

She understood his meaning; men of his station had no care for silly things like feelings and romantic love. Yet she was determined to allow Jade the opportunity to choose—to choose her groom, to choose how she wished to live her life.

"Do you believe in destiny?" she asked.

Lord Yu studied her, attentive and calm. "I've read the four famous essays that were directed to the notion of destiny," he replied. "'On the Destiny of Kings' by Ban Biao, 'On Fortune and Destiny' by Li Kang—"

"'On Doubtless Destiny' by Gu Jizhi and Gu Yuan, and 'On the Argument About Destiny' by Liu Jun," Haewon listed the rest, a little impatiently. "Yes, nauri, I have read those, too. So, do you believe in it?"

His large hand rested on the door of the gate, pushing it open just enough that they were no longer exchanging words through a crack. He took another step forward, leaned against the wooden frame, now only two paces away from her.

"I believe in fate," he said at last. "I was raised to understand that a gentleman bears his fate and follows it obediently."

"To *bear* fate," she said contemplatively. "I by far prefer the notion of destiny, for I am going to *choose* mine. And I hope my sister will, too, without anyone standing in her way."

"A young lady wishing to choose her destiny," he murmured. "Spoken precisely like a lady who has read too many novels, especially tales from two centuries ago."

Two centuries ago, women had much more freedom.

Four centuries ago, women had rights. They could freely mingle with men, have their own possessions, and inherit land.

She knew he was silently judging her, and for some reason, she couldn't level her gaze at him. Vulnerability chafed at her as she glared at the gleaming silk of his robe. "I'm convinced," she said, unable to hide the rawness in her voice, "that to live without a will is to deny the bird the sky, the flowers the sun. I was born with a will. Mayn't I use it?"

A long, peculiar silence fell.

When she dared to glance up, her breath hitched in her throat.

The rims of his eyes were red, his brows deeply furrowed. "To deny the bird the sky . . ." his voice rasped. For a moment he looked like such a bird. Looking for the sky. And he was staring at her, like she *was* the sky.

No, she was certainly imagining it. He couldn't possibly have feelings for her, as Young Master Byeongho had joked.

Lord Yu was a gentleman who had witnessed the failings of her family and showed no signs of forgetting it.

A gentleman so proud of his Confucian education and morality.

A perfect gentleman.

A perfect gentleman destined to marry a perfect wife and sire a perfect brood of dull, perfect children.

A gentleman whose world existed far, far above hers.

She nervously wrung her hands, then said lightheartedly, "The night is late. We had better both retire—"

"Give me the letter," he said, a bare whisper. "I promise, upon my honor, that I will deliver it intact, even if I do disapprove. I would rather you go and care for your sister."

"So you do disapprove."

"Marriage is a union between families. What the individual heart desires is of no importance."

"I just want *one* of us to be happy," Haewon blurted, her eyes locked with his. An unexpected burning stung her, like a long-buried hope that this man somehow drew to the surface. "And that person has to be Jade. I could be arranged in marriage to anyone, even a stranger I can barely tolerate. I have other things to bring me joy, and I make friends easily. But Jade—she keeps to herself. She raised us all, always denying herself her own needs and happiness. I am her only friend. I want her to be happy. Is that so improper?"

"Mistress Haewon," he said, with a tenderness that seemed so unlike him, "I give you my word. I will not open it. I shan't intervene. It wouldn't be my place to do so. Not when I, too . . ." He didn't finish. "I promise I will not intervene."

She swallowed. There was no other way to pass on the letter at this point. If she waited any longer, it might be too late. With Jade out of sight, the young master might forget her entirely.

"Then please, deliver the letter and leave the rest to fate," Haewon pressed. "If your friend's heart leads him to my sister, let it be. Let things unfold as they will. And if this so troubles you, simply deliver the letter and then forget my sister. Forget me, too."

She faltered, then at last proffered the letter to him. She waited for him to take it, but his dark eyes roamed over her face, his brows drawing together as though he was conflicted by some thought or memory. Then something shifted in his gaze, a look of certainty taking root. At last he reached out, but it was not the letter he grasped for; his long fingers folded around her hand instead.

Her heart leapt. A jolt of shock spiraled up along her arm, through her entire body, and she suddenly felt as though she were falling through open air, and it was difficult to breathe. Impossible to move. She could think of nothing but his hand, the warmth of his palm melting into her.

"I won't trouble myself over Byeongho's love life." His voice was soft. With his other hand, he took the letter from her. "But I have no intention of forgetting you."

A beat passed, then another. He was still holding her, and her heart was still spinning, her cheeks on fire—

"Haewon agasshi!" Maid Boram's voice called out. "Agasshi? Where did you go?"

Startled, she wrenched her hand from his. She turned sharply and hurried across the dark courtyard, trying not to imagine what Lord Yu's meaning could have been. She held Boram by the elbow, rushed into the room, then slid the door shut a little too hard.

"Agasshi." Boram frowned. "Why are your cheeks so red?"

Jade craned her head from where she sat on the bed mat. "Where did you go?"

Haewon made a reply, she wasn't sure what, and then she was pacing the room, her emotions a storm inside her. She paced while staring down at her hand. The warmth of him still lingered on her skin, like the faintest burn.

Why had he held her hand?

Why would he do such a thing?

She hesitated, then moved to the window, cracking it open just enough to look outside. The gate was closed again, as if it had never been open.

As if it had all been a figment of her imagination.

Chapter 18

THREE DAYS HAD PASSED SINCE THE ENCOUNTER WITH LORD Yu. Her heart still quickened at the memory, but she wasn't so naive to imagine that anything could come of it. She therefore dove into her transcription work at home, determined to forget the entire incident. A needless distraction.

Yet, every so often, her focus waned and she found herself thinking of Lord Yu again. Why had he held her hand? Had it been an accident? Or did he truly hold some form of affection for her? But that was ridiculous—when could he have possibly fallen for her? It was all too instantaneous. She shoved the questions aside each time and went back to her work, wishing she'd never met Lord Yu in the first place.

She had transcribed no more than two pages of a novel when Jade wandered into the room. She sat next to Haewon and was quiet for such a long time that Haewon finally stole a glance at her sister.

"What is it?"

Jade remained sitting, staring blankly ahead. "It has arrived," she said at last.

"What has arrived?"

Another long, long silence ensued.

Haewon set aside her brush and turned to face her sister, ready to pry the news from Jade, when she noticed the letter in her sister's white-knuckled grip.

"It is a letter from Young Master Byeongho," Jade said, and slowly a smile of sheer joy formed on her lips. "What should I do?"

Haewon let out a gasp, her heart thundering so fast her chest ached. Her sister's joy was *her* joy. She wanted to leap to her feet, embrace Jade, celebrate as soldiers did after an impossible victory. But it was too soon. This was only the beginning. Composing herself, Haewon rushed to ask, "What does it say?"

"He has read the romantic novels I recommended, found them most enjoyable, and wishes to see me again! He is asking to meet at Seogeomjeong tomorrow afternoon. I don't think I should go . . . I would much rather we exchange letters a few more times—"

"But of course you must go! See?" Haewon clasped Jade's hands. "It worked just as I knew it would." She forgot all about Lord Yu Seojun as her mind began to strategize. "We mustn't tell Maid Boram, that is for certain."

A little frown crinkled Jade's brow. "Seogeomjeong is quite a journey away."

"What is a long walk in good weather? That pavilion is where lovers meet—I've read of it often in poems. And he is right to choose that place, for to meet here in Gyonam or at Five Willows . . ." Haewon shook her head. "There would be too many eyes. And you know what they say: A lady is ever surrounded by spies. No, Seogeomjeong is the safest place to meet."

Jade clenched the letter, her anxiety evident.

"Write back," Haewon urged. "Ask to meet him in two days'

time instead. That is when Boram and Mother will drag Yeonhee to the creek to wash laundry. Most of the village women do their washing on that day, too."

"I suppose no one would miss us . . ." Jade still looked uneasy.

"I will go with you, and ensure that Young Master Byeongho does not make any improper advances."

Jade's face turned red before melting into laughter. "Oh, Haewon. I can't believe this is happening to *me*." Then the brightness of her expression blazed radiant. "If we are already breaking the rules for my sake, perhaps we might as well break another for yours."

Before Haewon could ask the meaning of this, Mother burst into their room, retying the coat string of her jacket as she said, "Retrieve your veil, Jade. We are going to visit the shaman." She clucked her tongue sharply as she struggled to arrange the ribbon neatly. "You are still filled with bad luck and we must ward it away. It has been announced that all but ten spinsters have been matched, and now Master Pyeongtaek's mother keeps insisting on a match with Jade. That woman vexes me to no end."

Jade obediently followed their mother out, and once they left, silence filled the house. Yeonhee had gone to tutor a few maids and wouldn't return until noon. Father was studying. Maid Boram was shuffling about carrying out her other duties.

Haewon was blessedly alone.

Her spirit felt buoyant with the good news Jade had shared. Unable to stop smiling, Haewon reached for her bowl of tea. It was cold now, but she still thoroughly enjoyed its taste, sturdy and robust.

After a few more sips, she steadied her mind and picked up

her ink-dipped brush. Her gaze flicked between the original novel and its copy as she resumed her transcription, keeping in mind the foremost rule Wol had taught her: Never write at the bottom margin of the page. Too many readers had complained that, over time, countless hands turning the pages would wear the ink away, leaving the words to fade into nothing.

She had yet to complete transcribing a copy this week, and she wanted to visit Five Willows and hated going empty-handed.

As she moved her brush, ink against the blank page, mountains rose and seas crashed through the expanse of her mind. Here, the concerns of the world could not follow her. She was already on a boat far away.

JADE BARELY SLEPT THAT NIGHT, AND THE FOLLOWING NIGHT, Haewon watched as her sister tossed and turned. When the sun finally arose, Haewon and her sister slipped out of Gyonam Village early in the morning, leaving behind the crowd of women off to pound laundry and gossip by the creek.

There was a heart-skipping sensation fluttering in Haewon's chest, this intuition that the day was filled with possibilities and new beginnings. It inspired a bounce in her steps as she walked. Jade, too, had recovered enough that she matched Haewon's long strides, the color high in her cheeks, her eyes glittering.

There could not have been a more perfect day for their . . . tryst? Escapade? Adventure? Haewon was still uncertain how to categorize this affair. But she and Jade had come to the silent agreement not to spare their possible ruin any thought. This was a golden opportunity, and it was worth the risk when the only other option was to stay still and watch Jade forced into a match by government officials.

A most *miserable* match.

Haewon took in a deep breath of air, determined to think of only good things this morning. The spring weather was too pleasant to think of anything else, anyway. Cool breezes left their skirts and veils billowing, and the sun warmed their bones. With the rain now falling several times a day, the trees were in full bloom, whole groves of them, clouds of white, pink, and yellow blossoms, branches dabbled with bright green buds.

"We're almost there," Haewon said, spotting the stream in the distance.

"Already?" Jade let out a nervous laugh. "I was hoping it might last a little longer. I'm terribly nervous."

Haewon herself was terribly nervous for her sister. But Jade had always been her unwavering support, and Haewon wished to be the same for her now.

"Here, let me have a look at you, eonni," she said, keeping her voice steady and sure. She whipped out a handkerchief and dabbed away the faint sheen of sweat from Jade's brow. "Bite your lips a little, to return some color to them. Good, and pinch your cheeks, too."

Satisfied, Haewon then adjusted her sister's veil back slightly, revealing more of her features and the sparkling hairpin that illuminated Jade's face.

"One last thing," Haewon murmured, carefully arranging the long veil over her sister's dress, draping it elegantly over the white jeogori, its collar trimmed in pale yellow, and the voluminous pink skirt adorned with embroidered flowers along the hem. It was Jade's finest gown made of a luxurious ramie fabric, reserved only for special occasions.

Jade's attire was a garden in full bloom, and as for Haewon, she'd chosen her most severe outfit, an old white jacket and an indigo-dyed skirt, befitting the background character she wished to play in Jade's great love story.

"Perfect," Haewon whispered, holding back a proud smile. "You look truly splendid, my dear sister. I think he will positively collapse at the sight of you."

Jade let out a nervous breath, her eyes gleaming. "I hope he is there, waiting for us. I think I'll be crushed if he's forgotten. He might have, you know."

"Well, we'll have to go see, won't we, eonni?"

Taking her sister's hand, Haewon led the way, the smile dropping from her face. If he was *not* there, she would personally storm over to Hwasadang and give him an earful. She would never forgive him, and she would take revenge on Jade's behalf and—

There were two gentlemen near Seogeomjeong Pavilion.

One was pacing about nervously, kicking at stones, dressed in a dramatic flare of colors, like an azure-blue river shimmering with the reflection of the spring wilderness. The second gentleman had leapt off his horse and was tethering the reins to a nearby tree, a tall and imposing figure who moved with the elegance and command of a prince. Haewon's stare pinned onto the latter gentleman, who was garbed in a robe of deep violet and a long overcoat of a sheer silk gauze that billowed as pale smoke.

Something had gone terribly wrong.

Shielding her eyes from the sunlight, Haewon stared harder, hoping her eyes had been mistaken. But it was no mistake. "Why is Lord Yu here?" she asked in a panicked whisper. Then she looked at Jade and a slow, creeping chill slithered down her spine at the sight of her sister's timid yet knowing smile.

"You've always done so much for me," Jade whispered. "You always think of my happiness. I wanted to do something for you."

"My happiness?" Haewon tried to sound pleasant. "What does Lord Yu have to do with my happiness?"

"Boram said you fancy him, and Lord Yu fancies you. She told me that you were only denying it out of pride and embarrassment. Remember what I told you?" It was now Jade who tugged Haewon along. "If we are already breaking the rules for my sake by meeting Young Master Byeongho, then why not break them entirely and allow you the same chance?"

Haewon's stomach twisted as they crossed the bridge, each step bringing her closer to him. To Lord Perfect—the man who never smiled, at least not at her. The one who was far too quiet, too rigid, too insufferably proper for someone so young. The one who seemed to take secret pleasure in judging her.

And then, here she was, standing right before him.

Chapter 19

The sky was vast and the weight of the heavens felt light as Shin Haewon walked alongside him, escorting their charges. Glimpses of her profile peeked out from under the veil—the arch of her nose, the soft curve of her cheeks—and when she looked ahead, sunlight pooled in her eyes, illuminating the light brown into a vivid shade of gold. He found it impossible to look away. For so long he had wondered who Magpie might be, the scribe whose letters he'd waited for as eagerly as he did for spring in the midst of winter, and here she stood, in the flesh.

"Nauri, watch your step," she said.

Seojun jerked his attention back and barely avoided the muddy patch of earth. "Thank you," he said, casting another glance her way, only to find her studying him.

"May I . . ." She hesitated, then continued, "May I speak plainly?"

His chest tightened at the familiar request. "I think you know no other way of speaking, Mistress Haewon."

The slightest of frowns crinkled her brows, then she fixed her gaze ahead once more as she asked, "Why did you come, nauri? Your friend does not require a chaperone."

"Byeongho ordered that I accompany him here, and to ask him no questions. He spoke with such unusual gravity that I thought it was an urgent matter," he said honestly. "I am as confounded by the situation as you."

"Hmm." She stared ahead again, her brows drawn, looking dissatisfied with his answer. "So there is no other reason as to why you joined . . . And you had no idea that *I* would be here?"

"None whatsoever."

She still looked dissatisfied, and it occurred to him that perhaps she believed he had come for *her*. He had held her hand that night in the garden, and perhaps she expected some form of an explanation . . .

But he didn't even know how or where to begin.

He could begin with the letters they had shared. And, indeed, it was what he desired above all else. He wanted Haewon to know him, to know him the way Magpie knew Black Lotus.

But he hesitated at this.

It was the same hesitation that had made him crumple every letter inviting Magpie to drink and converse with him in person. To meet the one to whom he had bared his soul, safely hidden behind anonymity, was a vulnerability he shied from. To be seen was to risk the very thing he feared most—to be truly known, only to disappoint.

"Mistress Jade," Byeongho's boisterous voice boomed, momentarily drawing Seojun out of his own conflicted thoughts, "would you like to visit the Seogeomjeong Pavilion up ahead? Or shall we stroll together for a little while longer?"

"I would like to walk," Mistress Jade replied quickly.

"I would, too. I think it would help calm my nerves. Indeed, I couldn't sleep all last night thinking of today. Of m-meeting you."

"Neither could I," Mistress Jade replied, and her voice remained so stiff and terse, it was hard to imagine that Jade had lost sleep over Byeongho at all.

As the pair strolled farther ahead, Haewon and Seojun fell farther behind. Her pace had slowed and he realized her attention was fixed upon a dot of white flowing downstream.

"What is that?" she asked, more to herself.

He didn't need to look closer to know. "Recycled paper."

"Recycled paper?"

"Past that grove of trees, you will see government workers there. This is where they come to recycle paper, as paper is too precious to destroy."

"I wish for only a quick look." She glanced over at her sister, hesitated for the barest moment before hurrying down the nearby slope and onto the riverbank. Seojun joined her as she crouched and waited, then at last caught a stray page, drenched but sturdy enough not to tear in her grasp.

As he had surmised, upstream a short distance away, workers were dipping the pages into the water, washing away the ink before spreading them on the rocks to dry. They appeared as snow resting on mountain peaks. Soon, the dried pages would be gathered and reused.

Haewon flipped the page around, drops of water dribbling down her wrist, disappearing into her wide sleeve.

He looked away. "The writing has already been washed away."

"Remnants of ink always remain on recycled paper."

"You seem to take a great deal of interest in paper, Mistress Haewon."

"I am around paper often," she said, and a quiet smile tugged at her lips. "I often wonder at how something as simple as paper can carry one's heart and mind in the form of a letter or a story, across land and water, right into the hands of the receiver. If the person is literate, that is."

He crouched next to her and examined the page she held, only to find himself distracted by the scent of her. She smelled of fresh wildflowers. And as her veil slipped back a little, he watched the loose strand of her hair brushing the side of her cheek. *She is Magpie,* he was reminded once more.

Shin Haewon was the scribe who had become as one in mind with his, the scribe he'd mistaken to be a gentleman friend. He'd only ever had gentlemen friends, the only friends he was permitted to know. As boys, he and Byeongho would study together, wrestling when their tutors weren't watching, freely butting heads like wild deer. But Magpie was a woman, and this reality formed a wide gulf between them, a valley he had no idea how to navigate.

"Did you know that before the Imjin War"—Haewon's voice startled him back to her, to the page in her hand—"we had some of the finest quality paper? There was a thriving industry in dochim."

He recomposed himself quickly. "Dochim?"

"*Do,* meaning 'to pound,' and *chim,* meaning 'hammering block.' Dochim." She laid the page on the ground, straightening its corners. "It's a process done after the paper is made. Workers stack alternating wet and dry sheets until they have a stack of a hundred pages. Then they place a special board atop it, press it down with a rock, and after a day, they pound it—two to three hundred times—until dry.

Then they repeat the process, alternating the pages, pressing, pounding again. After three or four rounds, the result is a glossy, smooth finish."

She sighed. "But after the war, many tools were destroyed. It caused irreparable damage to the dochim practice." Tracing the drenched page, she whispered, "Look at this. You can still see the handwriting. It is very faint, though."

글씨 못 썼다고 흉보지 마세요

"Scribes often mark the first page of forbidden books they transcribe with phrases like *Do not mock my handwriting*," she went on. "Scribes are often criticized for their script. I wonder how such a page ended up here?"

Seojun watched as a shadow crossed her features. She was one who valued knowledge, and he felt compelled to share what he'd overheard from his father. "I believe these are the books confiscated by the officers from the other bookshop a few days ago."

Her attention darted to him. "Do you think so? Did the king order this?"

"No, indeed, I do not think the king was involved. His Majesty is not this aggressive in his approaches."

"Then who could have ordered the raid?"

"Some high official, I suppose, who is either afraid of knowledge or sees the destruction of it as an opportunity to gain something." Seojun stared upstream at the recycled pages, each as pale as a soul scrubbed of all its thoughts and feelings.

You oughtn't to feel so downcast. The memory of his father whispered. *Fiction is more dangerous than wild beasts, for when a wild beast appears, people run. But when a lewd novel falls into someone's hands, they clutch it tightly.*

That was his writing, a cheap and vulgar scandal.

Seojun dipped his hand into the cold water, wishing the current could take with it the haunting, the ghost that refused to release him, the stories that beckoned him, humming in his blood. He wished he had never known this desire. This need to write. To write was to wrestle with despair and inadequacy. How many times had he tried to make his writing upright and respectable, only to witness—in utter horror and twisted fascination—as words escaped from his brush like darting fish, free and impossible to contain, impossible to guide. Writing had unveiled his most honest self, and his father—as well as the king, heaven's representative on Earth—had condemned such writings as a source of corruption. Seojun was convinced his writing was a reflection of his moral deficiency. So better for it to be washed away. For it to not exist at all.

"This storm of sensational novels," Seojun muttered, "does little to inspire a moral society." He rose to his feet, stared down at the abandoned page before turning. "Writing serves as a mirror, and when the writing of the people grows hurried, shallow, and chaotic, it shows a lack of any depth."

"I must say, Lord Yu, you are too harsh," she declared as they ascended the slope and reached level ground. "Perhaps fiction writing has become such, because the times are growing hurried and chaotic, and there are cracks in our beliefs, and Joseon people are searching for a world in novels to take them away from it all."

Resuming their roles as chaperones, they made their way over to the two lovebirds flirting in the pavilion. Haewon settled on a nearby rock shaded beneath a tree clouded with white blossoms. As for Seojun, he stationed himself right next to her, nervous and tense.

"Novels are honest," she continued. "And I believe, Lord Yu, that honesty—the story of the era and of the people *as it is*—is by far more valuable than the rigidness of old customs and rules."

Seojun gathered his hands behind his back, trying to hold on to his composure. Every word Haewon uttered was shocking, wildly improper, and very Magpie-esque. If he'd had any doubts that she was Magpie, the scribe who possessed intelligence and outlandish opinions that always left him enthralled, they were entirely gone now.

"You are silent, nauri. Why, do you disapprove of everything I say?" she asked teasingly. "Perhaps you do. But my father once put it this way: We can cling to withering classics, but all we will be doing is guarding an empty shell."

At this, Seojun had to look away, seized by the discomforting reminder of her family. *She* was near perfection, nearly all bewitching delight. But her family was her fatal flaw. "Your father is free-spirited in his thinking," he murmured, "though I suppose that is how one tends to think, when one lives isolated from power."

She arched a brow. "My father is studying for the civil service exam. Indeed, I am convinced he will pass it this time and secure a position in the government—"

"How many times has Scholar Shin failed?"

"Three. But nearly every gentleman fails at least thrice, I hear."

"Even if your father were to pass, he would never be placed in high office," Seojun said matter-of-factly. He had made inquiries into her background the past few days, and the more he'd learned, the more troubled he'd become. She belonged to a family that his father would never have considered associating with. "Scholar Shin comes from Pyeongan-do, the Gwanseo region."

"And what of that? Pyeongan-do is a lovely province."

He slid her a curious glance. "Those from the northern province like your father are always excluded from being appointed to key posts." It was an unwritten rule that *everyone* knew. "And for that matter, your mother . . . her lineage would be of no service to him. She is the daughter of a merchant—"

"A merchant who *became* a yangban noble."

"Many families purchase the yangban status these days. It holds no real weight. Not like it once did."

Haewon drew her shoulders back, a cold civility pinching her expression.

"I mean only this," he added quickly. "That you are intelligent, quite remarkable, and lovely. You have a mind that rivals my own—despite your lowly upbringing. I truly do have the highest regard for you."

"Well, that is certainly news. I was quite convinced you despised me."

Her words caught him off guard. Hatred was the furthest thing he felt for her. "How could I despise you? I am—I am most fond of you, Mistress Haewon."

She blinked. "*Fond* of me?"

His heart pounded; cold perspiration gathered on his back as he realized he would have to admit to his feelings for her. He'd never done anything like this before. But the dread eased away as he watched her sitting there, perched on a rock, surrounded by a cluster of tiny purple flowers. She sat there so proudly like it was her throne. And when a breeze tumbled by, blossoms showered down from the branches, catching on her veil like soft white adornments. Her eyes, ever dancing with light, were steadied on him, and he was convinced that he would never encounter a woman more beautiful than she.

"Unfortunately, Mistress Haewon," his voice rasped, "I have come to care for you, most deeply. For months I've thought of you."

Her brows pressed together, emotions racing across her countenance. First was a look of confusion and incredulity, which was to be expected. Any sensible woman would realize that his confession was akin to receiving a promise of a better life. Seojun then expected a look of joy to brighten her expression, or at least gratitude.

Instead, she appeared infuriated.

"*Unfortunately?*" she repeated, her voice cutting. "Yes, I suppose it is unfortunate for a great gentleman like you to fancy a woman like me, of such inferior birth. No, indeed, you really ought to try harder. To forget me, that is."

He frowned, utterly bewildered by her response. "You are—you are asking me to forget you."

"Yes. I could never reciprocate your feelings. I could never respect or care for someone like you."

Her words were arrows loosed at him, and they met their mark, leaving a gaping hole in his chest. "Someone like me?"

"Yes. Arrogant, so arrogant. You take such delight in looking down your nose at my family. And you despise novels. *That* I cannot forgive—"

"Mistress Haewon," he bit out as he felt a rare stirring of anger. *Magpie,* he wanted to say, *it is me, Black Lotus.* This truth was the most vulnerable part of him, a secret he had hoped to share when the opportunity arose. But he would simply tell her now, concern and caution be damned. "Do you know who I am?"

"I will not be interrupted, Lord Yu," she said, steel in her voice. "I think those like you who dislike novels are the most miserable. It is a reflection of your character and speaks to a rigidness that I cannot stand—"

"Do you know who I am?" he repeated, enunciating each word. Never had he met a more obstinate girl. "Do you know *why* I have been thinking of you for months?"

Her face flushed redder, outraged. "You have interrupted me twice now, but since you are so eager to know, I will give you my answer. I know enough about you, Lord Yu. I know all I need to know and, frankly, have no desire to learn more."

"Shin Haewon—"

"Let us end this conversation, Lord Yu." She rose to her feet, readjusted her veil as she said, with finality, "Truly, there is nothing more abhorrent than imposing your feelings on someone as reluctant as I."

The flash of anger sharpened into a searing burn. He was not accustomed to such rudeness. He couldn't bear feeling so defenseless, so humiliated. "You stare at me with contempt in your eyes as though I have spoken abominably, when all I have done is state the facts," he brusquely countered, and knew what he would say next was unkind, but he said it anyway. "It is fact that your mother's side is common by blood. It is fact that your father will never hold a position in court. And it is no less true that the novels you cling to are mere trifles. Do not pretend otherwise. You speak of them as though the world would end at their loss, as though their confiscation were a tragedy." He gritted his teeth, hating every word he had uttered, hating every word he had written, now the source of all his troubles. "But the world will go on. Nothing of true value will be lost."

Haewon fell quiet, her eyes red-rimmed as she turned away from him. She stared at the pavilion, where the lovebirds still conversed in total oblivion. "In truth," she said quietly, "I remain rather taken aback by your interest in me. We are so different, the two of us, and I think you could never truly care for me. Not in a way that is respectable and kind."

A muscle worked in his jaw. His heart felt numb near the site of her wounding words, around the awareness of the irrecoverable damage he had caused.

"Very well, then," he said. "I apologize, Mistress Haewon, for sharing my heart to you. I had no idea you would find my feelings for you so offensive."

"Is this how you open your heart to someone? I hate—" She closed her eyes, a spasm of pain tightening her features. Then the truth finally escaped her: "I hate how small you make me feel."

Guilt jabbed deep into his chest, but before he could say

anything, Haewon caught up her skirt and moved to leave. "Today is my sister's special day," she said, without looking at him. "I won't let anything spoil it. So, please, if you have any decency, please let us resume being strangers. You do not need to be amiable, or anything at all. Our conversation ends here."

Chapter 20

Jade glowed with delight for the rest of the day, and Haewon made all efforts to keep a smile pinned to her face, to hide her distress over the most unpleasant conversation she had ever endured.

Sleep evaded her that night as she recounted all that had transpired, and at first light the next day, Haewon grabbed her veil and discreetly set out. She traveled the usual path she took on her early-morning walks, but pressed herself farther this time until she reached a neighboring village nestled against the overlapping silhouettes of misty blue mountains. She was perspiring, the hem of her skirt dusty, by the time she returned home to greet her parents, who had just awoken.

But not even a long stroll could ease her inner turmoil.

Lord Yu's declaration still agitated her; his berating of her family still upset her, too. She felt justified in all that she'd said to him, yet the image of his sincere expression continued to haunt her.

For months I've thought of you, he had said.

What had he meant by that? They had only known each other for a few weeks.

She was desperate to confide in Jade, but her sister had gone with their mother to visit an ailing aunt and returned home too exhausted for conversation. The next day, when Haewon tried again to approach her, Jade was preoccupied, writing a letter to Young Master Byeongho. And letters were dangerous. She couldn't risk Jade sharing too much with the young master, for Lord Yu might hear of it and mistake her feelings for remorse, when she felt nothing of the sort. She was only confused.

Most violently confused.

It was at this precise moment, right at noon, that Mistress Wol appeared at her home, and by her outfit it was clear that Wol had traveled from afar, and on her own. She was disguised as a gentleman, garbed in a silky robe of lavender that shone bright in the sun. Blossoms sat on the brim of her hat, tilted at a roguish angle over her jade-spectacled eyes.

"Are you leaving for somewhere?" Haewon asked.

"Returning from somewhere." Wol slipped out of her sandals and stepped onto the veranda. "I went to visit a few book peddlers and thought to visit you."

"I'm honored—but why?"

"Must I have a reason to visit a friend?"

Haewon examined her friend skeptically. Wol preferred the company of books to people. The last time Wol visited had been years ago, when Jade was deathly ill. Concern crept in. "Is something the matter?" she asked.

Wol took off her hat, found her way to Haewon's room, and sat down.

"Do you want something to drink?"

"No," Wol said. "I shan't be staying long."

Haewon settled on the other side of the low table, gathering her knees against her chest as she watched her friend. "So? What brings you here?"

"Two concerns."

Haewon waited as Wol looked around, surveying the space. "Your room looks the same as when I visited long ago." It took a moment for Haewon to realize Wol was *searching* for something. "Lord Yu came by this morning to return books. He asked if you'd visited Five Willows of late."

Haewon froze, then she managed a smile. "Asked for me? Whyever would he?"

"Indeed, whyever would he? Did something happen between you two? Something *must* have for His Lordship to have stalked into my bookshop looking so—so heartbroken. What happened?"

Haewon could no longer hold back. She'd had no one to talk to about this matter and had been desperately itching to share it with someone, anyone. And so Haewon told Wol everything, from the storm and his dislike of her to his sudden confession at the pavilion.

Haewon shared this all, fully prepared to see Wol surprised and offended on Haewon's behalf. Instead, she saw Wol's expression crumple into a look she had never seen before. Her friend had turned pale, her brows knitted over wide, compassion-filled eyes, and the corners of her lips were pulled low. "You . . . you refused him," Wol whispered, her voice wobbling a little, as though they were speaking of a shivering stray left out in the rain and not Lord Perfect himself. "Your refusal must have made him so very unhappy. He usually conceals his emotions so well . . ."

"You are grieved for *his* unhappiness?"

"Of course I am sorry to hear how poorly he confessed to you," Wol added, her frown deepening as she appeared lost in thought. But what more was there to think about? "He is to be the master of a grand house. And his family is highly respected. They are treated like royalty. You do not regret having refused him?"

"No matter his wealth and privilege, I could never endure a life with a man who would, at best, propose marriage and resent me for the rest of his life for accepting it. In all likelihood, though, I think he never intended to make me his bride. And perhaps that is why I turned him down so easily," Haewon reflected, then let out a little laugh as she jokingly noted, "He likely planned on proposing that I become his concubine, as men of his standing do."

"Yes, most men would. But he is a gentleman. He would not have done that."

"All the men with concubines are gentlemen, and the most virtuous and well-respected ones have an entire harem—"

"Lord Yu is not like that."

"I was only making fun . . ." Haewon mumbled, then a troubling thought pinched at her. "Are you . . . are you friends with Lord Yu?"

Wol adjusted her spectacles. "No, but I am good friends with his sister, and what she shared with me . . ." She worried her lower lip, then glanced up. "He is not who you believe him to be."

"It doesn't matter who he is." Haewon straightened her posture as doubt niggled at her conscience. She hated the thought of being wrong. "It doesn't matter. The more I get to know him, I am sure, I shall hate him all the more. I'm sorry you like him. I simply do not and that is that."

"A pity."

"A pity?"

"Sometimes you come across people who have been searching for each other all their lives."

"As two enemies fated to despise each other."

"As two lost souls searching for their home."

A strange, painful lump formed under the ribs of her chest. Haewon let out a laugh, then laughed again, hoping to dislodge this ominous feeling. "I assure you, Lord Yu's feelings for me are no more than smoke, drifting wherever the wind wills. The wind brought him to me one morning, and by the afternoon, it will fly in another direction."

Wol arched a brow. "What is that look on your face? You looked troubled."

Haewon shifted under Wol's scrutiny. There was something about the way Wol looked at her, like she could see straight into her soul, catching every small detail, just as she did when proofreading manuscripts. Nothing could be hidden from Wol.

Sighing in defeat, Haewon confessed, "The truth is, while I don't regret turning him away . . . I do wish, for the sake of my own conscience, that I had responded to Lord Yu with more graciousness. It would have cost me little to be kind . . . But what use is there in regretting the past? My only consolation is that he will soon forget me—"

"EOMEONI! Where is Mother?! EOMEONI?"

Haewon flinched as the door was flung open. Yeonhee stomped in, her wild stare flying to Haewon, then pausing on Wol, then shooting back to Haewon. "*Where* is Mother?"

"I don't know," Haewon replied. "Could you not charge in next time like some—some soldier storming a fort—?"

"It's urgent!" Yeonhee shrieked. "Look at me! I told Jade to pluck my brows a *little* bit! But she plucked out *so* many and now *look*!"

Despite the stinging ache in her chest, despite Lord Yu's words still choking her heart, laughter escaped her. "My dearest Yeonhee," she said, "you look like a bandit leader with a scarred eyebrow."

A great sob escaped her sister, and she collapsed to the floor, grabbing ahold of a small mirror and examining her reflection again. "Stop laughing!" Her voice broke through the desperate heaves of grief. "I'm going to the capital tomorrow and how am I supposed to show up like *this*?" Another sob, and then Yeonhee stormed out of the room, yelling out for her mother again.

"You know I said I had two reasons for visiting?" Wol spoke calmly, Haewon's smile fading at her tone. "My second is your younger sister.

"You know I'm particular about who I let in to Five Willows. There was a strange fellow Yeonhee brought in after so elaborately vouching for his character. Her guest seemed more curious about the patrons than the books themselves, though. He also bore the most peculiar expression."

"How so?"

"With my patrons, whenever they browse books, they appear as though they're searching for a new world. But the look on his face was that of a man searching for errors. Perhaps I am fretting overly so, but I wonder if you know him? She kept calling him Young Master Wuyeong."

"I've never heard of him—" Haewon lifted her head sharply. "No . . . no surely it couldn't be him. Yeonhee had a gentleman admirer but promised to never associate with him." Haewon rubbed her temple, struck by a sharp headache. "I oughtn't to have trusted her."

"You should keep a better eye on her." Wol rose to leave. "I should go now. Tomorrow is the start of the five-day market—there will be no rest for me then." Pausing, she glanced around the room again. A beat of silence passed before she said cryptically, "Black Lotus used to write such long and elaborate letters to you . . ."

"Black Lotus?" Haewon echoed absently, leaning her forehead into her palm as she stared at the table, dread building in her chest. *Yeonhee, Yeonhee, Yeonhee. That foolish, reckless girl.* When Wol repeated her remark, Haewon finally looked up. "And, as you know, Black Lotus and I have stopped corresponding for quite some time."

Wol offered a tense smile. "You burned all the letters, I hope? With this edict reinforced, I think Black Lotus is more cautious than ever, and wishes to keep her identity a secret."

Guilt crept up her spine with stinging heat. As soon as Wol left, Haewon moved to retrieve her book of Black Lotus's letters, which was stored at the bottom of her wooden chest. She had destroyed the original letters but had made transcriptions of them. She hadn't thought there could be any real danger in that.

The lid of the chest creaked open, and when Haewon shuffled past the old dresses, her hand touched nothing but the wooden bottom.

Her journal was missing.

Chapter 21

SEOJUN FELT LIKE DEATH.

He had worked himself into a state of exhaustion. His father frequented his doorway, a heavy shadow that lingered. "You ought to eat some food with meat," Minister Yu would remind him. "Since you can only study when you are without illness, do not be stubborn, and be careful with your health."

Trays of food would come in, and then the trays would leave with the food barely touched. He had no appetite. He did not break from his studies, did not dare give his thoughts space to roam. The moment he did, he became instant prey to the most agonizing emotions he had ever experienced.

He studied from dawn until dusk. His plan was to know the Five Classics without reliance on commentaries, with a particular attention to the *Book of Documents*. Within the Five Classics, King Jeongjo was particularly fond of the "Great Plan," Kija's instructions in nine articles for how to run a state. The study he had neglected these past few weeks.

On nights when sleep eluded him, he made sure to keep his mind occupied, fixed his thoughts on the break-in that happened days ago. Between his study breaks, he questioned more servants, and even revisited the House of Bright Flowers in a futile attempt to gather information.

All the while, his manservant, Namgil—who had returned from an urgent family emergency—insisted that perhaps the robbery, the stolen manuscript, was nothing so sinister. After all, no blackmail and no literary censor had arrived.

Seojun nevertheless investigated and studied as though his life depended upon it. And for the most part, he managed to go an entire day without thinking of Shin Haewon.

And then there were days like today.

Days when, no matter his militant control, he could not ignore the echoes of birds trilling outside his open window, the wind carrying into his study the warmth of spring, fragrant with pine and flowers in full bloom. He let his focus slip, and his thoughts at once darted away like a deer that escaped into a vast forest. A forest that was filled with memories of Shin Haewon.

Sitting before the *Book of Rites*, its pages fluttering in the breeze, he leaned his head on his knuckles and could not progress past the first line. Hours flew by as he reviewed his every word and action at Seogeomjeong Pavilion, and her every response and twist of her features. Again and again.

She had refused him. Magpie *despised* him.

The memories swelled, and he dug his fingers into his eyes, desperate to push away the weight of her disdain. But it came crushing down upon him.

Why had he confessed to her? It was a regret that haunted him, constantly.

Why had he opened his heart to her?

Why couldn't he have chosen silence, as he usually did?

It could all have been avoided. He wouldn't be in such torment then.

Seojun watched, feeling utterly helpless, as time wasted away. Sunlight shifted, then withdrew. Shadows encroached as a chill bit the air. This was foolish. This was madness. Heaving out a breath, he rose to his feet and snatched up his hat, resigned to the idea that no work would be done this day. He needed to get away from here. To ride far, far away.

But before he could leave, he stilled at the faint creak of footsteps.

Seojun lowered his hat, recognizing his sister's tread. She hadn't spoken to him in days.

When a hesitant knock came, he returned to sit behind his low desk. "Come in."

His older sister entered, garbed in her usual widow's gown of a pure-white jacket and a white skirt. The mourning period for her husband had ended three years ago, yet she continued to wear it, as though in penitence for being a widow who'd fallen in love with another man. A grave crime in the eyes of the law.

"The servants are whispering about you. They are all worried." Gwideok sat before him, her voluminous skirt pooling around her. "Are you ill?"

Seojun ran a hand over his face. "You needn't concern yourself—"

"You are my brother; of course I need concern myself." She paused to summon a maid, who lit a floor lantern that filled the dark room with a warm glow. "Father keeps sending servants to ensure your well-being. You sent them all away, so Father finally came to *me* and asked me to come speak with you."

He remained still, his hands stretched out on either side of the *Book of Rites*, which had been opened on the same page since this morning. Frustration gnawed at him. For how long would this go on, this inability to function? To breathe, and to find breathing itself difficult? To go a day without fearing for his sanity?

Gwideok frowned. "What happened?"

What had happened . . . ?

He had met a girl. An intelligent, bright, and charming girl for whom he'd felt something beyond mere admiration. He had felt hope. Shin Haewon had inspired in him an excitement about life he had never felt before.

Slowly, the bitterness twisting him loosened. He tried to hold on to it, to remain angry, but the anger wouldn't stay. He could only sit before his sister, wounded and sad. Aching at the reality that his life would forever be absent of Shin Haewon.

"I feel," Seojun whispered, "as though I've been struck down by a speeding cart."

Gwideok waited in silence.

Rising to his feet again, he strode over to the window, pushed it wide open, and fixed a stare out at the shadowy courtyard garden of bamboo, pines, and plum trees. On most occasions he would remain reserved, even with his sister, keeping his thoughts and heartaches to himself. But he had glimpsed Gwideok's curious eyes and had realized, for the first time, how utterly exhausted he was. He was tired of always holding himself together. The truth was a burden he could no longer carry. "I confessed my feelings to a young lady."

"*You* did?" A long, stunned silence followed. "I never imagined . . .

You open your heart to so few! And even then, you never fully let down your walls. The lady in question must be quite the force to have toppled my infamously stoic brother. Well . . . are congratulations in order?"

A muscle twitched in his jaw. "She hates me."

Another long silence followed, then Gwideok folded her arms and asked pointedly, "What did you do?"

"Your tone of voice, nuwi, suggests you already see me as the one at fault."

"Of course I do. Why would a lady refuse *you* unless you behaved in a way that left *much* to be desired?"

"I didn't—" Seojun heaved out a breath, then paced before the window. "I don't know why. I mean, I have theories, but I'm unsure."

"What did you say to her?"

He shook his head, a burn searing in his chest. "I unfortunately fell for a girl of lower origins. Her family are rural folks, known for their moral laxness and crudity. They permit their daughters to visit places of ill repute; they do not discipline the youngest; the father encourages unorthodox ideas; and the mother, from what I've gathered, is the worst of all. She is the village scandalmonger and has spent what little fortune the family has on shamans, dresses, and shoes. So you see, nuwi, the young lady in question is one I ought never to have taken romantic interest in."

A beat passed before Gwideok replied.

"Please tell me you complimented her as you confessed your feelings, and shared none of your . . . practical social considerations."

"I told her most of what I shared with you." Seojun looked at his sister and was met by a flat, unamused stare. "It is the truth."

"You ought to have *lied*."

He frowned. "Lied? I have no regrets, none at all, for saying what are factual—"

"I am actually alarmed, Brother. It's almost remarkable that someone as intelligent as you would be so—so—"

"So what?" he asked dryly.

She waved her hand. "So *stupid*."

"You know Father. His expectations of me. You know what an immense sacrifice it would be, on my end, to consider her as a future bride. Gods, Father might even disown me over my choice. Being considerate was the least of my worries."

"You're right," she said sarcastically. "She ought to have been incredibly honored by your affection."

He paced the room, casting a warning glance at his sister. "Any sensible woman would have been honored by my interest in her, especially a woman in her station. She has everything to gain in my affection, and I, everything to lose."

"It looks to me like you are the one who lost everything."

He fell still.

"My little brother, who, since the age of five, has known nothing but his studies. No friends, save for Byeongho. Lonely, yet too guarded to reach for companionship. Tormented by the crushing weight of our father's expectations. Burdened by my failed existence," she said. And when he opened his mouth to protest, to reassure her otherwise, she ignored him and pressed on.

"A young man who has everything, yet takes up the brush to write stories, just to escape it all. My dearest brother, love is the closest thing to heaven. Isn't that what Byeongho always says? To win the heart of another is to gain a companion, and we are all in need of companionship. Be it a friend or sweetheart—" Her voice faltered. Emotion worked in her throat as she said, in a strained whisper, "This life is far too dark and lonely to journey through alone."

He set his jaw, refusing to heed his sister's remark. "Companionship is all well and good. But we live in the real world, not in a folktale where romantic feelings matter more than practical expectations."

Gwideok sighed as she rose to her feet. "I am reminded of the words from your good friend Magpie."

The mere mention of Magpie was physical pain. His heart bled and the muscles in his back spasmed, as though Magpie's name were an iron ball piercing through him.

"You shared a quote from one of Magpie's letters," Gwideok said, "and you said it had made such an impression on you."

"Which one?" he prodded, his voice gruff.

"*A person is a person, just as a flower is a flower,*" she quoted. "*Scholars rank one another, people and flowers, prizing the plum blossom over the common wildflowers, but to me, I love all flowers. They all bring delight. They are all beautiful.* Perhaps you ought to take Magpie's words to heart more, next time you consider matters of the heart."

Seojun looked away, the words of Magpie carving out a sickening hollowness in him. "There's nothing—" His voice broke. The memory of Magpie's letters shook him to the bone. He barely managed to recompose himself and say, "There's nothing that can be done now. She despises me. It's over."

"It is the first time in your life, I think, that you have been reduced to desperately wanting something from someone, with the likelihood of never getting it. My dear brother, you have been reduced to the position of mere mortal."

"The mere mortal I am now," he whispered, rubbing his brow, "would appreciate the dignity of sulking in solitude, if you'd be so kind."

"You are young, Seojun-ah. I think you will recover." She made to leave, then paused, a frown worrying her brow. "Before I leave, I did want to ask . . . Have you seen Maid Daebi?"

The air chilled around him. Maid Daebi, his sister's personal attendant. The same girl who had peered out from the shadows when he had found his study in chaos. The one who had hidden her dirt-lined nails.

"Isn't she always with you?"

"Usually, yes. But I haven't seen her since this morning. I know it's horribly inconsiderate of me to be sharing this now, but . . . I'm worried."

Facing his sister, Seojun collected his heartbreak and secured it in a box, to be opened later. He had learned at a young age to put his family first; their concerns came before his own. "Did anything happen to upset her?"

"I'm not sure why, but I saw Father raising his voice at her, questioning her. I don't know about what. And as soon as she was alone, your manservant Namgil accosted her, and he seemed rather upset with her, too. Demanded to know how she could have put him in such a position. They had a most heated discussion. All I heard was something about book thieves, and he also mentioned the Red Lantern—"

"The inn?" Seojun repeated, bewildered.

"Yes. And then . . . she simply left. I've been worrying about her since, but Father said he would handle it. I think he means to speak with you, too. He suspects Daebi might be up to no good. I truly hope that isn't the case!"

Seojun folded his arms. He had questioned Daebi a few times, each interaction yielding fewer answers.

"What are you thinking about?" Gwideok prodded.

He exhaled, gaze drifting toward his study door. "You know Maid Daebi best. How likely is it that she would, out of kindness, offer to wash spring greens for a fellow servant? Because on the night of the break-in, that was her claim."

Gwideok let out a sharp laugh. "Washing spring greens? She would never! She has no friends among the other servants—she thinks they're beneath her."

"You're certain of that?"

She clucked her tongue. "Perhaps she eloped, or something explainable like that. But yes, I'm certain. Maid Daebi's personal refrain has always been how cleanliness, decency, and decorum are inseparable virtues."

Seojun wandered out of his study, eyes fixed on the very spot where he had seen the maid, trembling, with dirt-lined nails. There was a strange thought floating on the outskirts of his mind, this instinct that the answer might be right before him. This feeling that the secrets lurking in his home were not as complicated as he was making them out to be.

Chapter 22

With growing franticness, Haewon had searched the house for the better part of the day, yet her book of letters remained missing. It wasn't the first time she had misplaced it, but this time, unease prickled at her.

Returning to her room, she stood with her hands on her hips and stared in confusion. Where had she put it?

A smudge of bright yellow winked at her from beneath the low-legged writing table.

She walked over and picked it up, the petal crumbling as she handled it. It was one of the many she had left pressed between the pages of her book. Then she surveyed the room and found another abandoned beside Yeonhee's wooden jwagyeong, the box that held small cosmetic pots and was topped with a collapsible mirror.

A hot burst of suspicion sparked in her.

At once, she turned on her heel and stalked out of the house, past the rows of large brown oongi crocks packed with fermented soybean pastes, soy sauce and pickled vegetables. She followed the voices to the kitchen yard, where she found her mother and Jade washing a small mountain of dallae, wild chives with red dirt clinging stubbornly to the tiny bulbs and stringy greens. Yeonhee sat on the nearby raised veranda, frowning into the small mirror in her hand. "I've already *tried* painting in my brows. I look even sillier now."

"Yeonhee-yah." Haewon approached her youngest sister. "Did you, perhaps, see my book of letters? The one I told you to never touch?"

"I asked Jade for brows shaped like willows leaves but instead they look like—like long, long spider legs."

"You kept saying your brows weren't thin enough. Anyway, they will grow out, as I've been reminding you since yesterday," Jade said calmly, then motioned at Haewon. "Your second sister is asking you a question."

"Yeonhee—" Haewon reached for her, but her little sister promptly pushed her hand aside.

"*Eomeoni*," Yeonhee whined, turning to her mother. "Do I really look strange? Does it look like I have no eyebrows from here?" She stood and took a few steps back. "Please tell me it doesn't look so awful, or I will die of mortification—"

"Oh, never mind how any of you look!" Mother snapped, violently washing the spring greens. "I am still exceedingly shocked and astonished. In fact I have never been *more* surprised! I heard just this morning from Mistress Jongsan, who was informed by Old Lady Mengbi, that Mistress Shinkyung—*Mistress Shinkyung!*—has secured a match for her eldest daughter!" She thrashed the sprouts in the water. "And her daughter is *four years older* than Jade! Indeed, it seems to me Jade will never get married. Our family is ruined. So it will make no difference whether you have brows *or not!*"

"Mother," Jade began in a voice of suppressed delight. Color had risen to her cheeks, as it did whenever she thought of Young Master Byeongho. "There's something I need to tell you . . ."

Haewon felt a painful pressure gathering under her rib cage. It would not matter whether the young master was enamored with Jade if her family ended up in ruins. And ruined they would be if her book of letters was discovered by the wrong person.

"Yeonhee-yah," Haewon said in a harsh whisper. "Stop ignoring me. What did you do—?"

"They're just letters." Yeonhee raised the small mirror back up, but she wasn't even looking at her reflection. She was staring ahead, and her hands were trembling. "I'm going to go fix my eyebrows. I think I can draw them better this time."

Haewon excused herself, murmuring to Jade that she would be back soon, then pursued Yeonhee down the veranda and into their shared quarters. She'd hoped Yeonhee had gone to retrieve the journal from somewhere and toss it over to her, but instead, she sat before the cosmetics box.

It was then that a thought struck her.

"What did you mean by *just* letters?" she asked. "What did you do to them?"

Yeonhee, despite her bravado, had turned a shade pale. "I didn't know it was *that* important."

"What did you do, Yeonhee-yah?"

At her silence, anger thrummed loud in Haewon's ears; it was all she could hear. "If that book is truly gone, I will never forgive you." Her voice broke on the last few words. "You ridiculous, foolish, *mean* girl, where is my book?"

"I am ridiculous, foolish, and mean, and you are perfect?" Yeonhee snapped, her voice rising in defense. "*You,* who writes scandalous love letters to Black Lotus?"

"They are not love letters."

"He's a man. Many speculate he is."

"Black Lotus is not a man—"

"But what am I saying, of course you're perfect." Yeonhee leaned forward with a brush in hand, drawing her eyebrows back in. "You never err. You are perfect and the whole world is a joke for you to judge and criticize. You're better than the rest of us. That's what you think."

"That is not what I think—"

"And I agree: Our family is ridiculous. This entire village is ridiculous. The way they go on and on about marriage and how the greatest honor for a woman is to bear a son. Well, I've met women who think differently. Women who are part of the Heretical Virgin Troupe. They have vowed to never wed, to never bear children, because they understand that there is more to a woman's life than—"

"I don't care! *Where are my letters?*" Haewon demanded, enunciating each word.

Yeonhee sat straighter, casting a nervous glance in Haewon's direction. Then quietly, she said, "I gave it to Young Master Wuyeong."

"You . . . you gave my book to someone?" Her whole body had gone rigid, and there was a ringing in her ears, all emotion numbed. "Why would you do such a thing?"

"We both share a love for books. And he didn't believe me, that you wrote to Black Lotus. I showed it to him . . . then it started raining, and he said he knew how to preserve it. I was hoping to go to the capital, retrieve it, and bring it back without . . . without you noticing. I'll get it back to you, I promise!"

"Do you trust him?" Haewon pressed.

Yeonhee rubbed her fingers nervously over the brass plates that decorated the wooden box. "I'm sorry. I'm *sorry*."

Never had an apology left Haewon so cold.

"I went to him yesterday. Met him at Five Willows." Yeonhee's voice grew small. "He—he had agreed to return it to me then. But he acted like he didn't even know me." Her eyes grew red as she blinked rapidly. "And I thought he loved me. I truly thought he did. My world lit up whenever he called me clever; no one has ever called me clever. I wanted so badly to please him, to make him look at me the way he does when I say the right things . . . And then one day, he started to take a great deal of interest in you."

Haewon stiffened. "Me?"

Yeonhee reached inside the box and desperately reorganized the items within.

"Yeonhee-yah." Haewon crossed the room and sat before her sister, waiting for her sister to be still. For her to stop searching for diversions. "You need to tell me everything."

Yeonhee blinked, finally drawing her hands out of the box and laying them on her lap. "Young Master Wuyeong, while taking a meal at the inn," she began haltingly, "had overheard strange rumors from a maid visiting the Red Lantern Inn. That Black Lotus's most treasured possession was a set of letters from a scribe named Magpie."

Haewon could hardly believe her ears. "Who . . . who is this maid?"

"I didn't ask."

"What else did you two talk about?"

"When he told me about this encounter," Yeonhee continued, "I . . . I told him I knew Magpie. That it was you—"

"*Why* would you tell him?!" Haewon cried, her voice rising a notch in horror.

"He was growing so distant! He was ignoring me most of the time, and so I hoped that telling him something shocking like this might win him back. And it *did.* He asked a hundred questions about you, and I was so overjoyed, I answered them all without . . . without thinking."

Haewon's stomach dropped. "So you brought him the book."

"Just to show him! Just for a glimpse!" Yeonhee cried. "But . . . now . . ." She swallowed hard. "Now, he won't give it back."

Haewon sat motionless. Her letters—her very soul—were now in the hands of a dishonorable stranger.

"He could expose me," Haewon whispered.

"He says that isn't his intent," Yeonhee rushed to say. "He said he'll return the book of letters, but only if you retrieve Black Lotus's original handwriting for him. Surely there must be stacks of it in Five Willows! Just one page, eonni, and this will all go away."

Dread surged through Haewon. "Why is he so intent on finding Black Lotus's handwriting? And Wol," she added, her voice thin. "If he is after Black Lotus's handwriting, he would know to approach Wol, too."

Yeonhee hesitated, then forced a smile. "He's summoned her to the Ministry of Justice, just to talk—"

"The Ministry of *Justice*? Is he a high official?"

"Only an inspector!" Yeonhee squeaked. "Don't fret. Wol will tell him whatever he wants to know, and then this will all be over."

Haewon clasped her hands together; they were trembling, yet she felt numb inside. "In short," she said, her voice faint, "you delivered my book of letters, in which Black Lotus and I shared our deepest, most private thoughts about forbidden novels and censorship . . . to a literary censor."

All Yeonhee managed to say to this was a feeble "But I didn't *know* he was one at the time!"

As soon as she could that day, Haewon hurried to Five Willows, hoping that Yeonhee was all wrong. That Wol would be there. That it was all a mistake. The collar of her dress was drenched in cold sweat by the time she arrived. She bent forward, clutching the pain jabbing at her side.

"I need to—speak with the merchant—for a moment," Haewon said through her gasps for air, glancing at Maid Boram, who sat crouched on the dirt road, bemoaning her sore legs. "You—rest here."

Haewon staggered into the shop, and when breathing became easier, she finally approached Merchant Hyoyang. "Ajusshi, is she here?"

"Eung?" The merchant paced about the front of the shop, hands gathered behind his back. "Who is here?"

"Wol."

"No. Well, who knows. My daughter comes and goes as she pleases."

"Ajusshi," she pressed. "So you have not seen her?"

He clucked his tongue as he waved his hand. "She's been away since yesterday. She sent me a note, saying not to expect her back anytime soon, but that she is well." Shaking his head, he gestured at a reader ahead. "Look at that man. He's been reading in my bookshop the entire day."

Haewon placed a hand over her throat, her heartbeat escalating again. Was Wol truly locked away at the Ministry of Justice, being interrogated?

She brushed past the merchant, wove through patrons, and arrived at the bookshelves at the far end of the shop. Slipping into the shadows behind it, she knocked quietly at the door, praying it would be her friend who greeted her. But instead, it was Wol's assistant who let her in.

"Wol hasn't returned?" Haewon asked.

"No, agasshi," the thug-like helper replied in his deep, gravelly voice.

Haewon nevertheless searched the aisles, then hurried into the transcription room, only to find it empty of scribes. "Wol?" she called out, hopeful as she approached the adjoining workroom, the door left open. Wol only left her door unlocked when she was present at Five Willows. "Wol?" she called out again, only to feel her heart sink as she stepped inside. It was empty, too.

No one was here, except for the painting of Wol's favorite poet, the Five-Willow Gentleman. Yet even the poet in the watercolor illustration stood with his back turned to her, staring off into the distance.

She was all alone.

And in the deafening silence, among the motionless stacks of books and manuscripts, Haewon remembered. *Just one page,* Yeonhee had said, *and this will all go away.*

All Inspector Wuyeong wanted was a few pages of Black Lotus's handwriting. She had always washed Black Lotus's original manuscripts upon transcription, but what if Wol had a few letters from Black Lotus, undestroyed?

She could search the workroom, and if she found what Inspector Wuyeong demanded . . . The threat hanging over her and her family would be gone. No one would ever know that Shin Haewon had transcribed books that no respectable lady would dare be caught reading—books women hid behind locked doors, tucked discreetly behind their embroidery work, or concealed within the covers of a Confucian classic.

She could escape whatever horror awaited her.

Guilt would undoubtedly plague her, but she could erase Black Lotus from her memory. Sever her ties with Wol. Leave her friends to the wolves, to the officials who would pin all blame on Five Willows for distributing forbidden novels. She would then live the rest of her life as she ought: behind walls, knowing nothing beyond the thickness and thinness of embroidery thread.

Haewon's gaze slid back to the portrait of the Five-Willow Gentleman, and though he was gazing off into the distance that she could not see, it almost felt as though he were looking at her, too.

He lives in contentment, and writes poetry to amuse himself and to express how he feels. Verses from his biography whispered by her like a breeze. *Worldly gain or loss does not concern him. This is his way of life.*

Haewon quickly gave her cheeks a light slap. "Good heavens, Shin Haewon, what are you *thinking*?"

Recoiling from her dark thoughts, she retreated from the workroom, still shaken. Her heart twisted as she took in the sight of the shop, its shelves and stacks of books, its dusty sunlight and air musty with the scent of aged paper. It was as familiar to her as her own room. Even if blindfolded, she would still find her way about, knowing how many steps to take, how many corners to turn to find her beloved books. Yunjidang's work, which had first given her mind wings? Three aisles down, to the left, on the third row, collecting dust under a stack of five other books. *Taekriji,* the bestselling travelogue she reread once a year? Always at the very front of the shop, with an entire shelf dedicated to copies of it. Yeonam's work, the giver of wonder and a good laugh? There were copies in the shelf right by where Haewon stood now. She knew every book in this shop, had read every page, and had painstakingly transcribed many of them.

It was home.

And every reader had pledged a silent oath in their heart the moment they had stepped into Five Willows, a vow of loyalty to one another and to the books here. It was this oath that strengthened her steps as she walked out into the front shop.

Wol would most certainly not identify Black Lotus, yet someone was bound to. Or worse, Inspector Wuyeong might uncover the truth himself. Somewhere in Haewon's book of letters, a clue could exist, a detail she herself had failed to notice. She had no idea what fate awaited Black Lotus once she was found, but the author deserved to know that there were wolves on her trail.

Out at the front of the shop again, Haewon hurried to the merchant, who now sat hunched behind his desk.

"Ajusshi, did Wol ever tell you who Black Lotus is? Or where the author might reside?"

Merchant Hyoyang stuffed his smoking pipe into his mouth and gnawed at it as he continued glaring at the reader in the corner.

"Ajusshi—"

"If Wol did," he said impatiently, "she would have told me in confidence."

"So you know?"

"No, of course not! I've asked her a few times, but she seems determined to take the secret to her grave."

Haewon stood frozen, gripping her veil as she stared through the open bookshop doors. Beyond the threshold, an ox-pulled cart rumbled past, weaving through the flow of white-robed pedestrians, but she barely saw it. Her mind was racing, searching for a way to reach Black Lotus.

"Why?" Merchant Hyoyang suddenly asked. "Is something the matter?"

"Your daughter—" Haewon hesitated. Wol had chosen not to tell her father about being summoned to the Ministry of Justice for a reason. "There is something urgent I must tell Black Lotus," she said instead.

"Then you'd better go tell the author yourself." Merchant Hyoyang returned his attention to the reader and continued his complaining. "Aigoo, aigoo. He knows I'm watching him, yet he keeps reading! Right before my eyes!"

"But I don't know who Black Lotus is, where she lives. How am I to tell the author myself—"

"Wol says you've already met Black Lotus."

Haewon's breath caught. "What?"

"That's what Wol said. It seems, at least, that you know more than you think you do."

Merchant Hyoyang shot to his feet, forgetting Haewon entirely as he stalked forward, shaking his pipe at the culprit like an accusatory finger. "You there, young man! Do you intend to read the entire book without paying?!"

Haewon couldn't move, summoning to mind all the women she knew, every friend and passing acquaintance, until a crowd of hundreds filled her head. Among them was Black Lotus?

Her heart beat so wildly against her chest it hurt to breathe. She *knew* Black Lotus. Her dearest, most precious friend had been nearer than she could have ever imagined. Had they conversed more than once? Had their sleeves brushed? Had they exchanged smiles?

She touched her brow, head spinning. She knew Black Lotus—the memory of their encounter lived somewhere in her mind. If she could just remember, then perhaps she could find her before it was too late.

Chapter 23

HAEWON NERVOUSLY TUCKED A STRAND OF HAIR BENEATH HER veil as she took in the sight before her. The capital looked so vast, so densely populated, its roads and alleys labyrinth-like, when searching for someone who didn't wish to be found.

But she sensed, deep within, that Black Lotus wouldn't mind too much if Magpie arrived at her gate. She had expressed as much in their last letter . . .

A painful knot formed in her chest at the memory. She had avoided thinking of the letter for some time now, for it pained her to recall how Black Lotus had so abruptly cut off their communication months ago. And so long as Haewon didn't think of the last letter, she'd managed to stave off the reality that their friendship had indeed come to an end.

Haewon pushed away her feelings with a heave of a sigh, steadied herself, and set her shoulders. There was no time to wallow in sadness. Reputations were at stake.

"Boram-ah." Haewon glanced at her maid, who had collapsed onto a wooden crate, wiping her brow with her handkerchief. "Do you know the directions to Myeongrye-bang District?"

Boram turned pale. "We are walking all the way there?"

"Merchant Hyoyang mentioned it a few weeks ago, that Wol had visited that district," Haewon said, more to herself, her mind racing to gather all the loose ends. "And on that very day, Wol shared that she'd had an audience with Black Lotus."

"I don't follow, agasshi. I think we had better return home—"

"We're right at the heart of the market; I'll buy you something sweet."

Boram shot up to her feet, smoothed out the wrinkles in her skirt, and straightened the ribbon of her jeogori jacket. "Follow me, agasshi, and I shall lead the way."

Leaving Five Willows behind, they hurried across the bustling Jongno Street toward a boy, his braided hair swinging to and fro as he walked, calling out, "Yeot! Sweet, sticky yeot! Come buy some taffy!" He had a rectangular wooden container hanging before him, two ropes looped around the box and his shoulders. Inside were rows of long, white yeot sticks.

"We'll buy one." Haewon dug into her pouch and paid, and soon they were winding their way through the crowd again, Boram very pleased with the chewy treat.

"You know—" Haewon held Boram's elbow, maneuvering her preoccupied maid away from rushing carts. "You know how all novelists write under a pseudonym?"

"Yes, agasshi."

"They hide their identity because novels are forbidden. And a writer's pseudonym is often inspired by a place they live near, or the place they were born. Where do you suppose the writer Black Lotus's hoching was based on?"

Boram bit the confectionary, twisting the stick until a satisfying chunk snapped off. Chewing, she said, "Perhaps where I am from. Shiheung Province is famous for their lotus ponds."

Haewon shook her head. She had always suspected Black Lotus lived nearby. There had been times when the author would send a response to Haewon's letter on the same day that Haewon had asked Wol to deliver it. She also remembered when Black Lotus had shared that she'd been born in Hanyang, and had been entrapped in the capital for what would soon be twenty years.

Black Lotus had never seen Nakdong River or the West Lake. *The only body of water I see frequently,* Black Lotus had once written, *is the lotus pond.*

Haewon flinched at this memory. "Is there a lotus pond nearby?"

"There is one near Sungnyemun Gate."

Her pulse raced, recalling the place Wol had traveled to the day she'd claimed to have visited Black Lotus. "And what about—" Her voice wavered under the thrill of excitement. "And what about Myeongrye-bang District?"

"Yes, there is one there, too."

"How do you know this?"

Boram quickened her steps to keep up alongside her mistress. "When you're a servant, you go all around the capital, delivering notes to this person and that."

"And you saw this lotus pond?"

"I've only heard of it. You're a hermit servant if you've never heard of Lotus Pond Mansion before."

"What do you mean?"

"Servants talk, agasshi, and whenever I meet them at the market, we exchange what we know—such as who belongs to a great family, where the best households are to serve in, and so on. And always, *always*, they speak of Myeongwoldang, the grand giwajip with the lotus pond." Boram paused to scrape the sticky sweet from her teeth. "Oh, you wouldn't know it. It's a mansion fit to rival the very residences of the royals. The servants there never cease boasting of its splendor."

"A residence fit for royalty . . ." Haewon echoed in disbelief.

"Yes, agasshi. They say it holds ninety-nine rooms, a hundred servants, and a warehouse vast enough to store eight hundred sacks of rice."

For some peculiar reason, Haewon's heart sank. She had never imagined Black Lotus living in grandeur. She had imagined the author living in a humble, dusty abode much like her own.

It didn't matter. Nothing she learned would sway her from the task at hand.

"We're here." Boram wiped her drenched brow after their lengthy walk, the sweet long gone. "This is Myeongrye-bang District."

Haewon glanced around, taking in the unfamiliar streets. She had never ventured this far before. Myeongrye-bang, like Bukcheon, was a district she had no ties to. It was a place dominated by wealthy and well-respected yangban aristocracy. None of her relatives lived here.

Haewon fidgeted with the ribbon of her veil as they continued deeper into the heart of Myeongrye-bang. Important-looking gentlemen in tall black hats and colorful silk robes strode by. High officials perched atop sedan chairs, carried by servants who called out "Make way! Make way!" as though the world were shaped to accommodate such masters.

Disappointment sharpened in Haewon. Black Lotus lived here,

and it was difficult to reconcile her hoped-for image of Black Lotus with the thought of a grand lady whose feet never touched mud, carried everywhere in a palanquin like the one passing by now, a vehicle that belonged only to the great families of Joseon.

The wood gleamed in the sunlight, illuminating its fine lacquer finish and detailed carvings. The window was drawn shut, concealing the woman within—a true lady never exposed her face in broad daylight. As the palanquin lumbered past, carried by four servants, it seemed almost to peer down at her.

As Boram paused now and then to ask for directions, Haewon followed silently, her heart sinking further and further down into the pit of her stomach. She realized she ought to brace herself. It hadn't occurred to her until now that, perhaps, she had idealized Black Lotus. Perhaps, all this time, she had projected what she had wanted to see onto the person. And the reverse could be true, Haewon realized, with growing dread. Black Lotus might look at Haewon and see only the flaws and their differences.

She closed her eyes briefly.

The world disappeared—the imposing sedan chairs and palanquins, the important-looking gentlemen, all vanished. A deep breath, and she was filled with the rich and earthy scent of spring, the vitality and lightness of budding new life. The gentle breeze carried into her mind verses from Yang Sa-eon.

"*T'aesan is mighty high, they say,*" Haewon whispered as she caught up with Boram, "*but it still is a hill beneath the sky.*"

At a corner, they turned onto a lane flanked by high stone walls, the path winding between two grand residences. The flare of the eaves cast deep shadows over them.

Climbing it and climbing,
there's no reason you can't climb all the way.
It's people who won't try to climb
who say, "That hill's too high, it's too high."

The alley twisted, then spilled onto a wide, open land.

Maid Boram gasped, or perhaps it was Haewon, her mind filled with a dizzying haze before the giwajip. The mansion rose upon a stone platform, stretching the full ninety-nine kan, the largest a nonroyal residence could be. Its wooden pillars soared, its black-tiled roof gleamed in the sun, its eaves curved skyward to ward off evil spirits.

Haewon clutched her icy fingers together, feeling as though she were standing before the gate of a palace. Then her heart stilled at what lay beyond. A serene pond greeted her, withered lotus husks poking out from the water. In steamy hot summer they would open white in full bloom.

"It's more impressive than I imagined." Boram blinked, then looked at her mistress. "Why, precisely, are we here, agasshi?"

"I have an urgent message for the mistress of the house."

"You *know* the mistress of this house?"

"I've met her before," Haewon replied, and left out, *I simply don't recall when.* "Please go announce my arrival, and tell them . . . tell them I am Magpie, and that I have a message from Five Willows."

A look of disapproval settled over Boram. "I thought it was your great secret."

"This lady knows who I am."

A look of suspicion narrowed Boram's eyes, but after a little shake of her head, she strode toward the small side gate. She did as Haewon requested, and soon, they were both permitted in by the gatekeeper.

The breathtaking courtyard was vast and ornate, brimming with the lush green of tall, swaying bamboos and a forest of trees. Bushes of camelias bloomed on either side of a small connecting gate, and Haewon could only imagine the splendor of the other courtyards held within the mansion compound. The sheer expanse of the place was more than enough for one family, even ten or twenty families. Her mother would often cope with not living in such a grand home by saying, *Take away all the windows and doors, and the mansion would be nothing but pillars!* Envy didn't even prick her heart, though—to covet such palatial grounds felt as futile as the earth envying the heavens.

"I wonder who is mistress of this house. Is she very grand?" Boram asked, glancing at Haewon. Then she let out a little gasp. "You look so ill, agasshi!"

"Do I? I feel perfectly fine."

She was, in fact, trembling. Her heart pounded and she felt herself on the verge of tears. She was about to meet the author who had become a friend most dear to her, a friend nestled so close to her heart. And she was terrified that the writer would not be what she had pictured.

"This way." The household attendant ushered them inside.

Haewon took off her sandals and stepped into the women's quarter. It was light and airy, with white-papered walls and warm wooden latticed windows. Sunlight streamed in and printed bright patterns over silk floor mats, vases, and lacquered furniture.

"*You!*" came a female voice.

Haewon's gaze shot up. A smiling lady sat before an embroidery stand. She was garbed plainly in white. A daughter in mourning, perhaps? Or a young widow?

"It's me, Gwideok. I introduced myself to you at the bookshop," the lady added, and then a quizzical look came over her face. "But it was over two years ago. I didn't think you would remember me."

"Of . . . of course I remember you, my lady," Haewon managed to say as she desperately leafed through her memory. This occurred often: other ladies recognized her, but she had recommended books to so many strangers. Yet a moment later, a vague recollection surfaced.

"Come, sit down. You wished to speak to me about Five Willows?" she asked, a line of worry forming in between her brows. "I'm sure I returned all the books. My brother returned them for me a few days ago. But please, you really must sit down. You are making me nervous, standing there and staring at me as though I am a ghost."

Haewon felt her knees grow weak; she slowly lowered herself onto a floor mat. Was this woman Black Lotus? And this was Black Lotus's chamber? Haewon gripped her trembling hands as she surveyed the room, then looked out the window, at the view the author must gaze out of while writing. A mutt happily scampered by with a ragged doll in its mouth. Then Haewon's gaze drifted upward.

She froze.

Yellow ribbons fluttered on a pine.

The normal practice is to tie ribbons onto a village sungwhangdang tree. The words she'd written to Black Lotus threaded through her mind. *But in volume seven of your book, you mention a woman tying prayer ribbons onto a pine tree. Shall I edit it to sungwhangdang tree?*

Haewon had been certain it was a mistake, fully intending to make the correction. But Black Lotus had replied, *Keep it yellow ribbons on pine.*

No one tied prayer ribbons to pine trees. No one.

Except, apparently, Black Lotus.

Chapter 24

Seojun stared at the yellow ribbons on the pine tree, catching glimpses of them fluttering above the wall that separated the men's and women's courtyards. A tradition his mother had begun and his sister had continued, tying her prayers onto its branches.

For my prayers to be seen by the heavens, she had replied shyly when he asked.

She never told him what her prayers were, but he'd known it the moment she took into her care the mutt he had brought home, much to his father's dismay. The creature was now her constant companion.

Seojun looked away from the window, returning his attention to the young maid behind him.

"As I was saying," he continued, "Maid Daebi, who recently left our service, informed me on the day of the break-in that she helped you rinse spring greens overnight."

"Not overnight." Maid Aji shifted uneasily. "It only takes two or three hours. She started at around midnight. I can't imagine why she was in the kitchen all night long. Perhaps she got distracted, had lots on her mind."

Silence fell.

He was beginning to think Namgil was right, that perhaps

the break-in held no sinister intent. But Seojun was stubborn by nature. When he began a task, he liked to see it through to the end.

A peal of laughter rang out beyond the courtyard wall.

He stilled at the sound. He hadn't heard his sister laugh in so long.

"Does my sister have visitors?"

"No, nauri." She spoke to the floor. "No, I don't believe so."

"A pity."

He wished she would meet with her other companions again. Go out to visit them as she used to. Invite them over; embroider and gossip. He shook his head, returning his thoughts to the matter at hand.

"I've been given to understand that Maid Daebi would never offer such assistance. If there is anything you are not telling me, now is the time."

Maid Aji chewed on her lower lip.

He pressed harder. "Maid Daebi will not be returning, so if concern for her is what's holding you back—"

"I saw her sneaking back into the house at midnight," she blurted. "She offered to wash the greens in exchange for my silence."

Seojun frowned. "And where had she been?"

"I think . . . I think she went to the gibang house."

"The gibang house?"

"She was asking earlier, asking the other girls for directions. Asking how long it would take to walk there and back."

Dread thickened in his veins. "Why," he began slowly, "would a maid go to an entertainment house?"

"I don't know. Perhaps . . . perhaps to see her sweetheart?" Then she rushed to add, blushing, "I warned her, doryeonnim, I did. I told her many times that she is unmarried, and if she were to become pregnant or cause a scandal, she would be dismissed."

"Do you know who her sweetheart is?"

Her face turned persimmon red. "I don't know for certain . . . but I know who she looks at often. I've seen her speaking alone with him, several times. Even saw them holding . . . h-holding . . . holding *hands*!" she blurted out, as though she had never witnessed anything more scandalous.

"And who is it?" Seojun asked, keeping his voice calm. "Whose hand was she holding?"

When Maid Aji uttered Namgil's name, he suddenly felt the beginnings of a headache.

Chapter 25

Lady Gwideok laughed again, her eyes wide with incredulity. "Truly?"

"Oh, I saw it with my own eyes," Haewon said, trying to hold back a smile.

"So you mean to say, a man attacked a storyteller because he couldn't endure the suspense?" Laughing again, Gwideok shook her head as she picked up her needle. "I oughtn't to be so surprised. Jeongisu storytellers always stop at the height of a plot, then demand the crowd pay up before continuing on. At least the storyteller wasn't injured!"

Haewon smoothed out the wrinkles in her skirt, her heart pounding hard against her rib cage. She was sitting before *Black Lotus*. "There was a case," she added, her voice sounding unusually small, "where a storyteller was attacked outside a tobacco shop. An outraged audience member grabbed a nearby tobacco-cutting knife and lunged at him."

A gasp escaped Gwideok. "A knife?"

"The man was so enraged by something that occurred in *The Tale of General Im* and flung his anger onto the storyteller."

"Good heavens, it must have been the scene when Kim Jajeom falsely accused General Im. I nearly threw that book across my room myself!" Gwideok sighed. "What strange power stories hold over us. Truly, I am a changed woman ever since I became a novel reader. Mistress Wol was the first to introduce them to me, and we became good friends. She is like a sister to me." Straightening her sleeves, Gwideok returned to her embroidery stand, fabric held taut within its wooden frame. Brightly colored threads wove together intricate patterns of flowers and butterflies. "You must tell me, Mistress Haewon, how did you come to love novels so much?"

The smile slowly faded from Haewon's lips.

Lady Gwideok spoke as though they were distant acquaintances, asking a question that Black Lotus and she had discussed in essay-length letters. Had the servant not relayed to Her Ladyship that *Magpie* had requested her audience? Did the lady not know? It could only explain why they hadn't reunited like two long-lost friends in the throes of rapturous joy. It was all, instead, very cordial.

Haewon picked up a sweet from the dessert tray she'd been offered. "My sister first introduced me to novels, tales that allowed me to explore even from within the confines of my room. And then Mistress Wol introduced me to the works of the female Confucian scholar Yunjidang. Have you read her writing?"

Gwideok glanced up. "No, but I have heard of her. Is her work any good?"

Haewon bit into the yakgwa, a golden cookie dipped in honey and ginger. Each bite ought to have been chewy and sweet, but she tasted nothing, her thoughts clinging to the yellow ribbons outside the window, waving to her from the pine branches. She had shared her love of Yunjidang with Black Lotus, too, but Lady Gwideok gazed at her as though she truly knew nothing.

The day I first read Yunjidang's work, Haewon had written, *was the day I learned that my mind could take wings and transcend everything I thought I knew to be true.*

As Haewon's thoughts tangled, a more dreadful possibility began prickling up her spine: What if Lady Gwideok did indeed know her to be Magpie but had simply forgotten the content of their letters? Just because Haewon had memorized the letters as one might verses from poems did not mean Lady Gwideok had cherished them with equal fervor. A sting of embarrassment burned her cheeks. Perhaps she had cared too much, while Black Lotus had several such acquaintances, and Magpie had never been anyone of particular significance to her.

"You ought to read one of her works," Haewon said weakly. She placed the cookie down and dusted her fingers onto the low table set next to her. "There's one line from her work that I will carry with me into death."

Gwideok's brows furrowed. "Oh? Well, then I must hear it."

"*Though I am a woman,*" Haewon quoted as pain and confusion expanded in her chest, "*the nature I originally received was no different from that of a man.* Yunjidang's writing is like an act of contemplation." She watched the lady still stitching away, and hoping to rouse in Black Lotus the memory of all their written conversations, Haewon went on. "Contemplating on the moral and spiritual equality between men and women. I never really imagined, until I read Yunjidang, that such thoughts could even be possible. For I was always taught, growing up, that women were inferior in all ways to men."

"Yes, have we not all grown up reading countless ladies' etiquette books?" Gwideok replied, oblivious to Haewon's turmoil.

"We women are not like men, those books ever remind us. We cannot distinguish between right and wrong, or the urgency of virtuous action."

"And you, Lady Gwideok?" The barest tremble slipped into Haewon's voice, and she tried not to sound overeager as she asked, "Why do you read?"

Haewon waited—she *yearned*—for the familiar answer. *There is an old saying,* Black Lotus had written, *about how scholars go to appreciate the mountains and rivers and sense at their core that they had fulfilled their purpose in admiring creation. A truly good book grants me the same feeling.*

Lady Gwideok instead gave a mischievous glance. "Because I am utterly bored."

Haewon smiled, but her heart constricted with a burning ache. There was none of Black Lotus's intensity of thought and feeling. It was as though the lady was withholding her true self from her. But why?

"I read voraciously, Mistress Haewon, so much so that I don't recall half the titles of books I have read. My brother supplies me—or rather, smuggles the books in to me. My father disapproves of novels. Considers them dangerous."

"Your brother is good to you."

"Oh yes, he is the best brother. My brother is like the moon—quiet, but always present. He would do anything for my happiness, and my father's, too."

"You should come to Five Willows again," Haewon said, attempting to recompose herself. "Then I can personally recommend books to you."

"Unfortunately, my reality is such that it is better if the world forgets me, and I dare not remind them of my existence," Gwideok said with unnatural cheerfulness, then hesitated. "I haven't ventured out of my home for some time, so you must forgive me if I say anything untoward. I'm unaccustomed to having company. Besides my family and attendants, I haven't had any in two years."

Haewon could barely hide her surprise. "Two years?"

"Two years, made bearable by novels." Gwideok ran her finger over a scar on her wrist, then nervously asked, "Have you heard anything scandalous about myself? Yu Gwideok."

"Your . . . your surname is Yu?"

"Yes, of the Munhwa Yu clan."

Yu. It was a common enough surname. And yet, there was a pinpricking sensation at the back of her mind. "I haven't heard anything, my lady."

"Good!" Gwideok tried to smile again, but it fell almost at once. She fidgeted with her sleeve, and Haewon's gaze fell upon her wrist again. She hadn't realized she was staring until Gwideok covered her wrist with her other hand.

Haewon jerked her stare away. "I beg your pardon. I didn't mean—I apologize."

"Oh, do not concern yourself." The lady patted her wrist. "It's from a few years ago. I nearly drowned. It was *quite* the experience. Nothing more than a . . . sort of sinking into blackness."

Haewon said quietly, gently, as one might approach a wounded bird, "How terrified you must have been."

"I felt so entirely alone, surrounded by cold and darkness. Almost sad. Then my brother leapt in after me. I thought he was a ghost at first, until he grabbed me and pulled me out."

The lady's words weighed heavy, and Haewon felt an urge to hold her hands, but remained still and listened.

"There was a rocky embankment on the shore," Lady Gwideok went on. "So my brother had to climb up. There were many barnacles all over it, which cut his arms and legs, and he was bleeding when I saw him rise up from the edge. I only have a few cuts here compared to him. He's—he was completely torn up—" Gwideok shook her head. "I am rambling."

"Not at all," Haewon pressed.

"You must forgive me for disclosing so much to you. I am not very good at exchanging pleasantries. I have the tendency of overwhelming my audience, and I haven't spoken of my past in so long I hardly know how to do so properly—"

"You can tell me anything, my lady," Haewon whispered. "It is as I always said in our letters—you and your words are safe with me."

Gwideok tilted her head. "Our letters?"

"Yes . . ." Haewon said, then anxiety prickled her skin. The lady appeared so oblivious Haewon was no longer certain of anything.

"My memory is so hazy of late; you must excuse me."

"I beg your pardon, my lady, but I must ask . . . when your servant announced my arrival, did they tell you who I was?"

"Only that a young lady was here from Five Willows. Why do you ask?"

Haewon felt her shoulders sag with relief. Lady Gwideok didn't *know* she was Magpie. Everything was so much clearer now! After taking in a few deep breaths to calm her excitement, she said, "Well, my lady, I have something to share. Would it surprise you that I know the title of your favorite book? That I know precisely which passage in *Yeolhailgi* is your most favored—?"

Lady Gwideok laughed. "*Yeolhailgi*? I fell asleep while reading that book. I'm not sure that I even finished it!"

Haewon froze. "Then . . . what is your favorite book?" she barely managed to ask.

"It will always be *The Tale of Pyeongsan Naengyeon*."

Cold panic surged through her blood, sending icy fingers creeping across her chest. Something was amiss. Black Lotus did not like this love story; it was, in fact, one of her least favorite novels.

The very reason Haewon had come to this house—to warn the writer of Inspector Wuyeong—died on her lips. She was no longer certain that Lady Gwideok was Black Lotus.

After a performance of nonchalance, Haewon waited for a lull in their conversation, and when it came, Haewon glanced out the window and feigned a look of surprise at the time, shared a few pleasantries, then said, "I had better leave now. My parents will be expecting me for our evening meal."

With that, a few more pleasantries were exchanged, and then Haewon stepped out into the courtyard.

"What a peculiar conversation," Boram said, and Haewon had completely forgotten the maid was there, sitting at the back of the chamber the entire time. "I'm still unsure as to why we came all this way, agasshi. And Lady Gwideok looked rather confused herself. You never told her the reason for your visit."

"I'm going to sit down for a moment," Haewon said, her knees weak. "I'd like to be alone."

Haewon staggered to the back of the women's quarter. And there she sat on the veranda, leaning her weight against one of the wooden pillars.

Her first thought was that she'd come to the wrong place, that this was not Black Lotus's home, but upon further consideration, that seemed impossible. How had the clues led her here, to the home of a woman who was not Black Lotus but was clearly a good friend of Mistress Wol? And how was it that this residence stood right before a lotus pond? Was it all a coincidence?

Yellow ribbons fluttered on pine tree branches.

No, she had found the right place, but had requested audience from the wrong person. She was certain of that now.

"I'm here," she whispered. "Magpie is here. But where are you?"

She glanced around again, at the peaks and waves of the rooftops, their black tiles gleaming in the sunlight. In one of the rooms, somewhere in this vast compound, had Black Lotus written that last letter to her?

I sit down this afternoon to answer your letter I received three mornings ago.

The words drifted toward her, on the wind, over the wall, through the swaying bamboos. Words from Black Lotus's final letter, their correspondence cut off as soon as the king's censure circulated.

How glad I was to get it, for I did not expect one so soon. You do not know how much pleasure I take in reading your letters. You take my most tangled and darkest thoughts; you spread them out in the sunlight for me, allowing the meaning to become clear. I have reread your letters so many times I almost think I see you.

Haewon closed her eyes, trying to steady herself. This had to be the home of Black Lotus. Lady Gwideok had mentioned two other family members—her father, who disapproved of novels, and her brother, who smuggled her books. Was the brother Black Lotus? She had found his home then, but for some reason, she no longer wished to know who he was. It was terrible, in fact, this realization that Black Lotus could indeed be a man. It meant they could never be friends.

Though I cherish my privacy above all else, I confess I would not be wholly against you discovering who I am. After all, you told me in one letter that you are so good at solving things, you must have been an investigator in your former life. Should you succeed, come and find me.

The author was a man. She would have to leave. But now she wished she'd been born a man, a scholar, who could take wine with Black Lotus, discuss books, and exchange ideas long into the night, without fear or shame.

I must return to my work now, and will end it with your request. You asked for a favorite passage of mine, so I send you one from the book you know is very dear to me, Yeolhailgi*:*

이 세상에 진실로 저를 아는 사람 하나를 만났다 하더라도
한이 없을 것이다

"*If there is one person in this entire world who understands me,*" she recited in a whisper, her mind drifting across the handwriting she'd committed to memory, "*I can live this life without bitterness.*"

A deep ache dug into her chest. Tears gathered at the corners of her eyes as she tilted her head against the column. She couldn't understand this grief pushing at her ribs, this feeling of loss. Dabbing at her eyes with her sleeve, Haewon shook her head. She was being foolish—

A voice drifted over the walls. Rich and elegant, with a depth that sent a lurch through her chest. Her entire body stiffened. For some strange reason, she could even smell his scent of sandalwood—imagined, yet she could still catch it in some faint recollection. She stood and numbly followed his voice beyond the wall.

"Find my manservant for me," the voice said. "I need to hear his explanation . . ."

The fluttering in her pulse faded just as fast as it had come. She realized who this stranger was, and how he was the first man to ever express his feelings for her, the first man she had disliked so much yet had thought of constantly, and the first man to so mortify her.

Panic surged through her.

She took a retreating step, gripped by a need to run away as every awful scenario flooded into her mind: He would spot her, peer down his nose at her as though she were his greatest enemy, as though she were a clod of mud staining his territory. She had wounded his pride and she knew how mean a humiliated man could become—

"Haewon agasshi!" Boram's voice shot out.

Haewon startled with a gasp. And she realized, with horror, that his footsteps beyond the wall had frozen.

"We had better leave now." Boram hurried over to her. "You said you would return home to help with cooking."

Her heart threatened to implode within her chest. With wobbly knees, she began her escape.

"Agasshi!" Boram cried. "Wait for me—oh! Where is your veil? Wait, let me go fetch it."

Haewon did not know how she managed to rush out of the courtyard and out onto the open road without stumbling, her knees trembling as they were. She had meant to wait outside the small gate, but it didn't feel far enough, so she kept walking until she could walk no farther.

She found herself in a wooden pavilion overlooking the pond. The weather was warm, but she was trembling. Her nerves were frayed. She had been in the mansion of the man she had rejected. A house that was a reflection of his family. She was so embarrassed, remembering her audacity, her outrage, at him pointing out the inferiority of her birth.

"Mistress Haewon."

That voice again. Her stomach knotted painfully as she turned around. She stood, pressed up against the banister. "L-Lord Yu."

He stood a few paces away, his cheeks flushed and his eyes stunned, his silk robe billowing in the breeze.

"You—you live here?" Haewon cried.

"I live here," he replied slowly.

Cold sweat dribbled down her brow. She tried stepping back but the banister dug into the small of her back. She wanted to run, but there was nowhere to go.

"Please, don't be alarmed," his voice rasped. "I only came to be sure I hadn't imagined hearing your name. I won't trouble you further. Only—" A frown knitted his brows, and he made a helpless gesture with his hand. "I wish to say that—that I am sorry for how things ended."

Haewon shook her head, a ringing sharpening in her ears. She had come searching for Black Lotus but was standing before Lord Yu. She pushed back against the banister, desperate to escape.

The wood creaked.

Then all at once, the banister let out an awful groan and the aged wood splintered.

A terrified yelp escaped her and she felt—oh gods, this had to be a nightmare—she felt her body arcing backward. Lord Yu was rushing for her, crossing over to her in a few long strides. She was falling backward. Everything felt as though it were occurring underwater—

And then she *was* underwater.

A shock of cold enveloped her. The pond wasn't deep, only reaching her waist, but the chill of it stole her breath. She staggered upright, coughing, stunned to her core. No one had pushed her and yet it felt as though the universe itself had, with a sharp, cruel, and deliberate shove.

Shivers ran through her as she gripped the heavy fabric of her skirt, staring down at the mud-soaked silk clinging to her torso.

If humiliation had a bottom, she had sunk well past it.

She wished the pond would swallow her whole now.

She wished she had never come.

"Doryeonnim! Oh, doryeonnim. You mustn't!" Female voices pierced through the haze of Haewon's shock, and when she looked up, it was to see Lord Yu leaping into the water. His servants had flocked around the bank, pale and aghast, as they watched their precious young master wade through the algae.

Haewon was certain she was imagining it all.

But then a hand reached forward, palm open and long fingers outstretched. Her chest contracted. Words from Black Lotus's letter wound tightly around her heart. *You will never be friendless. You will never be entirely alone.* Her gaze lifted, past the once-pristine robe now plastered against the hard lines of his chest, past the collar now speckled with mud, to the face of Lord Yu Seojun. The ringing in her ears grew louder.

"Come," he said, his voice as rough as gravel. His gaze was averted from her. "Let me assist you out."

He held her elbow, and despite the fabric of her sleeve between them, the heat of his hand burned into her skin. He continued to hold her firm as he guided her from the water, both of them nearly tripping more than once on the tangle of lotus stems and reeds. Once they reached the bank, Maid Boram raced to her side and threw the veil over her, hissing, "I can see *everything*, agasshi!"

It took a moment for Boram's words to register. Wet silk clung to skin, leaving little to the imagination. Horrified, she clutched the veil tight as she sank onto a rock, unable to look up at Lord Yu, grappling for composure as she felt her world tilting upside down. She scrambled to reclaim a modicum of decency as another, colder thought floated at the outer edges of her consciousness. At last, she managed to speak, but it was to the ground. "I apologize for—for all this."

"There is no need to apologize." He crouched to pluck off broken bits of stems and decayed lotus leaves from her drenched skirt, and the back of his neck was flushed a deep red. "You fell into the pond with such dignity and grace, it was quite a thrill to behold."

She would have liked to laugh at this; she might have, if not frozen from a growing shock that expanded in her like ice. She could not even muster a smile. And when the realization fully took hold of her, her hands began to shake. Lord Yu—could he be Black Lotus?

She was afraid her composure might break.

She had come, searching for him for a reason, but her mind was in such turmoil she could hardly think straight.

"Wol is at the Ministry of Justice" was all she managed to say. "She was summoned by an Inspector Wuyeong. You ought to go speak with her, at once."

His brows contracted briefly, then he looked up at her with perfect composure. "I shall see to it. You needn't spare another thought on the matter, Mistress Haewon."

Her heart twisted with inexplicable pain. She felt she'd lost her dignity in the pond, yet she sat here, staring down at the man who gazed at her with the reverence of a poet before the moon. A gaze so earnest and sincere that, for a moment, she could forget she was just a fool in a muddy dress.

Chapter 26

SEOJUN STOOD DRIPPING WET BEFORE HIS RESIDENCE.

For days, he had tried to pretend the Seogeomjeong incident had never occurred; he had tried to cut the memory from his mind. He could think of no other way to endure the raw heartache.

But then, from over the courtyard wall, he had heard her name being called. And he had known in that moment that he was a fool to think he could ever forget her. Shin Haewon had cracked open his carefully arranged world, and it would always remain so.

Before he'd known it, he had broken into a run across the courtyard, stunning every servant he passed. Lord Yu Seojun had been raised to uphold decorum, taught to be ever composed, to avoid acting rashly—and to never run. He had certainly never before bolted across Myeongwoldang. But all such concerns had fled his mind as he'd searched for her.

And he had found her.

And he had felt a pleasure so keen.

If, at any moment, she had crooked her finger, he would have knelt before her feet, willing to give up anything and all just to win even a sliver of her affection. Instead, she had backed away. All the blood had drained from her face, in utter panic at the sight of him.

Whatever delight he'd felt had splintered into heartache. Everywhere still ached.

When would this end? This sheer torment?

All he wanted at the moment was to be alone. To fall into a deep slumber and awaken only once he could finally breathe without hurting.

Seojun trudged into his residence, through the courtyard, and into his room, unmindful of his trail of wet footsteps. The servants moved silently around him, stripping off his outer and inner garments, eyes carefully averted from the scars carved into his arms and back. Water pooled on the floor, a steady *drip, drip, drip* that aggravated him. He felt himself unraveling, yet he didn't have the luxury to do so; there was an exam to pass, a break-in to investigate . . . and Haewon had mentioned Mistress Wol.

"Housekeeper Myeongsu," he called to the senior attendant as he was being dressed in a fresh robe, "send for my manservant—"

He froze. The realization struck an instant before she spoke.

"Namgil has been absent again since earlier today, doryeonnim," the woman said. "He left you a note this time. Shall I retrieve it for you?"

"Leave it in my study. I'll look at it later."

He massaged his aching temples, his mind circling around the events of this afternoon. Maid Aji had revealed that Namgil was Maid Daebi's lover, and with this revelation came a hundred questions, such as: Why were the pair involved in the break-in, and why would Namgil want his manuscript? Questions that frustrated him when he was still struggling with the most important one:

If Wol was indeed in trouble, why had Haewon come *here*?

Seojun paced, and as time passed, the sunlight bathing the chamber dwindled into strips of burning gold and elongated shadows.

Jade vases and mother-of-pearl-inlaid furniture glowed in the late afternoon light. It painted a picturesque scene of comfort, safety, and harmony. He could remain in his little world, never peer out the window, and pretend that there were no emergencies, no friends calling out to him for help.

But he cared too much to pretend.

After inspecting his appearance, ensuring no wrinkle, no loose sash belt, he then strode out of his chamber. Upon arriving before his father's study, servants announced him in, sliding the doors open.

The study room was spacious. In the summer, Minister Yu would have the large latticed windows opened, letting the breeze in. In the winter, the ondol floor would be warm, the air would be heated, yet Father would let it all out by opening one window. And in the spring, too, he often had a window open. In all seasons, ever since Mother's death, Minister Yu could be found gazing out the window. *The pine is eternally green,* he always said. *Every morning it looks newer to me.* Seojun had thought it strange, how his father could spend hours staring out the window at the same set of pine trees.

"Father," Seojun said, announcing his presence.

His father held court before a low desk, a folding screen stretched behind him.

"You seek out this elderly father of yours only when you have something to demand," his father remarked, his gaze never wavering from the letter before him. Four stones held the paper in place as his brush moved steadily across the page. After dipping his brush once more, he continued writing. "I hear that your manservant ran away, eloped with one of the maids. Is that why you are here? I think there's nothing much more to discuss. They are gone—what more can be done?"

"I think Namgil knows more about the break-in than he is letting on," Seojun noted, "but it isn't the reason why I am here, abeoji."

"Speak, then. I have little time to spare."

Seojun's muscles tensed. Minister Yu, these recent few weeks, was in a constant state of being disappointed in him. No matter what he said or did, his father always seemed to find something to criticize.

"It seems, Father, that officials at the ministry are making efforts to apprehend writers of forbidden books."

"And what is it to you?"

Silence weighed on his shoulders. He couldn't tell his father the truth, that he was Black Lotus. "Is it under your orders?"

"Of course not. I am too busy dealing with Catholics. More destroyed ancestral tablets. The spread of a belief that strikes at the very pillars of our Confucian society. But a group of officers has clandestinely taken it upon themselves to enforce the edict."

"Wol is being held for questioning by Inspector Wuyeong."

"Yes, so I've heard. A girl I told Gwideok to stop associating with."

"A girl Mother was fond of."

His father's lips pressed into a thin line. "That Wol girl will be fine. No torture is being used. I heard she was a menace, by all accounts. Charming all the officials. Apparently they're bending over backward to keep her comfortable." Father stilled. "These young and ambitious officers are, rightfully, intent on destroying novels. As the king always tells me, before we can even think to root out Catholicism, we must first put an end to fiction. Fiction is a clever thing, you see. A writer can hide anti-state sentiments inside their words."

Minister Yu continued to write, and Seojun stared, a dark thought looming over him. The destruction of books never ended with the written word, like the ban under the former king, King Yeongjo, provoked by the *Mingji Jilue* by Zhu Lin. The book had questioned the founder of Joseon, and by extension, the legitimacy of the dynasty itself. Those in possession of this controversial history book had been executed. Over a hundred people were implicated—from readers to book peddlers to transcribers.

They had been tortured, stripped, tied up in a straw mat, and laid in the blazing sun, and most put to death.

While Seojun couldn't imagine their present king spearheading such a bloody attack, he was certain of one thing: Censorship would not stop with fiction.

Finally Minister Yu finished writing. He dried the ink, slipped the letter into an envelope, and then at last looked up at his son. "Inspector Wuyeong requested to keep Wol in custody until she reveals who Black Lotus is. He's threatened to raid Five Willows otherwise." His father sighed. "An ugly business, this creation and distribution of novels. You would do well to stay away from these obscene books—"

"Do something to help her."

A quiet scoff, and then Minister Yu muttered, "You must first do something for me then."

Seojun braced himself.

"You must tell me the truth." The minister studied him carefully. "You're in love?"

Seojun tensed.

"What family is she from? The girl you were reported to have leapt into the pond for like a fool. No one of consequence, I'm sure." He shook his head. "You cannot hide from your father. I know. I have been informed by a little bird that she is the daughter of Scholar Shin, who is a *northerner*. No respectable gentleman would marry *any* woman with family in that region. And the mother isn't even true yangban aristocracy. So what were you thinking? What if word gets around?"

Seojun was speechless. It was as though he were listening to himself back at Seogeomjeong, his father uttering the very words he had uttered to Haewon. He now felt her full offense.

"You will meet with the Minister of Rites," Minister Yu said, as though finalizing the matter. "He wishes to conduct an interview with you before the engagement is formalized."

"Father, please," Seojun said, barely keeping calm. "I have lived my life according to your wishes. And even now, though I may appear to you as straying, you know I desire nothing more than to make you happy. I will meet with the Minister of Rites. I will get engaged and marry his daughter, as you wish it. But please—let Wol go. *You* may not be involved in Inspector Wuyeong's campaign, but surely you have influence to assist her."

His father tapped his finger against the desk. Once. Twice. "You look unhappy. But as you grow older, you will come to realize you cannot always have what you want. I, too, did not live my life exactly as I wished. I had to set aside personal desires for the greater good, as you must learn to do. You must think of what is best for your clan—what will bring honor to our name."

"I will, Father."

Minister Yu picked up his brush, snatched another sheet of paper, and muttered, "I will write to Inspector Wuyeong."

Once outside, Seojun wandered to the back of the residence and simply stood there. A crane landed at the pond's edge, and its long, skinny legs waded through the murky waters. The wind rustled through the leaves. Everything was as it had been, and yet entirely changed now.

He would soon be engaged. And once married into the family of his father's choice, Seojun knew he would also be tied down to the life of his father's choosing.

A heavy pall fell over him. Was this to be his life, then? Following in his father's footsteps: heading to his government office at dawn and working until dusk; joining in the clash between factions; purging rivals, betraying peers. So consumed by factional disputes, he would stop looking at life beyond the government office, forget his home, forget that an entire world lay outside . . .

Seojun ran a hand over his face.

He would worry about his gloomy and painfully tedious future tomorrow. Today, his heart was too sore for anything but the small problems. Like the break-in. Like Namgil's note.

Turning, he strode to his study. The housekeeper had left the folded piece of paper on his desk as he'd requested, too distracted as he was to deal with it earlier.

He picked it up now and unfolded it. The handwriting was hurried, the strokes lacking their usual neatness Seojun had once taken the time to teach his manservant.

I had no choice. I had to do it, to protect Daebi. I am leaving to join her. I wish you health and happiness. You have treated me with such benevolence and I am ashamed of myself. I cannot face you. All I can do, in return, is to leave you with this: It would have been impossible to open your two turtle locks with such speed without prior familiarity. Perhaps your locks were never truly yours to begin with. Indeed, I recollect you once telling me that most crimes are quite simple and ordinary. I think you were right about that.

Chapter 27

Haewon sat, swaying to and fro in a palanquin fit for a princess, feeling very much like a wet rag with bits of reed still tangled in her hair. The servants at Myeongwoldang House had offered to change her into a spare dress but she had begged to leave for home at once. To escape as far as she could from the home of Lord Yu.

Haewon folded her face into her hands.

How *strange* he must think her. Did he think she had intruded into his world, purposefully throwing herself into his path? The possibility appalled her. If only Boram hadn't called her name, if only he hadn't heard, then she might have slipped out of the mansion without his knowing. This disaster could have been entirely avoided!

And worse, he had been so kind.

She wished he had been anything but kind.

She wished he could remain the proud, reserved, and disagreeable gentleman she'd thought him to be. A man worthy of her thorny rejection. But now a cold shiver of a thought coursed down her spine. She was no longer certain of who Lord Yu was. In fact, had she known him at all? The last man in the entire kingdom whom she would have imagined to be Black Lotus—was Black Lotus.

She grabbed the handle, opening the latticed window, and gasped in a deep breath of air.

It *couldn't* be Lord Yu, it absolutely couldn't be *him* she'd written to . . .

But if Lord Yu were Black Lotus, their letters were now in the possession of Inspector Wuyeong. If the inspector ever thought to expose them to the public, anyone would look at such letters, between a man and a woman, and deem them love letters, more intimate and scandalous than an unmarried couple caught mid-embrace. It was the most intimate kind of association, the communion between two minds. Women had been publicly humiliated and men blocked from entering office for far lesser crimes.

The palanquin slowed, its rhythmic sway coming to an abrupt stop. So lost in thought she was, Haewon hadn't realized how much time had passed. Male voices called out, and with a jolt and rattle, Haewon felt the earth solid beneath her. The door creaked open, sunlight spilling in.

She winced as she stepped out, the world too painfully bright. Its edges too sharp. Villagers had stopped to gawk, their scrutiny upon her. A palanquin was a rare sight in Gyonam, and rumors were sure to spread. But Haewon couldn't be bothered to care. Her distress had reached its peak, a pounding headache as she stepped into her home. All she wanted was to be alone.

"Wh-whose family does that vehicle belong to, Haewon-ah?" Mother was instantly by her side, a trembling hand over her chest. "Why are you not answering your mother? Why are you staring so stupidly at the floor? Oh, good heavens, and what happened to your dress! Speak at once! I cannot endure this suspense!"

Jade swept in as though sensing Haewon's overwhelm and took their mother away. "Come, eomeoni. Let us ask Boram. Haewon doesn't look well."

Haewon barely managed to slip out of her sandals, her limbs feeling like water as she tried to haul herself to her room. She was desperate to wrap herself in a blanket and hide from the discovery she had made at Myeongwoldang—

Then all thoughts quieted.

Time itself seemed to slow.

Haewon retreated a few steps back and stared at the straw sandals lining the step below the veranda. Yeonhee's sandals were missing.

"Eonni," Haewon whispered, looking back at Jade. "Where is Yeonhee?"

"She was sobbing all morning," Jade called out, while maneuvering Mother across the yard. "But our little goblin seems to have finally settled down."

An uneasy sensation prickled Haewon as she turned and made her way over to their shared room. She slid the door open a bit too forcefully, a loud *clack* splitting the silence.

"Yeonhee-yah?"

Haewon stepped in and her attention fell on a lone note upon a table. She picked it up and her blood froze.

I am going to find Inspector Wuyeong.

I'm going to make things right between us.

I will not return until I do.

She carried the note with her, feeling dumbstruck as she looked around; Yeonhee had taken a few dresses, undergarments, her identification document, as though she meant to go on a long journey. Haewon felt her arms grow limp as she stood motionless. She did not mourn or rage; she felt nothing but a numbness, as though she were still underwater, trapped in the frigid darkness.

What followed, Haewon could hardly recall, as though she were caught in a trance. Noises and movements bled into each other. Her legs moved of their own accord; her hand pulled open Father's study; her mouth moved, forming words like the *House of Bright Flowers*, *book of letters*, and *Inspector Wuyeong*. Scholar Shin's wrinkled face paled; his scraggly gray beard twitched.

Mother's voice then joined the cacophony of noises, declaring, loud and shrill, "What do you mean Yeonhee is gone? She has run away? Yeobo, she is only sixteen!"

Jade held Haewon steady throughout as such confusion shrouded her mind. Yeonhee, run away? No. Surely not. She stared down at her hands, the note no longer in her possession. Her father had set out with it in a hurry.

"Here," Jade whispered, "you look faint, you ought to drink something."

Whatever she was given, it was strong, leaving Haewon rather lightheaded and untethered, as though she were observing herself from outside her body.

Slowly, Haewon became aware of the stillness and quiet. She looked around and discovered she was alone in her father's study. It was dusky outside, the trees shadowy, the land enveloped in blue mist.

How long had she been sitting here? Why had no one shaken her from this trance? She stepped out into the hall, her socked feet padding quietly across, and she paused before her parents' quarters. Her mother lay on her bed mat, groaning, a wet cloth over her brow.

She meant to step in, to go and offer some comfort, but a hand stilled her.

"I have never seen Mother so distraught," Jade whispered. "I would let her be for now, Haewon-ah; she is beyond hearing any words of consolation."

Mother groaned as she lifted a trembling hand into the air, which Jade instantly hurried over to hold. "What should we do?" Mother cried. "Oh, my girl. What shall we do?"

The same question petrified Haewon. She felt the brittle ice of respectability cracking beneath her family. The ice had held for them all these years, but now she saw patches so fragile they revealed the dark current beneath. And Yeonhee—with a few more missteps—would plunge them into the deep, freezing silence of shame.

What shall we do?

In Gyonam where everyone talked, where villagers were quick to draw conclusions and choose sides, Haewon had seen how neighbors became strangers, how gossipmongers became moralists who urged the community to condemn and to isolate. A family stripped of honor would then wither like a flower severed from its root until nothing remained of its former glory.

It had never occurred to Haewon that one day her family could be shunned in such a way. That one day, she too might find her family on the outside, starving for a little kindness and compassion.

She was desperate to save her family while she still could.

Later that evening, she joined efforts with Jade to find Yeonhee's hidden journal. They could not afford to be ignorant of any more of Yeonhee's secrets, and needed full clarity of Inspector Wuyeong's character, to better understand what their family faced.

It was dark out when they found their sister's new hiding place, the journal squeezed behind their large pinewood wardrobe.

"It might hold the specifics of Yeonhee's plans," Jade whispered, laying the journal on a table. She flipped it open and both sisters were greeted with a warning:

This journal is private!!!
Should you dare to read its contents,
may you suffer ten thousand deaths!

Guilt pinched at her, but Haewon nevertheless leaned in, reading alongside Jade. They paused now and then to dog-ear pages that mentioned the names of places and people that might aid their father's search.

Every page was sixteen-year-old Yeonhee, consumed by her feelings for Inspector Wuyeong. Tormented. Writhing, as though gripped by an illness. When would she see him again? Did *he* wish to see her again? Why had he stared at her like that? Did he feel the same way? Did he care for her more than he did his betrothed? When would he write to her again? He had touched her cheeks—what did that mean? He had kissed her, then had declared she was like a little sister to him. Why had he said that? Why was he no longer writing back? He had appeared suddenly again, lain with her, then had asked if she'd told anyone about their meeting. Why was he ignoring her now—

Haewon's hands darted out, quickly shutting the journal. She had been raised to believe that a woman's greatest worth resided in her chastity, and Yeonhee . . .

"I regret having opened the journal at all," Jade whispered, sickly pale.

"I, too, sorely regret it."

Footsteps crunched outside.

Exchanging wide-eyed glances with her sister, Haewon set the journal aside, leapt to her feet, and raced out of the room with Jade close behind. Had Father returned with Yeonhee? Was her family saved? Soon it wasn't only her and her sister, but Mother crowding the threshold door, holding a candle against the night—a sea of pitch darkness beyond.

A lantern appeared, illuminating Father's weary face. Him and no one else.

"Where is Yeonhee?" Mother cried. "How could you return without her?"

Haewon couldn't stem the disappointment grinding into her bones. This was a nightmare without an end. "Father?" she whispered.

His face was drawn and tired, the lightness in his step replaced by a weary shuffle. He entered the room and seemed to bring in with him a pall of despair.

“It appears,” Father began slowly, “that Yeonhee has run off to take justice into her own hands.”

“What does that mean?” Mother demanded. “Where *is* she?”

“She was spotted tailing Inspector Wuyeong, and last seen questioning his servants about a certain journal she wished returned to her. I think it must be this book of letters you so vaguely told me about, Haewon-ah.” He sighed. “Then she disappeared.”

“But *why*? All over a journal? I don’t understand! Yeobo, you must *do* something! Oh—” Mother gripped the back of her neck, taking a few staggering steps back. Jade rushed over to hold her. “I think I shall faint!”

Father massaged his temples, then sat before the low table where their untouched meal lay. He poured himself a drink, then simply peered down at his liquid reflection. “I went to Five Willows, since Yeonhee visits there often. You girls call it your second home, after all. But Merchant Hyoyang hadn’t seen her. Then this young gentleman approached me; he must have seen my distress. I didn’t know it was Lord Yu until he introduced himself.”

Haewon straightened in shock. She must have misheard.

“His Lordship shared with me that he knew this officer very well and offered his assistance—” Father looked up, his gray brows puckered. “Oh dear, Lord Yu asked that I keep quiet of his assistance. I forgot about that.”

Her pulse thundering, Haewon could only stare at her father. She was half convinced this was all a feverish nightmare. “Surely,” she barely managed to say, "surely you did not disclose our predicament to him . . . abeoji . . . ?"

"You *shared* everything with a stranger?!" Mother finally crumpled to the floor, leaning into Jade's embrace. "Oh, we are ruined! We are done for! Lord Yu will certainly feed us to the scandalmongers—!"

"Lord Yu is a good man. A better man than most. It is, all thanks to him, that our family was not already ruined by the gibang-house incident," Father noted, as a thoughtful look passed across his countenance. "Indeed, Lord Yu was very considerate of my distressed state. He took the lead, questioning shopkeepers and servants. Lord Yu has even arranged for me to have an audience with Inspector Wuyeong tomorrow. And I was feeling so ill with panic, I am ashamed to say I collapsed more than once. His Lordship assisted me—"

"And where is he now?" Mother stood up again, hands fluttering against her throat. "Where is this kind gentleman you speak of?"

Jade had moved to the window, then turned. "The moon is finally out, and I think I see someone. He's just leaving. Isn't that him?"

A gasp punctured the room, and Haewon realized, with terror, that the gasp was her own.

"*He* is here?" Mother cried.

"Lord Yu escorted me here. A polite young man," Father added, his voice heavy with fatigue. "He insisted that I oughtn't to travel alone in my condition, especially not with rumors of a tiger nearby."

"And you let him leave?" Mother cried. "Alone?"

"I did suggest he stay the night. I assured him we have welcomed travelers before him," Father supplied. "But he refused. The fortress gate will soon close for the night, so he insisted on staying at the inn."

"Aigoo! What does discretion matter when there are tigers in the woods? Tigers!" Mistress Myeongok's voice trembled. "What will our neighbors say when they find his dead body right outside our own home?"

Father rubbed his eyes, visibly exhausted, but Mother pressed on in a rising voice. "And if Lord Yu dies—for he surely *will* die!—we'll lose all hope of finding Yeonhee. Lord Yu knows this Wuyeong scoundrel, knows where to search. And if His Lordship is devoured alive, we'll have nothing. No connections, no answers, nothing at all!"

Father hesitated. "Yeobo, he turned down the invitation firmly. I cannot force him."

Haewon shifted uneasily. She tried not to imagine Lord Yu riding through the darkness, where danger prowled. But mostly, she recalled travelers complaining about the inn, of bedbugs leaping about on the straw mats occupants were made to sleep on. Her soul shuddered to think of Lord Yu, the gentleman who had likely been raised with the reverence of a prince, attempting to sleep in such a place.

"Father," Haewon whispered, feeling a sheen of cold dampen her collar. "Mother is right. You shouldn't have let him go."

"Indeed," Jade chimed in, "the roads aren't safe at night."

Father folded his arms as he stared ponderously at his drink. But at length, he stood. "Very well. I'll go bring him back. Though, mark my words, he will not be pleased."

As the door closed behind him, Mother collapsed once more,

muttering to herself in a frenzy. As for herself, Haewon felt as though she were going to be ill.

"We ought to return to our quarters," Jade whispered, eyeing Haewon. "It would be improper for us to be here when Father brings in the gentleman."

As they slipped into their room, Jade added, "We will remain in our room. You won't even have to see him."

Chapter 28

Haewon hid in her room. She stood with her back against the wall, listening to the rhythm of his footsteps, the low murmur of his voice through the walls as he addressed her mother, who was thanking him profusely and begging him to do all that he could to discreetly bring Yeonhee home. He sounded brusque, tense. His discomfort was evident.

"Agasshi!" Maid Boram gasped, rushing over to Haewon. "You are still in that dress from this afternoon? You will catch your death. Come, let me change you."

Haewon hadn't changed since arriving, too soon swept into the nightmare of her missing sister. "Thank you," she whispered as Boram stripped her down to her undergarments.

Boram left, then soon returned with a bucket of clean water, a little breathless as she spoke. "Good heavens. I *just* passed that tall, proud guest of ours. Your father was apologizing for dragging him here. And Lord Yu is staring at the door, as though he would like nothing more than to leave."

Embarrassment heated Haewon's skin as she crouched before the bucket in partial undress, wiping the bare sections of herself, her skin flushed a deep red.

"The ordeal the Shin family is putting that gentleman through!"

Boram went on, "Earlier today, you clung to him in the water like a clam onto a rock—"

Jade gasped, a sewing needle held midair. "You swam with Lord Yu?"

"I didn't *swim* with him," Haewon protested. "I fell into a pond and he assisted me out."

Boram huffed out a breath, taking the wet cloth to clean Haewon's back, her throat, behind her ears. "And now Lord Yu, heir to Myeongwoldang, a giwajip with ninety-nine rooms, has stepped into our Haewon agasshi's . . . tiny abode."

"I can't imagine why my name should be uttered in the same breath as his," Haewon said stiffly.

"I can't imagine why myself," Jade chimed in, and there was an odd glint in her eyes, as though she were privy to some great secret. Once Boram stalked off to retrieve clean clothing, Jade leaned forward and whispered, "Young Master Byeongho told me."

Haewon tensed. "Told you what?"

"You know how servants gossip. A few overheard a conversation at Myeongwoldang, and the story reached Young Master Byeongho. He told me a mysterious young woman had rejected Lord Yu. Of course, I instantly knew who the lady in question was. Oh, Haewon-ah." Her brow puckered, her eyes warming with anguish. "Is this true?"

"I meant to tell you," Haewon rushed to say, her voice lowered into a bare whisper. "But the opportunity never came."

"Have your feelings for him changed? Perhaps he is still besotted with you."

"I will tell you more later, eonni. But you needn't look so concerned." Haewon forced a smile as Boram returned. "It is over."

That was the truth. Lord Yu could not care for her any longer, not after how she had humiliated him, and certainly not after spending an evening with her uncouth and less-than-perfect family.

Her heart was heavy as she dragged herself into fresh undergarments. Boram proceeded to wrap her chest with a clean roll of jolitmal. The fabric cinched around her, a tightness she'd had to live with ever since her chest had filled out. Yet tonight, it felt even more constricting.

"Your parents have always offered room to elderly travelers, or couples, never a young man every family in the capital is vying to make their son-in-law." Boram chattered on as she continued to attend to her mistress. "I wonder what the villagers will say when they discover this. Though, I suppose that will be the least on their minds when they learn of Mistress Yeonhee!"

Haewon groaned, her head aching at the reminder.

"Perhaps," Jade said, "perhaps we will find her, before anyone knows better."

"Like I always say, every woman is surrounded by a neighborhood of spies." Boram now roamed about, picking up the undergarments soiled by the pond water. "People will know, if she doesn't return by tomorrow. Someone is bound to recognize her wandering alone in the capital, the longer she remains missing. Society is unforgiving of young ladies. Didn't the official who investigated Jade not say those very words?"

"Yes." Jade shook her head as she returned to her needlework. "He declared the virtuous woman is one of the greatest treasures of Joseon. And that it is better for a woman who loses her greatest possession to choose death."

Haewon scoffed. "I'm sure members from Father's clan will begin conspiring against Yeonhee as soon as they hear the gossip." She angrily pushed her arms through the straps of her nighttime dress and, once secured, shrugged into her white jacket. "But I will sooner push *them* into the deep water before they manage to lay a hand on Yeonhee."

"I'll bring you the rope." A sweet smile played on Jade's lips as she stabbed a needle into her embroidery. "So you might bind them up."

"And I . . ." Boram took the bundle of clothing and dumped it into a straw basket. "I will serve as your alibis. I will declare that Mistress Jade and Haewon spent their entire day"—she waved her hand—"toiling in the kitchen."

They all three exchanged smiles, each of them barely able to hide their fear and sadness. But Haewon knew, with certainty, that even if Yeonhee turned out to be the fifth great scandal in Joseon history, alongside the infamous Lady Eowudong, Lady Yu Gamdong, Lady Geumeumdong, and Lady Dongja, Yeonhee would always be swaddled in a kind of innocence. Haewon had carried Yeonhee on her back. She had washed her little sister's face. She had seen her joys and snotty sobs.

She *knew* Yeonhee.

Yeonhee would always be their Yeonhee.

Later that night, long after the twenty-eighth rumble of the Bosingak bell signaled the closing of the fortress gate, Haewon lay on her bed mat, staring blankly up at the ceiling while the others slept.

It was truly difficult to sleep when she was constantly wondering what the inscrutable, unsmiling giant was doing at the other end of her home. She wondered, too, how she might warn Lord Yu of the danger his reputation was in, without revealing herself as Magpie. He needed to know—by involving himself in the search for Yeonhee, it would bring him toe to toe with the very inspector who was searching for Black Lotus.

With a sigh, Haewon abandoned her mat and sat before her low table, preparing the paper and writing equipment. She lit a candle and leaned into the golden circle of light. After a few attempts, she composed a satisfactory note, dried the ink, then folded it in half.

Now lay her dilemma.

She could wait to deliver the note tomorrow. But her parents would expect her to remain in her room, and any chance of slipping away unnoticed would be lost with Mother and Father awake.

She could also sneak it under the study door, where Lord Yu was staying for the night, then flee.

Haewon folded her face into her hands, her heart thundering in her ears so loud that she couldn't *think*. This question would keep her up all night, and she wanted to be done with it. She never wished to think of Black Lotus and Magpie again.

Blowing out the candle, Haewon rose to her feet with the note clutched tight and padded across the dark room. She had to remind herself there was nothing to fear. Lord Yu wouldn't see her; she would be as quick as a mouse in the shadows of night, as quick as lightning itself, as quick as—

Boram tossed in her sleep, mumbling something about rice cakes and sweets. Then she fell motionless again.

Holding her breath, Haewon pulled the door open, wincing at every rumble and rattle of the doorframe. Then she stepped out and held herself still, listening for movement. There was none. Not a single murmur, creak, or shuffle. Everyone seemed to be asleep.

Her feet bare and her steps quiet, Haewon snuck across the wooden maru floor, the main living space where they would take meals together as a family. A few paces more, and she stood before the latticed door of the study, the hanji screen glowing a pale, moon-touched blue. Holding back the swell of her skirt, she crouched, note in hand as she stretched, about to slip it under—

The door suddenly slid open.

Haewon froze, staring at her fingertips, nearly touching a pair of silk white boseon. She glanced up, slowly, past the trousers, the silk robe that drifted elegantly over them. She dared not stare up any higher.

"Mistress Haewon?"

She shot to her feet. She hadn't planned for this! Then a most dreadful and horrifying realization dawned on her: She was in a state of undress. Bareheaded and in nothing but her nightgown, a sight reserved for only the closest of family members. She darted a glance around, searching for something, *anything*, to wrap herself in. But there was nothing.

"I . . . I couldn't sleep," he said, his voice tense, "so thought I might take a walk—"

She made the mistake of looking up, and her heart stuttered at the sight of him. His dark eyes were fixed on her, studying her intently.

"Why are you here, Mistress Haewon?" he whispered.

"Well . . ." She bit her lower lip, and his gaze fell, riveted on her mouth. Her heart threatened to explode from her chest. Why were they standing here, like a pair of newlyweds on their wedding night?

She tried to stomp the thought away, blaming all of Jade's romantic literature for putting *that* in her mind, but it wouldn't budge.

"Yeonhee?" Mother's voice startled the silence, echoing from the room across the main living space. "Yeonhee-yah, is that you?" Footsteps shuffled. "Yeobo, wake up. I think Yeonhee has returned."

Haewon's blood ran cold. The moment her parents stepped outside, they would see her alone with Lord Yu. Her mother would not hesitate; she would declare Haewon's honor compromised and hound Lord Yu to the ends of the kingdom until he took responsibility.

Lord Yu must have thought the same.

After a rush of muffled movements, Haewon found herself in the study. She was unsure if she had pushed him or he had drawn her in, but the study door was shut, and they stood pressed together, his back pushed up against the wall, and her clinging on to him, on the brink of losing her balance.

"I thought I heard Yeonhee." Mother's voice trembled. "I heard something, I vow I did!"

Lord Yu's heart pounded under the palm of her hand. Haewon tried not to pay it too much heed, along with the fact that they stood nearly hip to hip, the heat of his proximity scorching her skin. She could barely breathe, the air thick and warm. Their fingers were touching, both frozen on the brass door handle.

Just a few more moments, Haewon desperately reassured herself, *and Mother and Father will go back to sleep. I'll leave the study at once.*

"My dear . . ." It was her father, and the warm glow of candlelight moved across the paper-screened door, then settled upon the silhouette of a table. "You ought to speak quieter. Lord Yu is asleep."

Her eyes widened as the shadows of her parents lowered to the floor, and Lord Yu tensed beneath her. Evidently her parents had decided to lounge out on the maru. She shot a worried glance up, hoping to find an answer in Lord Yu's face, but he stood motionless, watching her.

The silence became stifling. The room felt entirely too small with him in it.

"She's my girl"—Mistress Myeongok's voice broke—"and I carried her for nine long months!" Sniffles, followed by the sound of her rummaging for her handkerchief. "It is terrible to be a mother. All three of them, they all grew up so fast; I was so desperate for them to stay young. At least when they were young I could shield them with my own body. But now they are grown! I am clueless as to how to be a good mother, and my greatest duty is to secure a good match for them—marriage to a man who will give them security and kindness. But now Yeonhee is missing, our whole family *ruined.*"

Haewon nearly pressed her forehead into the chest before her, as defeat sank into her stomach. It seemed Mother was in for a long conversation with Father. The only window in the study was tiny and situated high in the wall, so escape wasn't possible.

They were trapped.

Quietly, cautiously peeling herself off Lord Yu, she moved to her father's low-legged table, drew out a brush, and dipped it into the leftover ink. She wrote onto the moonlit paper: *I apologize for inconveniencing you like this. Yet again.*

Lord Yu settled on the floor next to her and gently took the brush from her. *Think nothing of it,* he wrote.

A deep ache burned in her chest. His handwriting—Black Lotus's writing—held such painful familiarity. Her gaze clung to his hand as he wrote on:

How are you feeling?

She was careful not to touch him, holding her sleeve back as she reached over for the brush. *I'm realizing how powerless I really am,* she wrote in response. *I can't seem to ensure anyone's happiness, not even one sister's.*

He wrote: *You will find your sister, or she may simply return home on her own.*

But even if she does return, what if rumors spread? She stared at the question haunting the back of her mind. The cold sheen of fear crept into her once more. *You know what will happen to my family. We will never be able to raise our heads in society.*

At his prolonged silence, she held the brush out to him. She knew it was rash to demand a reply. But, more than ever, she found herself in need of Black Lotus's words.

The night will feel long, should what you fear occur, he finally wrote, *but it will not be endless. All darkness has its end.*

She could barely read the words, the sense of despair growing. The night *would* in fact be endless. Jade would lose the opportunity to marry Young Master Byeongho—no matter how much he adored her, such a newly budded love could not withstand a family's downfall. Her mother would sink into the deepest, darkest pit of anguish. Her father would never leave his study and waste away. Yeonhee, if she ever returned home, would have to shoulder the guilt of it all.

Some families, Lord Yu continued to write, *when ruined, choose to let shame rot them. But you must take your family and leave the people and the area in which the scandal is rife, leave like the author of* Taekriji. *You and your family must find a new beginning. It is, I believe, the only way to be happy again.*

The thought of leaving her home filled her with sadness. Then she remembered the book he had mentioned.

"*Taekriji,*" she whispered, and the title summoned up memories. The book had mentioned a place with a high harvest and fertile land that boosted the economy, but also a place with good hospitality and beautiful mountains. She and her family would have to wander, like the writer. He had lived the ruined life before them, with no career, no reputation, no way to even feed himself. He had gone ahead of them, charted this territory, and he had come to the conclusion that Joseon was a wonderful country to wander about, lost.

I have only known Gyonam Village and parts of the capital for all my life, she wrote. Then she stared at the words, misery still weighing heavy in her chest, yet the barest sense of buoyancy fluttered. A crack of light in the clouds looming over her future. Taekriji *recommended places like Hapcheon, Gyeongsangnam, Gurye, Jeonju, Daejeon, Yuseong, and Hahoe.*

Seojun was still, his brows pressed in concentration. Then he held back his sleeve, and her gaze fell onto his forearm, a map of sinew and veins. His muscles drew taut as he ground the black stick into the inkstone with some water, the ink Father had made earlier used up. He continued to write:

Taekriji *praised the East Sea coast of Gangwon Province as one of the most beautiful places in Joseon. He wrote of it: "Once you tour this area, you instantly become a different person, and those who have passed through it still have the aura of a fresh world in their faces and demeanor even after ten years."*

Her chest burned. He was helping her spin an imaginary world, something to hold on to when night fell. *Thank you,* she mouthed.

He bowed his head, his expression unreadable.

The silence returned, and it was then she realized that her parents had left. The note she had composed earlier was nowhere to be found. She couldn't leave until she relayed the message, the sole reason she had ventured to the study in the first place. But where to even begin?

She picked up the brush, then recalled they were entirely alone. "Did you speak with Wol yet?" she whispered.

Startled, he glanced up at her, then at the door, and saw that the glow of the candle was gone. "No," he replied, his deep voice sending a reluctant shiver down her spine. "I visited the Ministry of Justice and they wouldn't permit me to visit her. So I went to speak with her father. That is how I came to cross paths with Scholar Shin."

"Father said you knew Inspector Wuyeong? How well do you know him?"

"Well enough," he murmured, then steadied his gaze on her. "Why do you ask? In fact, why did you come to Myeongwoldang to warn me about Wol? Me, of all people?"

Her heart pounded, her fingers icy as she whispered, "Inspector Wuyeong, according to my sister, is bent on looking for Black Lotus. He . . . he has obtained a book, a collection of letters." Then quickly, she added, "Transcribed letters. Not the originals. In any case, Inspector Wuyeong has it in his possession, and I fear he might find evidence in there that might identify . . . Black Lotus. I think you might know who this writer is. Please do not ask me why." She touched her brow. She was likely confusing Lord Yu. "I will not trouble you with further explanation. All you need to know is that Black Lotus's reputation is at risk."

She fumbled to organize her father's desk, clearing their pages of correspondence away. And when Lord Yu continued to remain silent, she finally looked up. His stare bore into her, his brows knitting together in intense study, then a strange look dawned over his expression, like the slow rise of sunlight stretching over the shadowed horizon. Every hidden brook and crevice, illuminated. With a voice barely more than a breath, he uttered a word that reached into the depths of her soul: "*Magpie*."

It was a statement. Not a question.

And with that, her heart seized. She startled back, wide-eyed, and his expression confirmed that he had known her secret for some time. "How . . . how long have you known?"

"Since I saw your handwriting," his voice rasped, "at Hwasadang House."

A pang of remorse struck her. Now she recalled his remark from Seogeomjeong: *Do you know* why *I have been thinking of you for months?* She should have waited for his answer or, at the least, ought to have pondered his meaning for longer than a passing moment. Haewon had to grip her hands, restraining herself from the need to hide her face behind them.

"And you kept my letters after all this time?" he asked softly.

He didn't sound upset, but she knew she owed him an explanation.

"I destroyed your letters as you asked, I promise," Haewon said. "But the fool that I am, I kept a record of them. I didn't want to forget your words." She did not, however, tell him that Inspector Wuyeong held those letters as blackmail. That man could still ruin her, for she had no intention of exposing Black Lotus's identity. Wringing a loose thread of her skirt, she added, "I'm not sure what the consequence will be of this book of letters, but I apologize nevertheless."

Lord Yu stilled the anxious hand of hers, then just as soon withdrew his own, leaving behind a burn on her skin. "I can hardly blame you; I kept yours, too."

"Oh" was all she managed.

A charged silence fell over them. The night grew too quiet. Haewon smoothed out her dress, her skirt rustling, then she nervously glanced his way. What was he thinking? What was he feeling?

Suddenly, he rose to his feet and wandered over to the far corner of the study, which was still not very far away. The study was much too small for two people who were not meant to be alone.

"You should go now," he said, his voice hoarse. "That would be wise."

He was sending her away, telling her to leave when—to her utter shame—she wanted to remain. Here, with the one person she had so desperately longed to befriend, who had become anything but a friend. She rose nevertheless, and with each retreating step, she felt the chilling darkness closing in around her.

"Rest well, nauri," she whispered, lingering by the door for a brief moment.

He did not look at her again, and so she left.

Chapter 29

It was agony.

The more time he spent with Haewon, the more a quiet desperation built within him. He wanted to reach out and feel the warmth of her hand in his. More than anything, that was what he desired. To simply hold her hand. But she had drawn the line, and he dared not cross it. He dared not, even as her arms pressed into his, as their hands touched in exchanging the brush, as her physical nearness burned through him. He had felt his composure unraveling the entire time, on the verge of losing his sanity.

As he lay on the bed mat that night, hands tucked under his head, staring up at the ceiling rafters, sleep evaded him. Every noise coming through the thin walls of the house left him alert, his heart beating at a pace that was not conducive to sleep.

The sky slowly brightened, and Seojun resigned himself to the fact that he wouldn't sleep at all tonight. He searched for distraction by perusing Scholar Shin's bookshelf, which was illuminated by the blue-gray skylight. Most of his collection comprised secondhand Confucian classics. He stilled at a book from a lending shop, evident at a glance by its cover wrapping of sambae. It was a work by Yeonam.

Slipping the copy off the shelf, Seojun flipped through the pages. It was a well-loved book, its margins and pages crowded with notes and drawings by readers. Some outbursts cursing the plot, and others cursing the reader for cursing at all, and others complaining about the scribe's handwriting, and still others complaining that the book was nearly illegible, with all its comments and commentaries, and all the drawings someone had thought it acceptable to cover entire pages with.

Mistress Wol found such defacement the bane of her existence.

To him, however, it was as much a part of the joy as reading a novel. There was a certain pleasure in encountering the thoughts of those who had come before.

The smile tugging at his lips fell as he came across the comment *This scribe's transcription work is riddled with so many spelling errors. I am tempted to correct it all with red ink. I recommend the copies transcribed by Magpie instead.*

Everyone in Five Willows knew of Magpie. Transcribers were more than simply copiers of texts—they edited as they transcribed, embellished as they went. Rarely were two transcribed copies entirely the same. Seojun read the comment below it, written in response: *Magpie's copies are always the first to disappear off the shelf.*

"Magpie," he whispered, the conversation with Haewon returning.

Haewon's book of letters was now in Inspector Wuyeong's hands. And considering Inspector Wuyeong's close ties to Yeonhee, he would not be surprised if the girl had shared, in confidence, that her elder sister was the infamous Magpie.

Seojun exhaled as he returned the novel to the shelf, the weight of Haewon's predicament settling over him with sudden, crushing force. Inspector Wuyeong would not care what became of Haewon or her family. A man who destroyed books was a man with no empathy. And if he exposed Haewon as Magpie, tying her name to works deemed heretical . . .

It would be a scandal far graver than Yeonhee's.

Sitting motionless, Seojun stared at the window, at the silhouette of branches swaying across the hanji screen. For the past few years, he'd had a reoccurring nightmare in which he was trapped beneath the sea. Frozen immobile by some inhuman force, he could do nothing but watch in a state of voiceless horror as the pale silhouette of his sister disappeared into the depths right below him.

That same helplessness settled over him now.

By daybreak, his head throbbed, his mind aching from all the thoughts. Plans, possibilities, things he could do, yet he was gripped by the pervasive realization that a woman's reputation was fragile. No matter his efforts, it might all fall apart. His mind teetered on the borderland of sleep, and soon he was no longer able to differentiate delusion and dream. A magpie was perched on the bookshelf, its harsh squawking ringing in his head, and pages from novels were falling from the rafters and melting into him like snowflakes.

A loud, piercing cry broke through his subconscious.

Seojun's eyes shot open. He was drenched in cold sweat, feverish, his head and arms draped over the low table. For a moment he wondered if the cry had come from his sister's quarters. She hadn't cried this loud in two years, since—

Then he remembered where he was.

Scholar Shin's books stared down at him. The small window hinted at the time, for the sky was the gray of either an early morning or a day overcast by clouds. Quickly, he refreshed himself, made himself decent, then stepped out of the study, only to find three women huddled around a note.

Dust motes danced in the dim skylight. The threshold doors had been left open, damp air breathing in and out across the maru floor, rain dribbling down from the eaves and pattering onto the veranda. There was a table laid right before the study door, arrayed with an assortment of food one would eat in the afternoon; it struck him he had slept well into the day, which had never occurred before. Disoriented, he looked around, and it took a moment to recognize Haewon, her eyes wide, her face utterly pale.

His blood turned cold. "What is the matter?"

Mistress Myeongok hurried forward. Everyone, including himself, had forgotten that her two daughters stood in plain sight. It was the height of impropriety. But in that moment, such concerns were meaningless.

"Oh, nauri! A courier came by this morning." Mistress Myeongok rushed to hand the note to him. "It was addressed to my husband, but he left early to meet Inspector Wuyeong. It is from Merchant Hyoyang of Five Willows."

Seojun was almost afraid to read it, but finally did.

Yeonhee just came by for a meal, and rest assured, I am quite certain she'll return to Five Willows. She left her identification document here by accident.

"We might yet find her! She cannot leave the capital without it!" Mistress Myeongok cried, fluttering her handkerchief about. The cloth, delicately embroidered with pale pink and yellow flowers, trembled in her hands as she drew a shuddering breath. "Oh, it is an agony that you must witness our family in such disgrace! Nauri, we must impose upon you once more. Indeed, with my husband gone, we have no other way—"

"I'll visit Five Willows. You needn't worry about that."

Grabbing his hat, Seojun strode out through the light shower and soon reached the stable. He had never felt his manservant's absence more keenly than now. With no one to assist, he untethered Jeolyeong himself and led the horse out. Once mounted, he eased the creature into a steady canter down the road, ignoring the rumbling of the skies. If Yeonhee was heading to Five Willows, he would find her. He would bribe any witnesses from gossiping, would even pay Inspector Wuyeong whatever he required to keep silent about both Yeonhee and Magpie. Anything to keep Haewon safe.

"Nauri!" a female voice called out behind him.

He reined his horse to a halt, then glanced back to see two women hurrying down the road, one at a run. Haewon reached him in no time, the color high on her cheeks, her silk veil flapping loudly behind her in the wet wind.

"It seems," she declared, a little out of breath, "that we are heading in the same direction!"

He didn't bother to dissuade her. If anyone was going to convince Yeonhee to return home, it would be one of her sisters.

"Hurry and find her," a distant voice called out. It was Mistress Myeongok, who stood farther away, waving her handkerchief. "We shall wait here, in case Yeonhee decides to return home!"

Then Jade called out, "I'll take good care of Mother!"

Seojun watched them for a moment longer, their humble abode appearing tiny against the sea of gray sky. Haewon's family remained, in many ways, as wild as he had first judged them to be, yet now there was a warmth to them, a loveliness he had not perceived before.

It was the father, Scholar Shin, who had surprised Seojun the most. Seojun was accustomed to men quick to shift blame, their words sharp with shameless cruelty, their viciousness a shield for their own fragile pride. Fathers who cherished their honor above all else and would never think twice about killing their own misbehaving daughters. Such men populated the government in droves. Yet Scholar Shin had been different. From the very beginning, he had blamed no one but himself for Yeonhee's disappearance, and had conspired not how to harm his daughter, but how he might shield her from cruel judgment.

It was only a glimpse into the family, but it was enough. Enough to see the roots of Haewon's warmth and kindness, her courage and her indomitable, unconventional spirit . . .

"Shall we go then?" Haewon looked up at him with that frank expression he'd come to adore. "To Five Willows."

Seojun dismounted, and leading his horse by the reins, he walked quietly alongside the young lady and her maid, who had finally caught up and covered her mistress with a straw cloak.

"Heavens, if Yeonhee would only return home today," Haewon exclaimed, "I will forgive her for causing our family so much distress."

"You would forgive her so easily?" Seojun asked. "Many would decide to withhold forgiveness entirely. Your sister stole your private letters."

Haewon paused thoughtfully, then met his gaze. "I believe we ought not to burn the bridge we might one day wish to cross. A burned bridge leaves no way back to the person we love." She then gave a little shrug. "And perhaps, if this incident had occurred a few months ago, I would have been entirely unforgiving. But I find myself . . . changed. We are only human; we are all capable of error. I, for one, am full of them. It is up to you, of course, to decide should the circumstance arise. Some bridges are meant to be burned down. But others . . . others are meant to be salvaged."

Appreciation for her warmed his heart, and he wondered if she would ever come to know how deeply he cherished her thoughts. "Hmm" was all he managed to say. He finally looked ahead.

They were passing through a grove of trees that were in full bloom a few days ago, now all bare green-budded branches, the earth carpeted with their pale, muddied blossoms. Puddles glistened on the road, and birds chirped in delight, bathing, flitting their wings, and splashing up droplets that gleamed bright.

He glanced back at Haewon, wondering what she was thinking of now. They had shared dozens of letters, and he had been so convinced he knew Magpie through and through. Yet as he continued to study the woman next to him, he realized he knew very little.

"What—" He cleared his throat, trying to steady the flutter of nervousness she always induced in him. "What was Yeonhee like, growing up together? All three of you?"

A faint look of amusement brightened her expression. "Yeonhee was passionate and playful. Curious and reckless, too. She yearns for so much from this life, and is the most loyal girl I know. Once, long ago, Jade was harassed by a village boy, and Yeonhee set out and struck the boy in the face. She is also the girl who laughs the loudest." Haewon caught her skirt as she walked around a deep puddle. “Her heart is as wide and deep as the sea. She will, at her own expense, strive to help her friends even to her own detriment.”

“And your elder sister, Jade?”

“She was the sunshine to me, and still is. She was like a mother when our own was overwhelmed by life.” Her lashes lowered. “Our family is not perfect. Indeed, we are far from perfect but—”

“No family is perfect.”

She offered him a wry smile. “No family is perfect, but very few families in your acquaintance, I’m sure, are as ill-mannered as mine.”

He held her gaze for a moment longer, memories stinging at his conscience. Memories he had wished to forget entirely. Of himself, holding his sister tight as he dragged himself across barnacle-encrusted stone, unmindful of his flesh tearing, the seawater turning red around him, until his manservant had turned pale and had yelled out that he was dripping blood.

“There’s something you should know,” he whispered.

“And what might that be?”

He rubbed the back of his neck. It seemed unfair, that he knew so much of her family’s vulnerability and shame, and she knew none of his own. “I trust you to keep this confidential.”

“Of course.” Haewon glanced behind to ascertain that her maid was out of earshot, then fixed her attention on him, all hints of amusement gone. “I promise.”

“My sister fell in love with a young man who was bold enough to woo a young widow, despite the law forbidding it, and they ran away. She later learned it was only because he attempted to blackmail our father for money, in exchange for her return. Father supplied it, and she was abandoned at an inn."

Haewon turned pale. "How devastated your sister must have been."

"As I said, my sister is widowed. Strictly forbidden from remarriage, from loving anyone else. When a widow dies for her husband, the government rewards the family. Her in-laws were hoping for that glory. They were pressuring her to take her own life. So you see, when she ran away with her lover, her father-in-law set out to preserve the family honor."

She frowned up at him, waiting with intense focus for him to continue.

"Her father-in-law cornered my sister, tried to convince her to die. But she wouldn't. So he pushed my sister off the seaside cliff."

"The near drowning," she whispered, to his surprise. "Your sister told me about it."

"She did? I suppose she's grown tired of her own silence."

"And the father-in-law left your sister alone afterward?"

"My father had an agreement with the in-laws. He would take Gwideok home; her in-laws would no longer make any attempt to harm her, on the condition that her scandal remain hidden. That she live as though she never existed. That was the cost of preserving her life."

Haewon shook her head, a sad look in her eyes.

"My sister has never recovered from the event. She won't step out, for fear of resurrecting the past. People have forgotten her very existence. She hasn't laughed—until you came. I am indebted to you," he said with all the warmth she inspired in him. "It's all I wanted, to hear her laugh again. I suppose that is why I am here. The same kindness and mercy I wish people to treat my sister with, I wish for your own. Your sister is alive and unharmed—that is what is most important, as of now. Wuyeong wouldn't think to hurt her; he would gain nothing in doing so."

"I hope not . . ."

He watched the way determination pressed Haewon's brows together. Busy, busy Mistress Haewon. How she would do anything for the happiness of her sisters.

As they entered the capital and approached Five Willows, he thought of the magpies and crows from a childhood tale, the story of how they had woven their bodies into a bridge so that Jiknyeo and Gyeonwu, separated by the vast expanse of the Milky Way, could meet once more.

He hoped the same for Haewon. That the heavens would take pity and intervene, and build a bridge of birds to bring her sister back home.

Chapter 30

Rain drummed on the rooftop, pattered against the latticed windows of the Five Willows bookshop. Pacing about, Haewon struggled to stay calm, her nerves fraying with every passing moment. They had arrived in the early afternoon and had waited for what felt like an eternity. Her damp dress had long since dried. Lord Yu, ever composed, stood browsing the shelves with quiet patience.

"The assistant said Merchant Hyoyang had left for a little bit," Haewon said, determined not to fuss about the impropriety, to not draw further attention to how entirely alone they were. Maid Boram was too riveted by a novel to pay them any heed, and the shop assistant was nodding off by the inner door. No other patron or scribe was in sight; the recent bookshop raid must have caused enough fear to keep them away.

Clearing her throat, she added, "But I'm sure Merchant Hyoyang will return any moment now."

Lord Yu flipped a page. "I'm sure."

Her heart continued to race. She rarely lost mastery over herself, but the merchant's absence, Yeonhee's disappearance, and *him*—that tall, handsome man standing in the same aisle as she—left her incredibly agitated.

She paced down the end of the aisle for the hundredth time

and took in the row of shelves. How long would she have to remain here, isolated with Lord Yu? How long before Yeonhee returned? Surely her sister would notice her identification document missing and panic. Wandering back to Lord Yu, Haewon absentmindedly picked up a book and flipped through its pages, releasing a cloud of dust. She sneezed.

A deep, warm chuckle broke the silence.

Her pulse leapt at the unfamiliar sound.

"You sneeze like a startled mouse," he remarked.

So accustomed to his reserve, she found herself frozen with shock, unable to register the moment. She stole a glance up at him, and then she saw . . . a *smile.* A boyish smile that softened his stern features. It was truly something to behold. The way the corners of his eyes crinkled, charming, kind. Her heart melted like a snow-covered field under the blazing sun. She'd never seen him smile before. At least, not like this, and not at her. He was impossibly handsome, more than she cared to admit. Heat slowly crept up her throat.

"Here it is," he said, pulling a book off the shelf right above her. He seemed in no hurry to step back after offering her his find. "The book I suggested to you, in many of our letters. An ideal read if you require a moment's escape."

A quiet fell over her as she held the book, the weight of it settling in her heart. The weight of all their letters, all their shared thoughts and feelings. Black Lotus's favorite book. The book that had changed the shape of his soul.

"*Yeolhailgi,*" she whispered.

She ran her hand down the thick hemp-fabric cover, and a

strangled laugh escaped her as she flipped through. "I fear a reread will be impossible. Look at all these drawings. Look at this one." She pointed it out to him.

Lord Yu peered down at the illustration from over her shoulder. The ink-drawn face with four eyes and a toothy grin smiled up at them. His brows knitted, and he murmured in grim observation, "It appears to be a self-portrait."

She burst into laughter, then quickly pressed a hand to her lips, lest she attract a brusque lecture from Maid Boram. In that moment, all Haewon's anxieties scattered, and she felt a lightness in her soul—as though, just for now, she could truly believe all would be well.

They continued leafing through the notes and sketches, swiftly turning past the more scandalous illustrations. She didn't think to feel embarrassed, and she forgot for a brief moment that Lord Yu was someone apart from her. He was simply there, beside her, and she felt as at ease with him as she did when lost in her own thoughts, safe within the walls of her room.

"Sometimes . . ." She shook her head, unable to stop smiling. "Sometimes I sit before a novel and wonder, 'Why is it we return to them? Why are we Joseon people so enamored by them?' I have truly witnessed ladies going into financial ruin to borrow books."

He cast her a thoughtful look. "My thoughts are . . . Novels move us in a way that Confucian classics cannot. The classics dictate how we ought to think. But novels speak to a longing that we are ashamed to admit."

A strand of her hair had slipped loose. She swiped it aside, but it fell over her face once more, tickling her cheek. "Longing? What kind—"

Everything in her stilled as a hand brushed her hair aside. His finger left a trail of warmth. Slowly, she looked up at him. His face had gone taut, and his hand still lingered in midair by her cheek. He looked disoriented, like he couldn't believe his own hand.

"I just—" His ears turned red. "I moved the hair because . . . it . . . it looked uncomfortable."

Their gazes locked for a moment too long. She could hardly even breathe, the way his gaze made her feel.

A knock came at the shop door, so sharp they startled apart. Her heart leapt and whirled, spinning like a leaf caught in a violent storm. By the time she found her bearings, she became aware of muffled female voices reciting verses, the key for entrance. The assistant let out a loud yawn, examined the visitors through the peephole, then removed the wooden bar.

A hand over her still-racing heart, Haewon peered out from behind the shelf and spotted a pair of young ladies wandering in. "It's not Yeonhee," she sighed, casting her companion a nervous glance.

"It is nearly evening. We've been waiting too long," Lord Yu noted, looking everywhere but at her. His usual composure had fractured; the tips of his ears still burned red, and he clasped his hands behind his back as though to physically restrain himself. Clearing his throat, he turned toward the entrance. "I will step out for a moment—"

"But it is still raining."

"Hardly. If Yeonhee was here earlier, there may be witnesses who saw where she went."

Without waiting for her response, he strode off, and she felt she could finally breathe. Knees weak, she leaned against the wall between two shelves. Her pulse beat, fast and unsteady, as she placed a hand over her cheek, where his finger had grazed. The sensation had burned into her skin, and she found, much to her chagrin, that she liked his touch.

She liked *him*.

Once, falling in love had seemed so simple, something that would occur as easily as the turning of seasons. Yet now, at eighteen, she realized it was no simple matter. One could fall in love with the wrong person—someone who belonged to the wrong family, held the wrong status; could fall in love early or too late, long after she had rejected him, after too much had occurred to turn time around.

"It is not to be," she whispered to herself, lowering her hand. She rubbed at a nonexistent stain on the cover of *Yeolhailgi*. "It is not meant to be . . ."

Even as she spoke these words, her shoulders sagged. She really, *really* liked him. Unbearably so. And she knew she would be thinking of Lord Yu for years to come. She would cherish their collection of moments and letters, going through them now and then to relive distant memories. For he was, without a doubt, one of those rare souls she could never and would never *wish* to forget.

Someone cleared their throat.

Her heart skipped. But when she opened her eyes, she found herself staring at a willowy, finely dressed gentleman. He caught her stare and offered her a most amiable smile as he adjusted his wide-brimmed hat. Disappointment sank into her chest. She already missed the company of her brooding, softhearted companion who bestowed smiles once every few centuries.

Drawing her veil low over her head, she moved away when the stranger spoke. "Have you ever seen a more dusty, disagreeable place as this?"

She stilled. "Are you speaking to me?"

"My proposition still stands," the stranger continued with smooth civility. "I reviewed those letters written between you and Black Lotus."

She frowned, confused at first. Then a jolt of understanding shot through her. The man standing by her was none other than Inspector Wuyeong, the man who'd made a plaything of her little sister.

"You need only obey my orders, and I shall spare you from ruin." He spoke soothingly, the patronizing way one spoke to a child. "Come now, promise me that you will do as I say, and I shall ensure that no calamity befalls your family."

She leveled a stare at him. She *would* control her tongue; one could not afford to upset the man who had dangerous secrets in his possession. And yet the moment she laid eyes on the cruel wretch, she at once failed to pacify herself and felt anger spark.

"You called yourself an investigator in a past life," he droned on. "Black Lotus invited you to find the author's true identity. I think you know who the writer is." He slid a studying glance over her, then his brows notched. A titter of a laugh escaped him. "You do know the identity of Black Lotus. I can see it in your face."

"Do you indeed?" she snapped.

"Now, now." He smiled again. He smiled far too often for her liking, and a type of smile she disliked—so shallow as to be meaningless. "No one is in our vicinity. Your maid is a few aisles down; the other two patrons are at the back of the shop. Tell me the truth, and no one will ever know that it was you."

"You seem to take a great deal of pleasure in forcing young women at your mercy," Haewon said tightly. "Is this how you treated my sister, too?"

"Ah, Yeonhee. That mischievous little dokkaebi."

Haewon squared her shoulders, held herself tall. "You had better tell me, at once, where my sister is, Inspector Wuyeong."

"Oh, I really don't know. That is the same answer I gave your father." He sighed. "Yeonhee was entertaining, until she grew tiresome. Did you know that? How tiresome that girl is—"

"You are fortunate that I was not born a man, Inspector. Otherwise, I would have not thought twice about striking you in the face."

Inspector Wuyeong grew pale and his lips thinned into a tight line. "Do you *know* what I am capable of doing? Cross me any further, and you will lose your reputation. You will lose *everything* you hold dear."

She met his glare, and as his rage swelled, a trickle of fear ran through her. It was like watching the sea heave before a storm, and she knew if she did not curb her tongue, the waves would rage high and come crashing down upon her and her family.

"Mistress Haewon," he hissed. "This is my last warning; I am not to be trifled with. If I put my mind to it, I will ruin you. You will never be able to lift your head again in society."

"I understand," she said, this time sliding a note of meekness in her voice. She even lowered her lashes. "I understand perfectly. Please, sir, spare my family."

"Then . . ." He took in a steadying breath. A sharp smile stretched his lips. "Tell me. Who is Black Lotus?"

The main door opened with a crash. Haewon jolted around to see rain-soaked officers in red uniforms gleaming like fresh blood. Water dripped from the brims of their hats, and the great plumes on their crowns swayed as they strode in. The tallest, most commanding figure among the officers prowled to the front of the pack. His lips twisted as he yanked a book from a trembling lady's hands and flipped through the pages with a sneer before tossing it over to an officer. "Seize all Catholic books! Confiscate all novels!"

Haewon watched in horror as the officers tore through shelves, wrenching books out. Volumes toppled in droves, pages ripped out, trampled beneath boots. Her heart splintered at the snapping of story-binding red strings, at the sharp rip of thick covers being torn off the flesh of stories. It felt like her very bones were being wrenched apart.

And watching her, with such smug victory, was Inspector Wuyeong. "Now will you tell me? You will, if you do not wish to be destroyed, as the books before you will be."

Haewon gripped her veil tight. She had grown up learning that respectability was everything. That it was the very air a woman breathed. And yet she could not shake away the conviction that there were far more important things in life.

"If I lose my honor, I will lose my place in the world," she whispered. "But if I betray Black Lotus, I very much fear I will lose myself. That is my answer to you, Inspector Wuyeong. And that is the only answer you will receive from me."

Chapter 31

The market was crowded despite the drizzling rain.

His robe damp against his skin, Seojun visited every merchant shop and street vendor, following the traces of Yeonhee. But his search was interrupted by a commotion up ahead. Like the sea parting at low tide, a path appeared through the crowd. Commoners had moved to prostrate themselves in the mud at the passing of a high official, and behind him was a line of officers.

"Excuse me," came a female voice. "Please, I *must* make haste."

Seojun looked and noticed, a few paces away, a young woman weaving around the bowed figures, her head veiled beneath an overcoat, the green silk gleaming bright amid the wash of commoners garbed in white. His attention narrowed upon a mark near the collar of the headdress: a single bird, embroidered. "Begging your pardon," she cried, "I didn't mean to step on you. I'm in such a hurry!"

Seojun returned his attention back to the scene before him, at officers pushing along empty wagons and carts. They were on their way to fill them, but with what?

A sudden uneasiness gripped him. Turning on his heel, he shouldered his way through the crowd, quickening his pace into a run until he stood before Five Willows. He was already too late. Officers swarmed the premises like flies upon a carcass.

"Is . . . is that not Minister Yu's son?" Voices sounded muffled in his distraction, his entire focus on the shop entrance, wondering if Haewon was still inside. "Ah yes. He is." Smudges of red-robed figures loomed next to him and clapped his back. "Yu Seojun! How tall and handsome you have grown! I always hear about your great achievements . . ." Voices continued to garble together. "You are your father's pride."

Panic thrummed as he watched officers stalk out with books and toss them into carts.

"Excuse me," Seojun insisted.

With Shin Haewon still inside, Five Willows might as well have been in flames. The fear gripped him just the same. Pushing his way through the growing crowd of spectators, then past the row of officers, he strode into Five Willows. A hand grabbed at him inside the shop, but then the officer at once snatched his hand away in disorientation.

Whispers arose among the officers. *Minister Yu's son.*

He shoved past a few more men, bumped into Merchant Hyoyang, who was bemoaning the situation, then drew closer to the center of chaos. Time slowed as he watched the books being lifted from the shelves, carried out in armfuls. Soon they would be scrubbed of ink, of all stories, left to wither under the merciless sun, their paper to be reused for *correct* and *proper* purposes.

Then he saw her.

Haewon moved through the wreckage, but she didn't see him, her face small and pale under the silk overcoat pulled over her head. Her eyes were red, her cheeks tear-streaked, her breathing ragged.

Instinctively, he caught her by the arm to stop her, then quickly released it just as she turned, startled, her face crumpling. "You came back."

His thundering pulse slackened as he took in the sight of her. She was here. She was before him, unharmed. Her veil still bundled her in anonymity. She and her family might not be ruined yet. He took in a deep breath, wiping his brow. His limbs had never felt so weak before. "Of course I did," he finally answered.

"The books," she whispered, "all these books . . ." She shook her head, a look of worry draining the remaining color from her face. "You need to leave. *He* is here."

Seojun looked up. Anger pulsed through his blood at the sight of Wuyeong watching them. But he managed to keep calm, his voice low, as he murmured to her, "The little bird. You once wore a veil with a magpie embroidered at the collar. Where is it now?"

Much confused, she stammered, "My veil? I—I'm unsure why you are asking. Let's not speak here. You should leave—"

"Where is it?"

She hesitated. "It was missing since two mornings ago. Yeonhee likely took it; she often does."

"Then I think, if you step outside, you will find that sister you are so desperately looking for."

"She is here?" Her shock and relief were palpable, so taken aback she seemed unaware of her own hand clasping his sleeve. She might as well have been tugging at his heart. "You are certain you saw her?"

"Yes," he rasped.

He watched her run to the door, then kept staring at the empty space she'd left behind. A sense of finality settled over him; it came in a wave of sadness and an odd feeling of emptiness, as though he had reached the end of a tale he'd wished would never end.

Once reunited with her sister, Shin Haewon would no longer have any need for his assistance. He would not see her again after this day. There would be no more late-night encounters. No more long walks down the damp country road together. No more Magpie and Black Lotus, the thread of potential scandal binding them together. No more, that is, so long as Wuyeong kept quiet. Turning now, he shot a cold glance at the man who was quickly becoming the bane of his existence.

"My lord!" Wuyeong's smooth voice called out. "I don't know what she's told you, but you'd be wise to keep your distance from her ilk. If I told you who she really was, why, you'd be flabbergasted—!"

Seojun moved forward in one swift movement, grabbing the nuisance by the collar. Knuckles white, he gave the man a fierce shove against the wall, sending more books toppling to the ground. Officers had paused their shuffling to stare.

"Stay away from her," Seojun snarled.

"I—" Wuyeong looked pale with shock. "I am merely doing my duty, nauri."

"Your duty? Is it your duty to harass young women?" His grip tightening around the man's collar, Seojun wanted nothing more than to shake some sense into him. "You are nothing more than a scoundrel, a sycophant who deserves a good thrashing."

Wuyeong grew a shade paler at this. "My d-dear Lord Yu, you are mistaken. Your anger is most misdirected. She's lied to you. Shin Haewon is no lady. She's—" A cursory glance around, and then he whispered, "Shall I tell it to you here? Who she is?"

Seojun released his grip, and soon they were in the privacy of the transcription room, which the officers had not yet touched.

With a clumsy tug, Wuyeong straightened his robe. He could not hide the tremor in his hands. "A book of evidence is already with your f-father, my lord. I will have to tell him all that I know, and truly, there is no other way to keep Mistress Shin Haewon's name from my lips if I cannot explain the identity of Black Lotus. She knows who the author is, I'm sure of it. They've exchanged over a hundred letters! Perhaps they are lovers! Either way, I must give your father a reason why I must interrogate Mistress Haewon—she is a gentleman's daughter after all, and I cannot simply do as I please. Indeed, the entire Ministry of Justice, and the king himself, will be so pleased with what I discover!"

Seojun stood taut. He thought of his father. Of his sister. Of their displeasure at the chaos he was about to bring to their door. But he had always known, for a long while, that no secret could remain buried forever. Especially not a secret that endangered others.

"If I tell you who Black Lotus is," Seojun said brusquely, "you must swear to me that you will leave her alone."

Wuyeong froze. "You . . . you know Black Lotus?"

A muscle worked in his jaw. Seojun hated the thought of delivering his fate into such a man's hand, but his father would soon discover the truth nevertheless. If Minister Yu possessed Haewon's book of letters, then it was only a matter of time before he recognized his son's turn of phrases, and the reference to the yellow ribbons on pine . . .

Looking away, Seojun stared at the dust drifting in the stormy light. "You asked for Black Lotus's identity," he said coldly, "and I will give you the answer. But you haven't promised me, yet, to leave Mistress Haewon alone."

"I swear it! I swear it upon the graves of my parents. Upon the graves of my ancestors!"

Seojun massaged his aching temple. It took him a few moments to bully himself into accommodating this mongrel. "I am who you are searching for."

"You are *whom*?"

"You asked for the identity," Seojun said with growing impatience, "and I am giving you the answer. *I* am Black Lotus."

Wuyeong scoffed, then his smirk vanished, his face going ashen. A flurry of emotions flickered across his features before settling into a grimace. "*You* are the writer?" He faltered, and as though realizing the greatness of his discovery, a smile trembled on his lips. "No, it makes sense. I see the way you look at that girl, that girl who goes by the name Magpie. I've read Black Lotus's letters. This is how you know each other so intimately . . ." Then a look of hesitation twisted his features. "If you are jesting, speak now. I will not be made a fool of."

The noose tightened around Seojun's throat. Yet he felt strangely calm as he repeated, "I, Yu Seojun, am Black Lotus. And I will admit all, provide evidence—on one condition." He met Wuyeong's gaze. "You will keep your promise and ensure that your knowledge of Magpie's identity dies with you. Or else, mark my word, I will make your life miserable for as long as I live."

Chapter 32

"Eonni."

Haewon stood outside Five Willows, her back rigid as she searched the crowd. She could have sworn she'd heard a familiar voice, but how could she have amid the uproar, spectators jeering at the officers as they hauled beloved books out by the cartload?

Dashing aside a bead of sweat, she continued to hurry, examining every face under a headdress. Her fear for her missing sister and her growing disquiet over Lord Yu's welfare solidified in her chest, a block of ice that made it difficult to breathe.

"Eonni!"

That familiar voice again, followed by a flash of bright green silk, an embroidered magpie marking the veil. A round, ruddy face appeared before Haewon, and within an instant, Yeonhee was in her arms. Yeonhee, the girl who swung on the geune-ttwigi swing, arching her frame skyward, eyes gleaming with terrified delight. Yeonhee, who had taken to leaping off, to see how far she could fly. Even a shaman, at her birth, had warned Mother to hold on to Yeonhee tight, that hers was a spirit that yearned to ride the seas and capture the stars. So Haewon clung to her little sister, afraid that life would push them apart again.

"My foolish sister," Haewon whispered, her voice shaking as relief washed through her. Then she held Yeonhee at arm's length and examined the girl. "You are safe; that is all that matters. Let's return home. Mother and Father are sick with worry."

Yeonhee's lower lip trembled. "But I cannot. Not yet."

"Not yet?" She gave her sister's arms a gentle squeeze. "I told you, our parents are sick with worry, and you still intend to leave again?"

"But I failed," Yeonhee cried. "I failed to retrieve your book of letters!"

Haewon blinked, unable to follow. "Whatever do you mean?"

"The Ministry of Justice is too heavily guarded. I tried but couldn't sneak in. The book of letters is stored inside an office there—I'm *certain* of it."

Shaking her head, Haewon didn't know whether to scold her sister's recklessness or embrace her for her courage. She instead readjusted Yeonhee's veil just so, tucking the jangot lower over her face. "Well, I am glad you are returned."

"Are you?" Yeonhee's voice shook with emotion. "I thought you must despise me."

"You know I will always love you. You may at times be silly, indiscreet, and a touch too impetuous," Haewon listed matter-of-factly, retying the veil ribbons under Yeonhee's chin. "But you are also as free-spirited as the wildflowers that flourish in the field, uncaring of where the bounds of polite society begin or end." Sadness tugged at her as she managed to add, her voice straining, "I rather adore that about you. You are Shin Yeonhee, and I will always want to be your sister, even in the next lifetime. There, all done."

Yeonhee's eyes gleamed with tears, and for the barest moment,

Haewon felt as though she had somehow reached her unreachable sister. But as soon as that look of vulnerability opened across Yeonhee's face, it was gone.

"So the officers are really taking all those books?" Yeonhee jerked her gaze away, at the scene beyond them. "Mistress Wol will be devastated. Has she returned yet?"

"Not yet."

"While I was at the Ministry of Justice, I overheard things. This whole raid was instigated by an official who was rebuked by the king for owning forty thousand novels. *Forty thousand!* How does one own so many novels? Anyway, the official who owned that great collection was demoted in rank, and was so ashamed, he is attempting to regain the king's favor by denouncing novels and inciting this raid."

Haewon finally returned her attention to Five Willows. A fresh wave of pain surged through her as she stared at the dark entrance of the bookshop. *If writing does not help edify the subject*—the king's declaration opened wide before her like a grave—*it is worse than if the writing did not exist at all.*

When the officers finally retreated and the crowd dispersed, Haewon lingered there with her sister. She knew it would be wise to return home. She ought to change with the times, to denounce novels in public while reading voraciously in private. But she couldn't abandon her second home. As though Yeonhee shared her heart, there was no hesitation as she followed Haewon into Five Willows.

Merchant Hyoyang sat slumped, his wilted figure casting a sad shadow against the bright orange glow of the setting sun. "Just let me be," he groaned, waving them away.

"Ajusshi, we'll help . . ." Haewon paused, chilled by this new echoing of her voice. It hadn't echoed before when the shelves were full, overflowing with stories. "We'll help you clean."

The shop had become a derelict, abandoned shack, and as they wandered deeper into it, collecting the loose pages laid to waste, Haewon found herself glancing around, half hoping to see Lord Yu. But he must have left, and surely, he was in no trouble himself. He was too great and privileged a gentleman to become entangled in such affairs.

"Are Mother and Father truly so upset with me?" Yeonhee asked hesitantly.

"They are more worried than upset. You know how it is: Gossip is malicious. Scandalmongers will take you down and the rest of us with you."

"They're all hypocrites, you know," Yeonhee said hotly. "They judge with gleeful harshness when others stumble, but when scandal lands at their door, they pray to the heavens that they be treated with kindness and fairness. Why are people so mean?" Her lips pursed as she picked up a torn book, pages hanging from the spine. "So cruel."

Haewon shook her head. "We are all hypocrites. We are all flawed. The sooner we face our own failures, the better. The cruelest kind of people are those who cover it up and become a judge of others. Or that is what I think, at least," she added, no longer so sure of her own thoughts as she once had been. "But I should hope novel readers are slightly kinder, wiser, and more empathetic. We have lived ten thousand lives through books, have endured ten thousand heartaches and joys. As I always say, I think those who do not read novels are the most miserable sort of human beings."

"Maid Boram is right, eonni," Yeonhee admitted. "You are full of dangerous thoughts."

A dry laugh escaped Haewon. "And you, my dear sister, *overflow* with them."

"Whyever are we like this?"

"I suspect there is some defect in our family. A flaw that runs deep in our blood."

"It is most certainly from Mother's side."

"Likely. Does she not always tell us the tale of our great-great-grandfather who once was a slave who rose to become a general?"

Yeonhee smiled like in old times, and Haewon kept close to her sister for a few moments longer. It was only when she was convinced Yeonhee wouldn't disappear that she let her gaze wander around. The emptiness weighed on her heart.

Haewon used to dream that one day, the streets of Hanyang might overflow with bookshops like Liulichang Street in Qing China. She had read the accounts by Hong Tae-yong, who had described his awe when strolling through the market district—so many books that his eyes grew weary and his neck stiff before he even finished browsing the shelves. She had often daydreamed of their own streets seeing such a day, when books were plentiful, when the printing press was no longer reserved solely for the government. When her neck, too, would become stiff from browsing the many shelves. What would it feel like? To be able to read until the soul felt full? To read without the shame and the fear of being caught? That bright dream, always lingering in the back of her mind, now felt like the spring blossoms that faded all too soon, trampled into the mud after one rainfall.

"Come," Haewon whispered, "let's find a broom—"

Footsteps creaked behind her.

Haewon stilled, her heart quickening as she slowly turned, certain it was Lord Yu. Her gaze instead landed on Wol. Her jade-rimmed spectacles gleamed in the windowlight, obscuring her eyes, which Haewon was sure were staring out with her usual fierceness. Relief washed through her. "You've returned!"

Wol's lips tightened as she took in the sight. Destroyed pages, the shelves bare. Gone were the books she had lovingly curated, many of which she personally had repaired. Then her nose turned red and quivered. Tears burst forth, shuddering, violent sobs. Haewon and Yeonhee rushed over to comfort their friend.

It was the kind of wailing one cried over a dead beloved. The raw, guttural sound of grief. An invading force had swept through her home, leaving the land burned and barren.

Chapter 33

The world had become an ocean, cold and silent.

Without thinking or feeling, Seojun went through the motions. He got off his horse once he arrived at Myeongwoldang, passed it off to the stable hand, and staggered toward the garden, unable to recover from the surprise. Moments before the inspector's departure, he had inquired how Wuyeong had first learned of the letters between Magpie and Black Lotus.

He'd expected the inspector to name Shin Yeonhee as the source. Instead, Wuyeong had explained that he'd overheard a woman at the Red Lantern boasting about Black Lotus's most treasured possession: stacks of private letters from a scribe named Magpie. The woman, Maid Daebi, had declared that they were, in fact, love letters. Yeonhee had only confirmed the details afterward.

Now everything made sense. All this time, he had been asking the wrong questions: *Why* would a maid and his manservant do such a thing? If fortune was what they were after, they'd had plenty to steal and of far greater value than a stack of pages. And *how* had they managed to open both locks, without being noticed by one of the many servants who had risen early? The questions had expanded in his mind a web of theories, involving book thieves and elaborate plans leading up to the heist. But now Namgil's note came to mind.

Most crimes are quite simple and ordinary.

Stripped away of the excess, Seojun was left with only the bone, and it was the memory of when he had first received the lock. It was a memory that rose before him like a door that he had been warned never to open and, therefore, had never thought to consider what might exist beyond it. But he slid it open now, and the burning brightness of a summer long ago seared into his vision, the silhouette of a man and a boy hovering there.

Such locks are crafted intricately to respect only the hand of the master. The man's deep voice echoed in his mind. *Even the most gifted of lock-picking thieves will struggle to open these two. Here, you've watched me unlock them, now it is your turn. Practice opening them yourself. The locks are yours.*

Seojun's steps slowed. He had arrived at the garden where his father stood observing the pine tree. Sunlight filtered through his three-tiered gauze hat.

Gritting his teeth, he announced his arrival. "Abeoji."

Minister Yu barely offered him a glance of acknowledgment.

At first Seojun only felt a hot trickle of suspicion in his blood, but that heat built steadily. Was his father involved in the break-in? How involved? And why? He could hardly hear his father through the clamoring of his thoughts.

"Though I am certain you will hold a position in high office one day," Minister Yu murmured, oblivious to Seojun's growing turmoil, "my dream for you is simple. I hope that you grow up to be like a pine tree, with integrity and fortitude. Do you know your great-great-grandfather, during wartime, survived by eating the bark of a pine tree?" He inhaled deeply, as though the fragrance might cleanse his soul, then exhaled. "The Joseon people are born under the pines, live with them, and die beneath them."

None of what his father said entered his heart. Everything he said now felt cheap with hypocrisy. Bitterness billowed as hot smoke, scorching the undersides of his ribs as he joined his father's side. He had no idea how to begin this fight. No elder had ever taught him how to confront his father. It felt almost sinful. And for a brief moment, he half wondered whether he ought to close his eyes and pretend this never happened, as a good and filial son would do.

But he was not one to look away. If his suspicion was correct, then his father's foolishness had set into motion a series of events that now endangered Shin Haewon and her entire family.

"Abeoji," Seojun implored, "did you instruct my manservant to steal my keys?"

From the corner of his eye, he saw his father go still, then his expression tightened and his brows shot low over his troubled eyes. It was the face of a guilty man.

"You were behind it all along," Seojun bitterly concluded. "Did you take delight in my complete ignorance? In watching your foolish son search for answers, chasing after his own tail?"

Minister Yu expelled a weary breath, as though he had known this moment would come. Just as Seojun had known that his secret could never remain hidden.

"I had a second pair of keys made by the locksmith. You were only sixteen."

Birds landed nearby, but Seojun saw none of it.

The quiet space between them grew like a dividing wall.

"My own manservant stole my keys that night," Seojun retorted, struggling to keep his composure as memories swept in over his head. Memories of the shock, of how violated he'd felt, as though his room were no longer his own. Memories of his sleepless nights. Of wandering the streets wondering if he was being watched. And memories of his father's indifference throughout the ordeal. "Why were my keys stolen if you already had the second pair?" he ground out. "You turned servants against me, but why was that necessary—" He stopped, the pieces falling as quietly as ash around him, and when understanding came, he felt as though something in him died. "You wished to make it appear like a break-in, rather than a father stealing into his son's room. You wanted me to be afraid."

"As you *ought* to be. You *should* be afraid. I saw Mistress Wol lingering outside in the morning—before you left for the gibang house," Minister Yu explained with a strained formality, as though determined to cling to his innocence, "and so I had Maid Daebi eavesdrop for me. She told me everything. That you are Black Lotus. I went into your room long after you left to verify if it was true. I only meant to scare you, to make you stop writing. So I staged the break-in, and I had your manservant steal the keys."

Seojun remained motionless, his stare boring into the courtyard. "You could have simply spoken to me."

"You hid your writing from me in the first place." Minister Yu's voice rose a notch. "An *entire* identity! How could I trust you?"

"In doing what you did, you sent Inspector Wuyeong after me. He knows everything now."

A muscle worked in his father's jaw. "It was Maid Daebi, that gossiping wench. I dismissed her the instant I learned of her light mouth. Things got out of hand, I know. I regret that."

"But you do not regret breaking my trust."

His father's voice turned defensive. "You will never understand everything. You will never grasp the depths of a father's concern. I work in the Ministry of Justice. I have discussed matters with the king at length. I have heard, with my own ears, the king's contempt for novels. Over and over again, His Majesty and the officials have spoken of you—of Black Lotus. Writers like yourself, young men with superficial knowledge, who disdain the classics and instead indulge in stories that lead to moral decay. Again and again, the king and his men speak of how novels are like obscene music and women—they corrupt, they lure men away from the rightful path." His father's voice wavered for the first time. "And when I realized it was *you* they were all condemning, I felt a terror in my bones. I wanted to protect our honor. I had to do something. If a man cannot control his own household, how dare he serve in government? How dare he think to shape policies and uphold justice?"

Seojun gripped his hands tighter.

It was like the stories his mother had told him as a child.

Do not cry, do not disobey your parents, or a tiger will creep into the village and snatch you from your blanket. The tiger will drag you into the mountains where it feasts on misbehaving children.

He had learned to behave as a child for fear of being devoured by the unknown.

But he was no longer a child.

And he was no longer terrified of what lay beyond the shadows.

Seojun spoke, not in anger, not in mourning, not in outrage.

Calmly, very calmly, he said, "The one thing I cannot forgive is betrayal. And you betrayed me, abeoji. After all my efforts to please you, after all I sacrificed—my happiness, my dreams, my choices—all for you. And in the end, *you* betrayed me. And in doing so, you hurt others as well. Others I hold dear."

"I sense you waiting," his father murmured. "Waiting for me to retaliate."

"You always do."

"I have enough shame not to do so," his father said, looking ten times older as his shoulders finally sagged. "My only hope is that you will not hate this foolish father."

Seojun clenched his jaw, restraining his sharp words. He had always thought his father's voice was like thunder. That his words carried the weight of mountains. But now, he saw a man who trembled like a leaf in the wind. He had never seen his father look terrified before. And in this moment, he felt gripped by this urgent need to hurt this man. To hurt him *more*. To punish him for the betrayal, and mainly, for the sheer disappointment.

This was his father?

This was the man he had spent his whole life trying to please?

This broken, immoral man?

He could hurt him. Crush the old man's heart until it was dust grinding beneath his heel. For Seojun knew his father's greatest weakness: himself. Seojun was the only son, the child his father had yearned for in his old age. A son he had poured all his failed dreams into.

He could break his father's heart.

He knew how—

Yet a strange warmth held him back, a warmth that very much felt like Haewon's hand on his back. *We are all capable of error,* she had told him. He thought of her desperate conspiring with Jade and Boram, doing whatever they could to protect their own. Most of society would call Yeonhee's actions unforgivable. And yet, he had seen it with his own eyes: her home, her parents, Haewon's own heart, thrown open to welcome Yeonhee back. Shin Haewon, who had so fiercely defended her sister in the gibang. Who fought for her again. Again, and again, and again. The sight had moved him then. It moved him still.

A burned bridge leaves no way back . . .

His father's actions were more than a mere error. But Haewon was right; this was a bridge he did not wish to burn. Despite his rage, despite his resentment, he could not imagine a life without a father. Once, his father had been the ground beneath his feet, and the sky above. That would never be true again—but still, Seojun knew, with a painful certainty, that he wanted to watch his father grow old, to be by his side until the very end.

He suppressed a sigh as he studied Minister Yu, his eyes downcast, shoulders wilted like an old man. He was indeed an old man. When had he aged so? He saw his father's wrinkles and brown age spots. He realized his father's head didn't quite meet his shoulder. When had he outgrown his father, once a giant to him in every way?

"I could never hate you," Seojun finally said, defeated. "I would rather die than hate you."

Minister Yu shuddered. Then, slowly, hesitantly, he clasped

Seojun's hand in both of his own. He patted the hand once. No words were said, but no words were needed.

"Your mother told me, before her death. Harmony is to be cherished. It was her wish that our family live harmoniously. It is, is it not, a pillar of the Confucian way. I have broken it, and now when I enter the netherworld, I shall have no face with which to greet your mother."

Seojun stared at their hands, wondering when his father had ever held them before.

"The king will summon you. Undoubtedly. I know Inspector Wuyeong and he will not hesitate to report you. And for the king to learn of your misconduct, so soon after the edict was reinforced . . ." Minister Yu's grip tightened. "The king will not be pleased. His Majesty might deal with you severely to set an example."

Seojun dragged his gaze to the pine trees his father so loved. Such a burden weighed upon his shoulders. He could not act without his actions shaking the roots of his entire household. "My only regret," Seojun whispered, "will be bringing you and Older Sister further unhappiness."

Minister Yu heaved out a breath, clucked his tongue. "How has everything gotten so tangled? Why is loving one's child so simple, and yet so incredibly difficult?" A pause, and he averted his gaze. "The missing manuscript . . . I took it to read for myself."

Seojun froze, bracing himself for criticism.

"I enjoyed it. It entertained me and I lost sleep," Minister Yu said simply. "But if you wish to protect your family, your sister, you must never write again. You must promise the king this, then perhaps his wrath might be alleviated from you—and from our family." He withdrew his hands from Seojun's, and they stood alone once more, like two lonesome trees on separate mountains. "And that Shin girl, you were seen with her again at Five Willows—"

"You may deride me, abeoji, but I will not have you say a bad word about her."

"So you do love her." Minister Yu studied his son, his brows furrowing. "Indeed, I hope you have no intention of proposing to her. You must promise me that you will not."

"It is of no use making such promises," Seojun muttered. "She won't have me."

His father's brows shot up. "*She* will not have *you*?" He appeared disoriented, even curious. "Why ever not?"

"I'm not good enough for her."

Minister Yu nearly choked. "*My* son? Not good enough?" His incredulity hung between them, and then a strange, most unexpected look of bemusement tugged at his lips. "How like your mother. She had nothing to her name, yet rejected me thrice . . ." His thoughts seemed to hang upon these words, reminiscing about the days gone by. At length, he shook his head and his expression stiffened once more. "Either way, you will promise me to never propose marriage to that girl."

"I will not, abeoji."

Minister Yu gave his son a long, examining stare, then let out a harrumph of disapproval as he looked away. "I am disappointed in you."

As I am in you, Seojun withheld himself from saying, for he saw past the facade; he saw the cracks in his father's countenance, the signs of a man defeated. A father deeply aware that he had nearly lost his son.

As Seojun walked away, he felt a terrible lightness to his soul. A freedom that did not feel quite liberating. He was on his own now, for he had chosen his own path, a path that strayed from the course set out for him in his youth.

Such thoughts burdened him as he strode down the corridor, and he was about to enter his study when a voice rang out.

"Seojun-ah!"

He glanced to see his older sister, attired as usual in her widow's gown of pure white. Unaware of the heaviness he bore, she brushed past him and intruded into his study, then paused to examine the shelf that displayed precious vases.

"Nuwi." Seojun waited by the door. "I wish to be alone."

"The most curious thing arrived a moment ago. Shall I tell you about it?"

"Tell me later."

"So you do not wish to know about this note? It is from the Shin household. Very well, I shall go then—"

In a few long strides, Seojun was before his sister, his heart pounding. He barely managed to speak. "What note?"

A smile tugged at her lips. "I had no idea why Shin Haewon visited me the other day, but I am beginning to suspect that there is something occurring between the two of you. She is the woman, isn't she, who rejected you?"

"Gods, must you remind me? I feel beaten down already," he said while taking the note from her. It was a message from Haewon, addressed to his sister, of all people.

Dear Lady Gwideok,

Rain has drizzled down endlessly since the morning. The lanes around your living quarters must be muddy indeed. I hope you are in good health?

Haewon continued to ramble, writing in circles, until at last, she wrote:

Forgive my boldness, but I write to you as I have no other way to reach your brother. I knew, the moment we spoke, that you were someone I might confide in—just as you confided in me. I cannot share in detail just yet, but a disaster nearly struck upon my family, and your brother was of great assistance. Please let him know that my sister is safe at home now. And please express to him how grateful I am, and will always be.

His chest felt tight as he reread her note. Her handwriting held such a spell over him, as though the strokes were the silhouette of her soul on paper. It was the closest he would ever be to her now.

"Will you write back?" Gwideok's voice drew him back to reality. "I will prepare an envelope, mark it clearly as a note from me. It will be a good disguise to hide your response. Bring your note to my quarters when you do," she ordered, before taking her leave with a mischievous twinkle in her eyes.

He, himself, felt not an ounce of whatever it was that amused his sister so.

Sitting alone before his desk, Seojun picked up his brush to write upon a blank sheet, then froze; he had written to Magpie dozens of letters, but he had written none to Shin Haewon. A sudden constraint gripped his hand, and all he managed to write was:

Dear Mistress Haewon,

I am truly glad to hear that your sister is safe at home, and hope you and your family are well, too. If there is anything more you need from me, I am, and will always be, at your service.

Yu Seojun

The ink had long dried and he was still holding his brush. There was nothing more he needed to write, yet so much more he wanted to share—about his father, the crushing disappointment, the worries, and his affection for her. How deep they ran, how painful to silence. But he was a gentleman. Honor, decorum, and prudence forbade him from imposing his feelings on a lady who had shown no wish to receive them.

At long last, he sent the note to his sister, and in the stillness that followed, he was convinced there was no longer anything to look forward to in life.

Chapter 34

THROUGHOUT THE FOLLOWING WEEK, THE CAPITAL BUZZED WITH whispers, and Haewon overheard more than a few refer to a "delightful new scandal." Lord Yu Seojun, the brilliant gentleman who was to enter the Royal Academy in the first rank, had been summoned by the king. No one knew exactly why; the affair was carefully hushed up. One of the main figures in this drama, Inspector Wuyeong, had been relocated to another post far outside the capital, shamed into secrecy.

Speculation therefore spread as wildfire.

Some claimed the king had ordered Lord Yu to atone for his misconduct (whatever that may be) by writing a formal letter of apology in the pure classical style, to which he had allegedly agreed. Others whispered that Lord Yu had refused and chosen a life of political isolation instead. A few went so far as to say he would be sent to a remote island in military exile, though this was widely dismissed. After all, Lord Yu was the son of Minister Yu, and the king would not dare openly oppose a member of the Old Doctrine, which held the bureaucracy, military, and local governance in its grip. He could not risk losing their tenuous support.

Such tales spread far and wide throughout even Gyonam Village, trickling in through the whispers of servants. Haewon learned bits and pieces through Jade as well, who discreetly tried to fish as much as she could from Young Master Byeongho while their families exchanged wedding gifts. But the young master knew little himself. The affair was shrouded in mystery, and Yeonhee—who was staying with their aunt in the far north to evade any further scandal—had written to declare that Haewon ought to simply write to Lord Yu and ask him herself.

Haewon couldn't, of course.

She wasn't his friend, nor his sweetheart. She had no right to correspond with him any further.

But she remained terribly ill at ease.

"What of you, Wol? Have you heard from Lord Yu?" Haewon asked when she visited Five Willows one morning, settling herself before a transcriber's low-legged table.

Wol glanced up from a book. "Only once."

Her pulse leapt, quickening with hope. But hope for what? Her emotions of late were in disarray. "What did Lord Yu write?"

"Oh . . ." Wol gave a little shrug as she set the book aside and picked up the next. "He inquired after my well-being. That is all—" Clucking her tongue, she shook her head. "This copy will not do. It is entirely impossible to read with all these scribbles."

As Wol continued to examine the stack of returned books, Haewon felt a weight sink into her chest. She had come to Five Willows to transcribe books for Wol, to fill her empty shelves, but now all she could think about was *him*.

"I wonder if he will ever write again," Haewon whispered, unable to withhold her concern. "I fear he will not. How can anyone endure the king's rebuke? His pride barely endured His Majesty's criticism of his work, even while he was hidden behind a pseudonym."

"You needn't look so glum." Wol tossed a book aside and picked up the next. "I thought about it, and of late, I'm beginning to think Black Lotus will write again. Surely the longing to write is like the waves at sea; you can't stop it, and you certainly can't escape it."

"I hope you're right."

Haewon went back to her transcription work, to the book she was copying, *Yeolhailgi*. After Lord Yu had given it to her off the shelf, she'd held on to it under her veil throughout the raid. She flipped the page now, and her heart quieted at the lines she knew had been waiting for her. Lord Yu's favorite line in the entirety of the book.

"*If there is one person in this entire world who understands me*," she read under her breath, "*I can live this life without bitterness.*"

The words slid through her like thread, weaving themselves into the fabric of her soul. It was then she understood, with some astonishment, the extent of her own feelings for Yu Seojun—the one who had truly understood her. Not the surface she presented to the world, but the deepest, most honest parts of her. Parts of her she hadn't even known existed, unfolding before her eyes as she'd written to Black Lotus. A friend before whom she could lay herself bare without fear. A friendship that felt like refuge after a long day's wandering in a world too sad, prejudiced, and lonely.

A heavy sigh escaped her. Haewon half expected Wol to remark upon it, for she had been sighing all day, but instead she found herself alone. Wol had disappeared somewhere.

"There are books to be transcribed," Haewon reminded herself, about to flip the page when a trace of ink caught the edge of her gaze—like a fleeting face in the crowd. A startling familiarity that conjured up a rush of memory—of lush green trees and bright blue summer skies, eating wild berries while reading letters by the stream, the surrounding world a magnificent mystery . . . Her breathing grew uneven as she leaned in and studied a note in the margin, a single note squeezed in among the scribble of other comments:

Magpie,

The word burned into her. There was only one who would ever address her in such a note. A desperate ache wrung her heart tight as she read on.

You are the kind of soul
one finds only once
in a lifetime, and
travels the next thousand
searching for again.
I would do that for you.
I could live and die,
searching each lifetime,
for you.

The bookshop blurred, a wash of color and light as more tears welled in her eyes.

She felt such a rush of love for this man.

Upon rising to her feet, she paced, overwhelmed and at a loss. What was she to do with these feelings? These emotions that overflowed in her heart and she felt she might drown in. Pausing before a little window, she stared out as a helpless, unbearable ache pulsed in her chest. She tried not to picture what it might be like to meet Lord Yu again, what it might feel like to talk to him, to exist in the quiet warmth of his presence . . .

She found herself wishing, as she watched a lone bird glide through the azure blue, that she too could sprout wings. To glide above all her worries, over the walls and the mountains of societal rules and customs, to simply follow where the wind took her. For now, she realized, she had words, and words could fly. Words were meant to soar, to rise from the heart as the truest and most earnest expression of her deepest thoughts. Words were meant to be carried from one soul and shared.

Wandering back to the table, Haewon found herself drawing out a fresh sheet of paper and picking up her brush. She began to write:

Dear Lord Yu,

How have you been faring? I know I ought not to write directly to you, so you can imagine how anxious I am to hear that everything is all right with you. As for myself, I am well—

Haewon paused. Throwing aside the draft, she took out a new page. She breathed in deep and wrote down the truth:

I miss you, Yu Seojun. I miss you terribly.

The words stared back at her. They felt too bare and vulnerable, yet she nevertheless folded the note and slipped it into a spare envelope she found in Wol's office. Then she stepped out of the shop and onto the dusty road.

"Agasshi?" Boram hurried out after her. "Are you leaving already?"

Haewon surveyed the street. Urchins darted through the market bustle, ragged and tanned, laughing. After stopping one, she crouched before the boy with raven-black hair braided down his back, and held out a coin.

"Would you be so good as to deliver something for me?"

He nodded and took the coin in his grubby hand.

"It's a letter. I need it delivered to Lord Yu Seojun—"

"Agasshi!" Boram cried, shuffling closer. "Did I hear you correctly? You are sending a letter to *him*? What if someone finds out?"

"They will," Haewon said, "if you declare this news any louder."

"*Agasshi,*" she pleaded.

"Deliver it to Lord Yu," Haewon repeated, "at Myeongwoldang, located in Myeongrye-bang District. Come back and find me later, and I'll buy you a warm meal."

The boy must have carried out such a task before, for he asked, "Who do I say it's from?"

"From . . ." Haewon hesitated. "From Magpie."

Boram fussed over Haewon's headdress, smoothing out its wrinkles. "If I may speak plainly—and I daresay someone must—a young lady ought not to be so forward. Such things invite *nothing* but regret!"

"Perhaps I will regret this," Haewon said under her breath as she stood up. The boy had long disappeared into the crowd. "But what is life without its little misadventures?"

Chapter 35

THE EVENING DREW NEAR, AND THE SKY HAD DEEPENED INTO A golden blue, the clouds a drifting scatter of light. Strolling homeward, Haewon heaved out what felt to be her hundredth sigh; the weight remained heavy in her chest. She wanted to lie down and curl up under her blanket, to cradle her aching heart. The courier boy had returned late in the day to claim his meal, and as he'd wolfed down his brothy gukbap, he had shared his account of the delivery. Boram had turned out to be right.

"I am all astonishment." Boram sniffed, two angry spots flushing her cheeks. "Lord Yu *knew* it was from you. But the boy said so himself, didn't he, that His Lordship read the letter with *perfect* indifference? Oh, heavens, and I still have not recovered from what the boy said next. The Minister of Rites was at His Lordship's home! The father of Lord Yu's betrothed! And he *left* to dine with the man! Just like that!"

"At all events," Haewon said lightly, even managing to tuck her hurt behind a smile, "Lord Yu and I have each resumed our proper station, he to his world, and I to mine. It is just as it should have always been."

Boram scoffed with all the indignation of a scorned lover. "We should have known better. My mother always did say the hearts of men are fickle. They will fall in love fast and forget us just as soon, while we pine away for years."

"Then you must prepare yourself, Boram-ah. I think I shall become quite intolerable."

"Oh, agasshi . . ." She sniffled. "You hide your heartache too well." Shaking her head, she dabbed at the corner of her eye. "But I fear you're the sort who will pine forever, and fight your parents until they permit you to live as a spinster. Oh!" she cried. "To think, you shall live the rest of your years alone, among dusty books, your eyes growing dim as you spend entire days transcribing novels. It's too tragic. I cannot endure the thought of you suffering so."

A genuine laugh escaped Haewon. "Well, that doesn't sound too tragic. It sounds rather delightful—" She came to an abrupt halt, realizing why she'd felt so bare this entire time. A frustrated groan escaped her. "I left them at the shop."

"Left what?"

"I forgot my transcription work there. I promised Wol I would transcribe three copies of *Yeolhailgi* in the next few days."

"You would walk *all* the way back to Five Willows? At this late hour? Agasshi. We can retrieve it another day—"

"I really must. I think I will lose my sanity if I have nothing to keep my mind occupied."

Boram continued her protest as she followed, trying to keep up with Haewon's long strides back down Jongno Street. In no time at all they arrived before Five Willows. There was a great steed tethered to a post nearby, watching them.

"I won't be long," Haewon said, then hurried into the shop.

Merchant Hyoyang was counting coins and paused to let out a great yawn. Haewon quickly passed him by, knocked on the back door, and then was permitted into the secret bookshop by Wol's assistant. Wol was also present, casting Haewon a nod before returning to her fervent dispute with a book peddler, haggling over the cost of new and used novels.

Haewon found her transcription work, just where she had left it. After wrapping the items and hiding the sack under her veil, she rejoined her maid outside. "There, wasn't I quick?"

"Let us go at once, agasshi, and leave this miserable day behind." Boram sighed, gazing wistfully ahead. "If we leave now, we'll be home in time for the evening meal. Mistress Myeongok said she'll have roasted pheasant and tofu soup prepared tonight, the perfect meal to pair with the fresh greens I seasoned this morning. And Jade said she would steam the rice cakes made with the seoki mushrooms sent by your aunt from the Mount Kumgang region. I hear it tastes so good that even duteop rice cakes cannot match this."

Haewon meant to leave for home, she truly did, but she kept glancing back at the tethered horse. A distant memory lurked around the edges of her thoughts as the creature hoofed at the earth, lean muscles rippling under a silky black coat, tail swishing languidly through a cloud of gnats.

"Agasshi?"

The memory continued to drift, a haze that thickened until she felt as though she were standing in mist. The road beneath her became the mossy forest floor. A curtain of rain fell from a canopy, and suddenly, her mind was in a drenched forest prickling with pine trees. A gentleman sat leaning against a trunk, nursing his wounded arm, the blood fresh against his cerulean-blue robe. His dark gaze lifted to her, and instantly, she knew who this horse belonged to.

"Boram-ah," Haewon whispered, her voice unsteady, "I forgot one more thing—"

"*Agasshi!*" Boram whined. "If we don't leave now, there will be no rice cakes left for us."

"Here, buy yourself something to eat. Anything you want."

Boram stared wide-eyed at the coin. "I can spend all of it? You said you were saving to purchase new shoes for Yeonhee—"

"I'll transcribe more books. Go. I'll return shortly."

Heart thundering, Haewon stumbled back into Five Willows, rushing over to Merchant Hyoyang. "Ajusshi"—she could barely restrain her eagerness—"did you perhaps see Lord Yu enter this shop?"

"I wouldn't know." Merchant Hyoyang yawned again, tears springing from his eyes and tumbling into his beard. "I am busy all the time. Utterly exhausted now."

Haewon stared past him, wondering if she had missed Lord Yu in her hurry to collect her transcription work. She must have. She *hoped* she had, and also hoped he was still there. A mixture of panic and anticipation constricted her heart as she made her way into the secret shop beyond, once permitted entrance again. She inspected each aisle this time. Shadows and golden sunlight striped the floor. The empty shelves and empty space stared back at her.

He was not here.

He had no reason to be here. There were no books to browse, and Wol was still preoccupied.

A maddening ache pierced her chest. Her spirit wilting, she dragged herself out into the open, the market clattering around her. She was most certain that the horse belonged to Lord Yu, for there was the unmistakable constellation of small white spots scattered across the creature's hindquarters. *Like the Bukdu Chilseong.* She remembered thinking this very thought in the forest, weeks ago, while trapped under a canopy with His Lordship.

But where else could he be?

Haewon surveyed her periphery; then on a whim, she slipped between Five Willows and its neighboring merchant shop, down the passage that opened onto the desolate Pimatgol Alley, a hidden pathway walled in by the backs of other shops. She didn't notice him at first, and when she did, she slowed to a halt, never imagining to find him thus.

He sat pale and motionless on a crate, his forlorn figure draped in the shadow cast by the great eaves of the Five Willows shop. His shoulders were slumped, long arms hanging over his knees, his head lowered and his brooding gaze fixed. The hard lines of his face were made sharper by the fading light, and his brows were knitted over eyes that appeared tired, lost, and very sad. The gentleman who seemed to never lose mastery over himself now looked utterly disheveled. His hat hung from the hat string tied around his neck, resting behind his back, as if he'd pushed it off in the heat of frustration. His robe was wind whipped and mud splattered.

As she took a step forward, Lord Yu at last turned his eyes and looked at her. She fidgeted with the books in her arms as she stood before his uncomprehending shock.

"Haewon-ah," he whispered incredulously.

"Are you . . . are you waiting for Wol—?"

Three long strides brought him to her, and he halted, uncertain. "The courier boy gave me your note, and I knew you must have written to me from Five Willows," he whispered, his gaze intent upon her. "I came here as soon as I could. I thought I had missed you."

"So you read my silly letter . . ." She lowered her lashes, playing with the knot of the travel sack. "You must find my conduct very unbecoming of a lady."

The silence intensified, and she sought desperately for something to say to relieve the tension of the moment. But before she could think of anything, her mind went quiet as he reached out and tucked a strand of her hair back beneath her veil. She looked up again, the reflection of herself held in the pool of his eyes, illuminated by the golden skylight.

"I find your conduct, Mistress Haewon, to be utterly—outrageously—bewitching," his voice rasped. He lifted the wrapped books from her arms and tucked them into his. "You needn't answer me now, but I hope there is room for me in your heart, or I fear I shall wander entirely lost forever."

Her eyes burned. This moment felt too dreamlike to be true. She must have fallen into another tale entirely.

"And it will become my greatest regret if I do not tell you this," he spoke on, his frown returning. "I wish for you to know that I truly regret the words I said to you at the pavilion."

"But you were not wrong," Haewon whispered. "To be associated with my family would leave you open to censure—"

"It would be no sacrifice to be with you; it's what I choose and what I want. It's what I desire. And rather, the sacrifice would be on your end, to bind yourself to an insufferable man like me, and to a family riddled with secrets and errors." He looked away, a muscle working in his jaw. "My father nearly ruined you, though unintentionally so."

She blinked up at him, and when he shared what he had learned, she felt only compassion for what he must have endured and must still be enduring. She took a tiny step forward, closer to him, and he flinched as though in surprise. "Well, nauri," she said, and mustered the courage to ask, "do you still want me?"

Something leapt in his gaze. "Yes. More than life itself."

"Then I must beg your forgiveness for not recognizing you sooner," she barely managed to say as her throat tightened with emotions, nose tingling, eyes growing damp. "You are, to me as well, the kind of soul one finds only once in a lifetime, and travels the next thousand searching for again—"

He closed the space between them, and her heart raced like a restless horse set loose across the overflowing grassland, pounding with painful intensity. His hand reached out for hers, running his thumb across her knuckles.

"Someone might see," she gasped, even as she chose to remain still, her pulse skipping at the sensation of his hand, which was much rougher than she'd imagined, so much larger than her own. "We will be most scandalously compromised."

"Then I might have to marry you, Mistress Haewon."

The heat that burned her cheeks flared to the tips of her toes. "You mustn't make such jests."

"It is no jest," he whispered. "Haewon-ah. Shin Haewon. I wish you could see my heart. I wish you could see how I feel for you."

Her breath caught as he drew her close. He was looking at her, she at him, and there were stern etiquettes to abide by, some wise wisdom like *Save the tryst for darkness*. But he was looking at her, and she could think of little else, and he seemed to forget everything, everything melting in the warmth of their proximity. The sensation of his fingers, the rough pad of his thumb drawing circles against her inner wrist.

"You have nothing to prove," Haewon said, so quietly he had to lean forward. Her breath against his cheek, the red flush crawling up along his neck. "For my heart is already yours."

"Mine?" he whispered.

"Yes."

His head turned, just the slightest bit, and it was all that was needed for his lips to brush her jaw. He hesitated for the barest moment before his lips brushed against hers in a gentle and undemanding kiss. It was utterly scandalous, but his lips were against hers, and it was all she could think of, her heart racing with a wild thrill she'd never before experienced, a mixture of joy and anticipation that beat too fast.

"Agasshi?"

Haewon startled free from Lord Yu's embrace, then swept a glance around. It was only them in the alleyway, and His Lordship appeared as flushed and disoriented as she felt. It was as though they had been shaken awake from a reverie.

"Agasshi!" Boram called again from the other side. "I purchased a few rice cakes for us both! Where are you?"

Haewon touched her lips. It was improper to even associate with a man, to even permit him a glance at her full face, yet here they were, kissing in public, in broad daylight. The shock of the moment continued to thrum in her veins.

"May I—" He faltered. "May I walk you home?"

"Yes," she said breathlessly, her face growing even hotter. "I would like that very much."

When they stepped out of the alley, Maid Boram gawked, her eyes growing as round as saucers. She did not say a word, though. Her shocked silence bore into Haewon's back as she walked alongside Lord Yu. They walked with enough distance between them that, to any onlooker, it would seem no more than a lone gentleman leading his horse ahead, and a mistress and her maid scurrying home. No passersby would notice the impropriety as Haewon, at last giving into temptation, peeked at Yu Seojun from under her veil. He was watching her, too. She bit her smile and looked away, an uneasy joy swelling in her heart.

A joy that felt almost too much.

She inhaled a deep breath, her chest expanding with the scent of spring, then another as she took in the familiar scenery around her. Over the many years, she had walked this path alone during her early-morning strolls. She had watched the grove of trees changing with the seasons. The branches snow-dusted in winter, clouded with blossoms in spring, lush green in summer, shivering bare in autumn. Then the winter would return. She had daydreamed during these walks, imagining herself carving out her own destiny, and walking that off-course path alone, for who else would follow? Now it occurred to her she might have gained a companion on this journey, to appreciate with her the shifting landscapes of life and its changing seasons—together.

"We're arrived," Boram declared, wiping at her perspiring brow. "We had better hurry inside, agasshi, before you are seen with—with—" She cleared her throat, flicking a nervous glance about.

Haewon guarded her face from displaying her disappointment. She was wishing she had lived farther away, to have more time to spend with Seojun, when she felt him draw near. His hand touched the side of her jangot cloak, slipped under; his knuckles grazed the length of her bare wrist. A shiver ran down her spine.

"Your m-mother is likely worried sick about you, a-agasshi," Boram stammered, her face turning bright pink as she kept her stare trained ahead. "We should leave; that would be wise—"

"No, Boram-ah," Haewon said, the entirety of her attention centered on his hands, which were still caressing her. "Mother is too preoccupied with Jade's wedding to notice my absence."

"Well, you cannot—" Boram tried to look everywhere but downward at their entangled fingers. "What if you are *seen*?"

As though Boram's anxiety had summoned them, a gang of ajummas was stalking down the road, pots on their heads as they gossiped in boisterous voices.

"*Agasshi!*" Boram cried in a harsh whisper.

Haewon bit her lower lip. "I should go." She at last moved to follow Boram, but Seojun's hand slid around her wrist in a gentle grasp. She could have easily pulled away, but she didn't want to.

"*Stay,*" he whispered. "Don't leave me just yet."

"Oh, heavens, I vow my hair will turn gray soon," Boram squealed. Then she wiped her brow again and shot Lord Yu the stern, measuring look of a protective matron. "Take good care of her, nauri. I'll keep an eye out for you both. And—and I'll take those books."

After tethering his horse, Seojun took Haewon and led her down a path, deep into the pine forest where shadows crawled up along the trunks, only the treetop peaks still drenched in light. The sky had deepened into a quiet purple, flocks of birds now singing their dusk chorus.

When at last she faced him, Haewon found herself staring up into a pair of eyes fixed intently upon her. She leaned against a tree trunk as he stepped closer. A nervousness fluttered awake as she watched his gaze drop to her lips, his eyes darkening, or perhaps it was the fading light. She had never experienced this before; it was all so new.

"I've been dying to know, nauri. There are so many rumors about what happened between you and the king," she rambled, to ward off the building sense of vulnerability. "But I'm not sure what is true."

"I wrote the apology letter."

She winced. "You apologized for writing?"

A ghost of a smile played at the corners of his lips. "I wrote a most long-winded letter, in which I apologized for being unable to apologize, that my sin was too grave for me to even consider apologizing, but that I do apologize for causing His Majesty trouble."

She stifled a laugh. "And how did the king respond?"

He drew her veil back slightly, as though wanting a clearer look at her face. "The king sounded both irritated and amused with me. In the end, my father is a Noron faction leader. His Majesty is unable to punish me too severely, but will keep a tight rein on me nevertheless."

She frowned. Would this truly be the end of Black Lotus?

"It is to be expected. I am to enter the Royal Academy, so His Majesty wishes to ensure that my essays do not imitate the free-spirited novel writing style."

"All this must agitate you so . . ."

"I'm unsure how I feel," he whispered. "In truth, I can think of little else right now but you."

"*Oh.*" Her pulse quickened as he leaned in. An unfamiliar, molten sensation curled at the pit of her stomach as his nose grazed the crook of her neck, trailed down along her jaw, then his lips brushed hers in soft and polite kisses.

She hoped he wouldn't stop.

Slowly, the nervousness drifted away. She melted into his embrace that felt so familiar, so safe, as though his arms had held her just so, many lifetimes ago. It was then that a new boldness roused in her. She slipped her arms around his neck, and she touched him, exploring the expanse of his back, tracing the slopes of his taut muscles. Her hands drifted along his high, stiff collar, caressed the back of his bare neck. His skin was hot to the touch, damp with a thin sheen of sweat from growing exertion, as though he were under immense restraint.

She had no idea what possessed her then, but as he kissed her, she took a little nip at his lower lip. And the moment she did, Yu Seojun unraveled right before her. A helpless sound escaped him. This time, he pulled her in closer, so close that she felt melded to him. His mouth pressed hard, burning against hers, coaxing her lips apart and kissing her in a way she never imagined possible of a gentleman like him: insistent, intoxicating, and urgent.

Desire pooled and consumed all sense of time. It couldn't have been more than a few minutes, but her hands and toes had grown cold in the deepening chill. And when they finally broke away, chests expanding as they both tried to catch their breath, Haewon blinked and realized they had been kissing for perhaps too long.

"I didn't realize the time," Seojun said, appearing flustered as he studied the sky. "You—" His voice wavered. Clearing his throat, he tried again. "You should return home before night falls."

Haewon could not will herself to leave. She wanted to stay. Just a moment longer. To stay long enough to unfold and read his mind as she had his letters, to hear his thoughts unconfined by the space of a page or the restraints put in place by their pseudonyms. He was hers now. Her gentleman. And she had waited too long, grown too curious, to let him go without asking the many questions she had—particularly the one that had preoccupied her for the past few days.

"I really must know something before you leave," she said, and almost of its own accord, her hand grasped the corner of his sleeve. "Will you keep writing novels?"

"Novels . . ." he murmured. "In truth, I've forgotten why I began writing them in the first place."

"Is that so? Well, this I can tell you. I still remember how I felt when I first read your work. I recall it most vividly."

His gaze steadied on her, a raw and vulnerable look opening across his expression. "And what did you feel?"

Tilting her head, she smiled as the memory returned, a surge of happiness that flooded the horizon of her soul. "It was as if I'd fallen into a trance," she began as she strolled over to a nearby pavilion. "Sitting in front of a rice bowl, I forgot to eat; standing in front of the basin, I forgot to wash my face. I remember thinking, *Where am I? Is this my room?* As far as I was concerned then, I was journeying through Mount Jiri, standing before the Buril waterfall!"

He chuckled as he sat on the raised pavilion floor, right next to her. "Is that so? I'm not sure that you'd be so eager for me to write if you knew the cost. If I am caught again, I would most likely end up isolated from high positions."

"And why should I care? But do *you* wish to be in power?"

"It is what my father wishes of me."

"But does Yu Seojun wish it?"

"Not particularly." He leaned back, his arms propped behind him. "What I've always dreamed of is a quiet life, perhaps a government post somewhere far from the capital, somewhere scenic."

"Somewhere that the author Lee Junghwan would recommend in *Taekriji*?"

"Precisely."

"And you would write, then?"

"Perhaps one day. But today—there is such a weight in my heart, a stifling pall that will not leave. The mere thought of writing suffocates me now."

For a moment, his gaze grew distant, his thoughts lost in a place that not even she could reach. Then he turned to her. "And you, Shin Haewon?" He reached and took her hand, carefully studying the light blue veins threading across the top of it, examining with keen interest the writing calluses marking her fingers. "Will you continue to transcribe?"

"Would you permit me?"

His brows drew together. "You would stop, if I asked it of you?"

"No secret remains a secret. I wouldn't wish to become a disgrace to your family . . ." she admitted. "But if I am honest, I would simply be more cunning and find ways, as I always do."

A smile of relief broke across his face. "Imja," he addressed her, an endearment that sent a ripple through her soul. "I would much rather never call you mine, and live life without you, wandering without a home forever, than to bind you to a life you were not meant for. You are, and will always be, the mistress of your own life."

"The mistress of my own life," she repeated softly.

A quiet settled between them. She had imagined, while walking here, how it might feel to be promised Myeongwoldang, to be mistress of such a great giwajip. But this was something far more precious to her. To find someone who held her dream, her deepest longings, with as much gentle kindness as though it were his own.

"It is late now. I don't wish to worry your parents," he whispered, pausing to press another slow, lingering kiss upon her lips. "I'll escort you home."

Fingers entangled, they strolled down the path, and Haewon took in the sight around her. The sun hovered on the horizon, the forest now a silhouette of shadows. The stream out in the clearing shimmered pink with the reflection of floating clouds. The cacophony of birds, the spring wind and the rustling greenery, seemed to crescendo in a beautiful melody as she walked together with him. Her heart was full, and she found herself unable to stop smiling.

Truly, she wished to write this moment into a book and live inside it forever.

Epilogue

Dearest,

In your letter, dated the third, you asked that I think of you. Since arriving at my new post as magistrate, I've done little else, and for that, I feel quite ashamed. I think of you endlessly . . . which is to say, perhaps far too much.

The sun rises and sets, the years have come and gone, and the more I have come to know you, the more deeply I have loved you. I know you will be joining me this month. A wiser man might take comfort knowing this, but alas, I am not that man. I deeply long for you. Please, put me out of my misery and visit me in my dreams.

Your husband,
Yu Seojun

PS. One day at my office, burdened by paperwork, I finally picked up my brush, and by the month's end I found that I had finished writing the final volume. I am sending you the manuscript for your perusal, and please extend my apologies to Wol for the delay. It seems inspiration required a quarter century to arrive.

Names Glossary

Heroine: Haewon—Heh-wun

Oldest Sister: Jade (birth name: Yeonok—Yuhn-ok)

Youngest Sister: Yeonhee—Yun-hee

Mother: Mistress Myeongok—Myung-ok

Father: Scholar Shin

Hero: Lord Yu Seojun—Suh-joon

Father: Minister Yu

Older Sister: Gwideok—Gwee-duk

Hero's Best Friend: Young Master Byeongho—Byung-ho

Bookshop Owner's Daughter: Mistress Wol

Literary Censor: Wuyeong—Woo-yung

Author's Note

Behind Five Willows is set in the time of the marriage edict, a policy that was enforced in February 1791, and by June, 281 spinsters were identified. I took the creative liberty to suggest that this push to marry off all these 281 spinsters was ongoing into 1792, which is when the novel takes place. The main policy I focused on in my book, however, was the Restoration of a Pure Writing Style edict of 1785, later referred to as *Munchebanjeong* (문체반정). This edict was reiterated in 1786, 1787, toward the end of 1791, and once more in 1793.

As the Munchebanjeong edict is a complex policy, I wanted to dive a bit deeper into it. This policy prohibited the importation of Catholic books and Chinese books, including novels and historical works. It also banned the creation and circulation of fictional writing. The reasons behind this edict are complicated, and for the purpose of this author's note, I'll simplify them to three causes.

The first underlying motive, suggested by some scholars, is that King Jeongjo's aversion to fiction was a reaction to his relationship with his father, the controversial Crown Prince Sado. Sado had a fondness for novels, and this trait likely came under fire as one of the reasons for the prince's misconduct. And as Jeongjo grew up under his father's tragic legacy, he may have rejected novels as a way to distance himself from it.

The second motive stemmed from Jeongjo's commitment to reinforcing Neo-Confucianism as the foundation of the state. He viewed writing as a mirror that reflected society's values, customs, politics, and culture. Writing, in his perspective, held the power to preserve Confucian order. But with commercialization growing and social unrest splintering the late Joseon society, there may have been a surge of interest in alternative ideas and a desire to break from the rigid Confucian ideology, as well as the hunger for freer forms of expression.

This shift likely alarmed King Jeongjo. The popularity of "vulgar" themes and unorthodox literary expressions challenged the ideals of Confucian morality. Fiction, in this context, was seen as a seed of disorder. By suppressing it through the Munchebanjeong edict, Jeongjo aimed to create an upright society.

The third—and perhaps the main—motive was entirely political. During Jeongjo's reign, the royal court was dominated by the king's rivals, the Old Doctrine faction (Noron), while other factions, including the Southern faction (Namin), were marginalized. Jeongjo supported a policy of impartiality, which sought to distribute power more evenly among factions. The literary crackdown became one way to achieve this balance and protect the Southerners, the faction he favored.

For example, in 1785, a few scholars of the Southern faction attended Catholic mass, an illegal act at the time. Instead of punishing them directly, Jeongjo redirected blame toward books associated with Seohak (Western science, technology, and religion).

Then in 1791, the Jinsan incident escalated tensions. Two Catholics of the Southern faction, Kwŏn Sangyŏn and Yun

Chich'ung, burned their ancestral tablets as the Catholic Church in Beijing deemed the practice of ancestral worship to be idolatrous. In the eyes of the law in Joseon Korea, however, this was considered rebellion against the throne. When the Old Doctrine faction tried to use this incident to purge their rivals, Jeongjo again manipulated his Munchebanjeong policy to protect the Southern faction by emphasizing the dangers of the current literary culture rather than targeting the Southerners, many of whom were Catholic converts. King Jeongjo stressed that, before even attempting to ban Catholicism and other Western ideas, the state had to first ban fiction, and in order to ban fiction, the state ought to first prohibit books from China. The literary culture at large, rather than Catholicism itself, was therefore presented as the greater threat.

However, it is important to note that censorship rarely ends with fiction. While King Jeongjo had employed Munchebanjeong to weaken the Noron faction and consolidate royal authority, the political pendulum swung in the opposite direction after his death. The Noron faction retaliated with the Sinyu Persecution of 1801, targeting Catholics—realizing that to purge Catholics would be a natural means of purging their rival Southern faction. So while the Sinyu Persecution was framed as a movement to eliminate unorthodoxy, the persecution was a political purge at its core, resulting in the deaths of Southern faction members, as well as many who had nothing to do with this political rivalry. Approximately three hundred Catholics were beheaded, and thousands of others were arrested, tortured, and sent into exile.

As illustrated, the reasons behind the Munchebanjeong edict were layered, but its outcome was clear: Writers were affected. King Jeongjo began to enforce this policy in earnest by the end of 1791, and the two most notable writers who were affected by it were Pak Chiwŏn and Yi Ok.

Pak Chiwŏn (pen name: Yeonam, 연암, 燕巖) was the author of the masterpiece *Yeolhailgi*, and his controversial writing style was so immensely popular that King Jeongjo deemed him to be the central figure responsible for the corruption of literary culture. However, as Pak Chiwŏn was from a prestigious Old Doctrine family, he was shielded from the king's punishment.

In contrast, Yi Ok (pen name: Munmuja, 문무자, 文無子) came from a humble background, and therefore experienced much harsher consequences. As a student at the Royal Confucian Academy and a successful examinee of the Classics Licentiate Exam, he was discovered writing in a style disapproved of by the king. In 1792, Yi Ok was exiled. He ended up abandoning his aspirations for civil service and lived the rest of his life in isolation, devoting his life to writing works of fiction that literati scholars disdained. But while reading Professor Youme Kim's paper about Yi Ok's life and listening to Professor Park Su-mil's lecture series on this writer, I became so fascinated by Yi Ok that he ended up becoming a source of inspiration for this book.

One thing that struck me about Yi Ok's life is how easily his writing could have disappeared, like that of the many writers of his era who lacked prominent descendants to preserve their work.

Fortunately for Yi Ok, he had Kim Yŏ, a friend who believed his writing was of worth. Kim Yŏ used his own resources, pushed past all the criticism, and took it upon himself to collect and compile Yi Ok's writings. And it is thanks to that one friend that Yi Ok's writing endures today.

Acknowledgments

WRITING THIS BOOK FELT LIKE COMING FULL CIRCLE. AT thirteen, I fell in love with *Pride and Prejudice* and began writing fanfiction. The joy I felt writing stories about Elizabeth Bennet and Mr. Darcy grew into a dream to publish my own original stories. So it was, without a doubt, Jane Austen who first sparked my love of storytelling. And writing *Behind Five Willows,* after all these years, has felt like a return to that first love. I'm so grateful to everyone who played a part in bringing this story to life.

To my editor, Emily Settle, thank you for all your hard work and wonderful feedback. Your love for this book helped it shine, and working with you has truly been one of the greatest gifts of my publishing journey.

To my champion, Amy Bishop-Wycisk, what would I do without you?! You've been with me every step of the way: cheering me on, offering encouragement, and guiding me in so many ways. Also, thank you for being the cool and chatty agent I can hide behind at events (hehe).

I also wanted to share this: It was actually both of you, Emily and Amy, who inspired the characters of Magpie and Mistress Wol. I imagined them as editors and agents in their own ways, both involved in discovering good books, shaping stories, and encouraging writers. You've both helped me see the worth in my own work, especially during times when I doubted it, so thank you for being such an inspiration.

Many thanks to my publishing team at Feiwel and Friends, including my fantastic publicist, Chantal Gersch, my marketing manager, Gaby Salpeter, and the Fierce Reads marketing team; copyeditor Nicole Brugger-Dethmers; cover artist Shotze; managing editor Dawn Ryan and production editors Helen Seachrist and Mariam Chaduneli; designers Rich Deas, Beste Doğan, and Maria W. Jenson; and production manager Kim Waymer. I'd also like to thank Jim McCarthy for joining the team and for the excitement you brought to this project!

To my research buddy, Eunice Kim, thank you for always being there to brainstorm with me! I still remember those early conversations about this book over Korean food in NYC. Your thoughts have been so precious to me. And to Sarah Mughal Rana, you have no idea how much I appreciate having a friend like you to confide in about my publishing highs and lows.

To Sharon and Gee, you both mean the world to me. Thank you for letting me spam you on KakaoTalk with all my publishing-related questions and thoughts. And to Charles, I'm grateful that you are you, and that you're my little brother. To Cristina Lee, thank you for your friendship. I'm always so grateful for you! Whenever I try to write about friendship, I often think of ours.

My immense gratitude to all the librarians, booksellers, and reviewers who have supported my works. I wrote this book with all of you book lovers in mind. And to my readers—I could go on and on about how much every one of you means to me. This book, in particular, is dedicated to those who had to endure Chapter 42 from *A Crane Among Wolves*.

I'd also like to credit the lovely translation of the *Yeolhailgi* quote in Chapter 6 to Jinwoo Park. Thank you for taking the time to help me with a line I struggled so hard to translate myself. Credit also to Sung-Il Lee for the translation of Hwang Jini's "Meeting in Dreams," Peter H. Lee for the translation of Hwang Jini's "Do Not Boast of Your Speed," David Hinton for the translation of a quote from the *Analects*, Kil Cha and Michael J. Pettid for *The Tale of Unyong* excerpt translation, Sejong Cultural Society for the translation of Yang Sa-eon's verses, and LAC Poetry for the translation of Tao Yuanming's "Biography of the Five Willows Gentleman." I'd also like to note that the pen name Black Lotus was inspired by Jean-Michel Othoniel's *Black Lotus* exhibition at Kukje Gallery. And thank you to Tifa, your one comment on Instagram ended up inspiring the early chapters of this book.

To my professor and classmates from my Jane Austen seminar at the University of Toronto, you still live rent-free in my head, even though many years have passed. I'll never forget how our class split into the most heated debate over which *Pride and Prejudice* adaptation was superior: the 2005 film or the 1995 TV drama.

To my father, thank you for first introducing me to *Pride and Prejudice*; you were watching the 1940 adaptation on TVO with me, and when you noticed how obsessed I was with the film, you bought me a copy of the book. And to my mother, who has read all my books and has always been my number one cheerleader—I love you both so much.

I also want to thank my in-laws for babysitting in order to carve out writing time for me. To my kids, thank you for the constant and most-needed reminder: to step away from my writing desk and live life.

A special thank-you to my husband, Bosco; thank you for being my safe space. Thank you for always fiercely guarding my writing time. Thank you for your kindness and for always going out of your way to make sure I never run out of coffee when I write.

I'm grateful for the many resources that made it possible to write this book, especially:

Han Hee-sook, "Women's Life During the Chosŏn Dynasty"

Kim Yong-shim, *Munchebanjeong, This Is How I See It (문체반정, 나는 이렇게 본다)*

Ksenia Chizhova, *The Subject of Feelings: Emotion, Kinship, Fiction, and Women's Culture in Korea, Late 17th–Early 20th Centuries*

Christopher Lovins, "Testing the Limits: King Chŏngjo and Royal Power in Late Chosŏn"

"Early marriage of women" *(여성의 조혼)*, published by Hankookmunhwasa (한국문화사)

Lecture series on Yi Ok by Professor Park Su-mil (Hanyang University)

Miyoung Kim, "Modernity in Korean Literature Based on the Study of *Ch'unhyang-chŏn*"

Youme Kim, "The Life and Works of Yi Ok"

Jamie Jungmin Yoo, "Networks of Disquiet: Censorship and the Production of Literature in Eighteenth-Century Korea"

Jo Gye-yeong, *Birth of the Book* (책의 탄생)

The annotated edition of *Pride and Prejudice* edited by David M. Shapard

And lastly: I thank Jesus, my lord and savior, for being near to the brokenhearted.

About the Author

Julie Anna Tang

JUNE HUR is a *New York Times*–bestselling and Edgar Award–winning author of YA historicals, including *The Silence of Bones, The Forest of Stolen Girls, The Red Palace, A Crane Among Wolves,* and *Behind Five Willows*. Born in South Korea, June spent her formative years in the USA, Canada, and South Korea before studying history and literature at the University of Toronto and working at the city's public library. Her work has been featured in *Forbes*, NPR, *The New York Times*, CBC, *Vogue Korea*, and KBS. June resides in Toronto with her family and can be spotted writing in coffee shops.

junehur.com

Thank you for reading this Feiwel & Friends book.
The friends who made *Behind Five Willows* possible are:

Jean Feiwel, Publisher
Liz Szabla, VP, Associate Publisher
Rich Deas, Senior Creative Director
Anna Roberto, Executive Editor
Holly West, Executive Editor
Kat Brzozowski, Senior Editor
Emily Settle, Senior Editor
Dawn Ryan, Executive Managing Editor
Kim Waymer, Senior Production Manager
Foyinsi Adegbonmire, Editor
Rachel Diebel, Editor
Brittany Groves, Assistant Editor
Maria W. Jenson, Designer
Beste Doğan, Designer
Helen Seachrist, Senior Manager, Production Editorial
Mariam Chaduneli, Production Editorial Assistant
Chantal Gersch, Publicity Manager
Gabriella Salpeter, Marketing Manager

Follow us on Facebook or visit us online at mackids.com.
Our books are friends for life.